LONGARM WOKE WITH A START AND ROLLED FROM THE BUNK TO HIS FEET . . .

His hand moved by instinct to scoop up the butt of the Colt when a soft voice from the darkness said, "I hope I didn't disturb you, Custis."

"Jessibee?" Longarm asked.

"I hope you weren't expecting someone else. If you are, perhaps I'd better go."

"No, no!" he said hastily. "Wait, I'll light the lamp."

"Don't" she said. "The moon's just behind a cloud right now. We'll have all the light we need . . ."

TABOR EVANS

LONGARM

AND THE BANDIT QUEEN

A JOVE BOOK

First Jove edition published February 1980

10 9 8 7 6 5 4 3 2 1

Printed in the United States of America

Jove books are published by Jove Publications, Inc.,
200 Madison Avenue, New York, NY 10016

Chapter 1

The icy bite of the twilight wind cut through Longarm's clothes and crept down inside the leather tops of his stovepipe cavalry boots, curling his toes and numbing them. He wondered if they might not be turning blue. His hands, on which he wore thin leather gloves—the only pair he'd found when rummaging in his saddlebags—felt like they were blue, too. Longarm wasn't about to pull the gloves off to find out. His fingers were so chilled that he was afraid one or two might come off with the gloves.

A stray gust sent an icy thread trickling down his collar to rustle the hair on his chest. *Damn me for a double-dyed jackass!* he thought as he pulled the lapels of his long, black Prince Albert coat closer together. *If I'd thought it'd be this cold so far south along the Arkansas in September, I'd have brought my sheepskin instead of leaving it hang in Denver where it ain't doing nobody any good.*

Letting go the reins of his Texas-bitted cavalry mount, Longarm slapped his palms together to bring back some feeling. They flexed enough, with a little beating, to let him slide one hand inside his tight-pulled coat lapels and fish a cheroot out of his vest pocket. He chomped his strong teeth over the tip of the cheroot, clamping the thin cigar in his mouth while he fumbled a match from his coat pocket.

He made two tries at flicking the match into flame with a thumbnail before remembering that he had on gloves. *For all they're keeping your hands warm, old son,* he told himself, *you might as well not be wearing them.*

Lifting a foot out of the stirrup, he hoisted his leg upward high enough to bend it, and struck the match on his bootheel. The puff of blue smoke that he loosed to mingle with the chill air, almost as visibly blue as the smoke itself in the fading light, made him feel a little bit better.

But not enough to mention, his thoughts ran on. *Billy Vail's just too damn tight with voucher money lately, telling me to get a remount at Ft. Gibson instead of letting me stay on the train all the way to Ft. Smith and renting a livery horse there.*

By now, the fragrant smoke from the cigar was beginning to soothe Longarm's spirits somewhat.

But I guess it ain't all Billy's fault. It's them damn pencil-pushers back in Washington. They set on their padded swivel chairs all day and figure how to cut off a penny here and whittle away a nickel there, and I wind up freezing my butt for fifty or sixty miles on a cavalry nag traipsing across the ass-end of the Cherokee Nation, when I still ought to be at least halfway warm in a coach seat on the damn train.

Which don't mean it ain't Billy's fault that I'm here in the first place. I got about as much business being down here between the Creek and Cherokee Nations, trying to pick up a smell of Jesse James's trail, as a butchering-sized hog has trying to fly. Seems like every day that goes by and the James boys stay hid out, the hotter everybody gets about finding them. Hell, I'll stand by what I told Billy when he put me on this case. I'll put up a mint-new double eagle against his plugged two-bit piece that Jesse's right close to where he calls home, over east in Missouri. And he ain't going to be found until those neighbors of his start flapping their jaws. Trouble is, nobody's listening when I try to tell them what only seems like good sense to me.

Ahead of him, Longarm caught the glint of a campfire's light flickering among the trunks of the big sweet gum and blackjack oak trees that grew thickly on both sides of the river trail. The trail meandered more or less parallel to the banks of the Arkansas River as it flowed sluggishly southeast toward the line between the Indian Nation and the state of Arkansas.

He picked up the reins and twitched them to send his mount in the direction of the promised warmth. There was still a good distance between him and the fire. He

6

nudged his horse with a spurless bootheel to speed it up a bit, anxious, now that he'd seen the blaze, to stop and settle down beside it, and share its warmth with whoever had built it.

He'd covered most of the distance to the flickering spot of light, zigzagging between the trees and skirting the heavy brush, when a scream split the darkening night. For a moment, Longarm couldn't be sure there was a connection between the scream and the fire. He was still too far away to see anything but a suggestion of dark shapes silhouetted against the glow that spread around the fire. There were three or four figures moving around, but he couldn't tell whether they were those of men or women. Just to be on the safe side, though, he slipped his Winchester out of its sadddle scabbard and flicked off the safety. Then he dug both heels hard into his horse's flanks, and the animal spurted forward.

Twenty seconds and two or three screams later, Longarm was close enough to get an idea as to what was going on around the campfire, as the diminishing distance sharpened the blurred edges of the shapes of four men and a woman. As the distance continued to lessen, he saw that the men had been chasing their companion, and as he watched them, the men wrestled the woman to the ground. Three of them held her—one holding each of her legs, the third stretching her arms above her head. The fourth ripped away her skirt and underclothes, and fumbled at his belt.

By now, Longarm was close enough to see more than silhouettes. The men became defined as bearded, butternut-jean-clad individuals, but the woman was only a stretch of bare flesh, tinted deep pink by the lurid firelight. Dark pubic hair broke the sweep of her skin between waist and legs. The man who'd begun fumbling with his belt had let his jeans drop now, and Longarm could see his protruding erection as he dropped to his knees between the writhing woman's widespread legs.

Her screams increased when she felt him probing to enter her. She twisted as best she could, trying to avoid his eager efforts, and her body arched against the strain her captors were putting on her arms and legs. The kneeling

7

man struck her with his fist, and the woman's screams stopped abruptly, as did her struggles. One of the men said something. Longarm was too far away to make out the words, but he heard the raucous laughter that followed the remark.

That was enough for him. Rape was rape under any circumstances, and rape wasn't something that Longarm's personal code would countenance. It was also against the law, and he was the law.

He pulled up the horse with a sliding of hooves. Shooting against firelight was tricky, as he'd learned through long experience. He caught the kneeling man in his sights, and squeezed the Winchester's trigger.

For a split second, the kneeling man froze, then the impact of the high-velocity .44-40 slug toppled him over. He fell across one of the woman's pinioned legs. His companions let go of the now-sagging limbs they'd been struggling to hold still, and clawed for their guns.

Longarm reduced the odds with a snapshot at the man at the group's head. His shot was quick, and the flickering firelight made sighting chancy. His target crumpled, then floundered on the ground. Longarm swung the Winchester, but the other two were on the move even before he'd started shifting his aim. Before he could trigger a third shot, the two remaining rapists were running into the deep shadows among the trees around the vest-pocket clearing.

While Longarm was searching the dappled shadows for a shot at the running desperadoes, the man who'd been his second target struggled to his feet and hobbbled, bent double, into the sheltering woods. Longarm was in easy pistol range now. He sheathed the Winchester and dropped the horse's reins over its nose. The cavalry-trained animal stood placidly.

Longarm dismounted, drawing his Colt, and struck off to one side of the fire. He had no way of knowing where the three men were, but instinct and experience told him they'd probably not gone far. The odds were that they'd taken shelter among the big boles of the gumwood trees and thick foliage of the scrub oak that surrounded the little clearing.

Longarm could see them in his mind's eye, shielded

8

behind a protecting tree trunk while they waited for him to enter the revealing circle of firelight to bend over the body of the woman, who still lay unmoving on the ground beside the blaze. The twilight had slid into darkness during the moments it had taken for him to reach the fire, and the ensuing minutes that had been consumed in his brief surprise attack. Neither moon nor starlight penetrated through the thin gray overcast that had veiled the sky when it had last been visible. Longarm stopped to let his eyes grow acccustomed to the gloom, and to listen for sounds of movement.

There was a constant rustling in the wooded area. The wind was still brisk, and it whined softly as an undertone to the shushing it caused among the autumn-hardened leaves, still green and thick, but dry now after the sun of summertime. Bit by bit, his ears grew used to the forest murmur, his eyes to the freshly dark night. Directly in front of him, a twig cracked under the pressure of a booted foot. Slowly, Longarm edged ahead.

He felt his way, lowering each foot slowly as he stepped forward, putting his weight on the foot gradually, ready to pull back if the springiness of the loose leaves that blanketed the ground was interrupted by the hard line of a dry tree limb or twig. His caution saved him a bad fall, for he was still balanced on one foot when the foot he was advancing touched the ground briefly before the earth crumbled away under its pressure. Still, he had to shuffle to keep from pitching forward, and the sudden movement set up a soft rustling in the vegetation underfoot.

A line of fire cut the darkness in front of him, and the sound of the shot and the ugly, high-pitched whistle of lead zipping past, mere inches from his chest, sounded at almost the same instant.

Longarm hit the ground, squeezing off a shot toward the spot where he'd seen the muzzle blast as he fell. Two gunshots cut the night now, a few feet apart, but they were high. When he'd gone to the ground, Longarm had fallen into a shallow ditch. He rolled, measuring it by feel, finding that it was no ditch, but judging from its size and shape, a grave.

For that woman they were about to rape, he thought.

Figured to get rid of her after they'd had all they wanted from her.

He lifted himself to his knees, and reached out one hand in front of him, encountered the earth that had been lifted from the grave. It was as good a breastwork as anybody could ask for. Longarm put a shot into the darkness from behind the shelter of the dirt pile.

Two shots replied, and he answered them instantly, shooting to the side of the muzzle blasts. One of his slugs found flesh. A cry of mixed anger and pain sounded from the darkness.

"Son of a bitch winged me!" a man's voice grated. "Shit on this! Whoever that is, he's better than I am at sharpshooting in the dark! I'm getting the hell out of here!"

"Not without me, you ain't!" a second voice replied. "Come on! Lucky we didn't unsaddle before we went for the woman!"

There was a loud pounding of feet on dry leaves and the slapping of scrub-oak branches against bodies. The noises faded, then there was an angry exchange of words in tones too low for Longarm to make out what was being said. Finally, the drumbeat of hooves thudded noisily beyond the waning fire, then faded into the distance, telling Longarm that his antagonists had ridden off with more haste than caution.

Longarm waited until the hoofbeats died, to make sure, before he stepped out of the shallow grave, that the three riders weren't going to regain their courage and circle back.

Unreplenished, the fire had waned to little more than a bed of red coals from which an occasional flicker of bright flame burst when the heat ate into a sap-pocket. The woman was still unconscious. Longarm studied her with a frown.

She was young, younger than she'd sounded to him, but the noises she'd made had been dragged out of her in fear and rage. He put her age at somewhere in the middle twenties. Her face, in repose, was unlined—a square-shaped face, with a firm jaw under slightly over-full lips. Her nose was upturned and small, with wide nostrils, under full, heavy brows. Her cheekbones were high, her

10

brow unlined. She had thick black hair that grew in a half-circle around a narrow forehead, and streamed out loose on the ground under her shoulders.

Her clothing was still disarranged. Her white shirtwaist was rumpled, its collar ripped half off, and the corduroy riding skirt that had been pulled away by her attacker had fallen or been pulled high; it covered her breasts in a rumpled mass that hid their contour. Her body was bare from the waist down. A gently rounded stomach glowed in the firelight. Below a thick black vee of pubic hair, her thighs tapered plumply to calves still covered by high-laced boots, with thick stockings folded over their tops. Her knee-length underpants lay in a tattered wad at one side.

Across one of the woman's legs, the man whom Longarm's rifle slug had killed lay sprawled, his arms thrust upward. Blood stained the side and front of his butternut shirt, where the bullet had taken him. His narrow hips and buttocks were bare.

Longarm pulled one of the dead man's arms aside to get a clear look at his bearded face. It was not one that he recognized, either from a past arrest or from any of the wanted flyers at which he'd looked recently. In death, the face might have belonged to anybody, a storekeeper or a farmer. It had lost whatever villainy it might have possessed while the man was still alive.

Longarm grabbed the corpse by its limp wrists, and dragged it away from the woman. Then he eased her skirt down to cover her thighs before he took stock of his surroundings.

At the edge of the clearing, two horses were tethered to a bush. Both were still saddled. Behind them, a mule was also tied up; it bore a lightly loaded packsaddle. There was nothing in the clearing, except the dying fire and a small stack of chopped tree limbs at one side of it, to give any sign that the group had intended to make camp there for the night. There were no bedrolls, no cooking utensils, not even a water bucket.

Longarm brought his own horse up and tethered it where the others stood, then he threw a few of the pieces of cut wood on the coals, hunkered down, and stripped off his gloves. In the flurry of action he'd set off, he'd for-

11

gotten about the cold wind. In the clearing, the trees cut the force of the breeze, though its presence was still indicated by the waving of the treetops. Thoughtfully, Longarm took out a fresh cheroot and lighted it while he continued to study the little glade.

From the evidence, it was impossible to tell whether the woman had been traveling with the four men, or had encountered them on the trail and been forced to accompany them to the secluded spot. Longarm gave up on the puzzle. When the woman woke up, he'd get the answers to his questions.

He did not have long to wait. The young woman sighed, and her arms moved fitfully. Then her eyes snapped open. A scream started from her lips when she saw Longarm squatting beside the fire, but she choked it off before it had gained enough volume to emerge from her mouth as anything louder than a surprised gasp.

"You startled me," she said, struggling into a sitting position.

Longarm let a small frown gather on his brow, though it was hidden by the wide brim of his flat-topped Stetson, as he tried to put a location to the odd intonation in her voice. It was not from the South, nor was it one that carried the casual overtones of the West, or the flatness of New York. Rather, it was a nasal voice, produced in her head rather than flowing easily from her throat. Longarm had heard words inflected that way before, but not very often; the predominant regional accent of the West reflected the soft, elongated vowel sounds of Southern speech.

She went on, "Something happened that I don't remember. I don't remember you at all."

"No reason why you should, ma'am. Far as I know, you never did lay eyes on me before, any more than I've seen you before now."

Her brows knitted thoughtfully as she struggled to remember. "Then, what happened to me?"

"You got hit. Real hard, judging from the length of time you've been out. You don't need to worry about anything, though. Nobody laid a hand on you while you were unconscious. You're all right."

12

Longarm studied her while she was looking around the clearing. She was a bit older than he'd first judged her to be—in her early thirties, perhaps. Her eyes, which he was seeing for the first time, were dark brown. Her gaze, darting around the little glade, fell on the dead man who lay on the ground at one edge of the clearing.

"My God!" she gasped. "He was—he was the one—"

"He was the one that hit you," Longarm filled in when her voice trailed off.

"More than that." She began to tremble as memory came rushing back. "He was one of the guides I hired at Fort Smith. He—they—there were four of them. And they were going to rape me."

Longarm nodded. "That's about the size of it. I watched it all, from the time they commenced chasing you around until I got busy and changed their ideas."

"Is that a polite way of telling me that you killed him?"

"Well, now, I wasn't trying to be polite, ma'am. No more than I usually am, to a lady. But now that you remember what was going on, it won't bring back more bad memories than you've already got. The reason you don't know how all of it come about is that you'd been knocked cold just before I dropped that fellow there."

"My God! What kind of place am I in? You're saying you shot that man in cold blood?"

"No, I wouldn't exactly say it was cold-blooded. I was mad as hell, if you don't object to me swearing a mite. I don't like to see four men ganging up on anybody, let alone a woman, trying to hurt her."

"Hurting's one thing. Killing's another. I've never been raped, and I don't suppose it would be a very nice experience, but at least I'd still have been alive when they finished. That man lying there is dead!"

"Yep. Just about as dead as anybody'll ever be."

"You killed him deliberately, with a gun, instead of just stopping him from—from what he wanted to do."

Longarm was losing his patience. He looked into the woman's angry eyes for a moment before he replied, "If you'll recall, ma'am, there were four of them. And they weren't the kind I'd want to walk up to and try to reason with, seeing as how all of them were wearing guns."

13

"He should have been tried in court, not summarily executed! Even the most disgusting criminal deserves a trial before a judge and jury. You deprived him of his life without giving him a chance to defend himself!" Her eyes were fixed scornfully on Longarm's apparently emotionless face.

"Oh, he defended himself. Him and his three friends all had a few shots at me before I winged two of them and they lit out."

"But they didn't—"

Longarm's temper finally let go. "Now, you just be good enough to keep quiet a minute, ma'am."

She looked at him questioningly, and started to say something, but Longarm was already standing up, his back to her. He went to the fire and selected a branch, choosing one that had a good flame at one end and was long enough to serve as a torch.

"You follow along with me, if you feel able to," he told the woman.

"Follow?" She shook her head. "I don't understand."

"You will," he assured her.

Longarm waited for her to stand up. She got to her feet by kneeling first. The loose, unfastened skirt dropped away. She stood up quickly and grabbed for the skirt, which lay on the ground. Draping it around her waist, she fumbled for a button or snap, but whatever had secured the garment had been torn off by the dead man. She settled for holding the skirt with one hand as she took a step toward Longarm. He led her toward the edge of the glade.

"Where are we going?" she asked suspiciously.

"Not far, just a few steps over here. There's something I want you to see."

Wordlessly, still puzzled, she followed him as he led the way to the shallow grave. By the light of the burning branch, they could see a short-handled spade sticking in the ground beside the pile of dirt that had been taken from the long, narrow excavation.

"Good God!" she gasped, as the significance of the hole's shape dawned on her. "You've already dug a grave for the man you killed! I suppose you're getting ready to bury him out here in this wild place, without even a prayer?"

14

"You're a little bit wrong in what you're thinking, ma'am." Longarm kept his voice to a low-keyed, conversational pitch. Very matter-of-factly, he went on, "You see, it wasn't me that dug this grave. Those men did, sometime after you got here, after they'd made their plans for you while you were on the trail from Fort Smith. They weren't planning on letting you go free to testify against them, if they got caught after they'd finished with you."

"You . . . you mean, that grave was intended for me?" she asked. Her voice was suddenly subdued, its scolding tone gone, and she spoke almost in a whisper.

"Well, now, you stop and think back a minute," Longarm suggested. "After you and those four rascals stopped here—they said it was time to stop, didn't they? Getting too dark to see the trail, or something like that?"

"Yes. Something like that. They said it was gettting dark and the horses were tiring. We'd left Fort Smith quite early, so I believed them."

"And after you'd stopped, one of them chopped up some wood, and another one acted like he was taking care of the horses, and one or two of them went off, maybe to look for water? I suspicion he told you there was a spring off this way close by?"

"Yes," she agreed. "Jasper—that's the one who's dead—said it was too wet closer to the spring for us to stop." She shook her head. "He wasn't gone long enough to dig a hole this big, though."

"Oh, I don't know." Longarm pulled the shovel out of the soil and pushed it back in, experimentally. "Real soft dirt. Mostly just a thick layer of old, dried leaves and suchlike. And you can see the hole's not real deep." He held the torch so the woman could get a better look at the shallow pit.

"I—maybe I'm mistaken about the time. Perhaps he was gone long enough, now that I think back."

"And while he was gone, I bet the other three kept you busy with stories and jokes and so forth?" Longarm suggested.

Slowly, she nodded. "Yes. Yes, they did. How did you know that?"

"You ain't the first woman that's trusted the wrong kind

15

of men, and maybe dropped out of sight along some lone-some trail. Maybe wound up in a hole like this one, where nobody's likely to find the body for a dozen years or more. Mostly, the kind of men I'm talking about run in bunches of three or four, and it don't much matter how they do what they got in mind, or where it happens. They pretty generally follow the same style."

"From the way you talk, you know a great deal about the way these rapists—and I suppose they're robbers, too—about the way they operate. How do I know you're not one yourself?" she challenged.

"I guess you don't, at that." Longarm pulled out his wallet and flipped it open to show her his deputy U.S. marshal's badge. "Maybe this'll set your mind at ease a mite."

"You're an officer of the law? A U.S. marshal?"

"Deputy marshal," he corrected her.

"And you actually shot that man," she went on, as though he hadn't spoken. "Shot him without making any sort of effort to warn him to stop? Without making an effort to arrest him? You just pulled your pistol out and killed him?"

Longarm's patience ran out. He snapped. "Now, that's all I want to hear from you along those lines! I wasn't close enough to use my sixgun, or they'd all four be dead now, instead of just one! They were four-to-one against me, and all of them packed iron. The way that fellow was going after you, once he shut you up with his fist, he'd have been on you and inside you before I opened my mouth. Warning him wouldn't have stopped him. All it would have done was to give one of the others time to kill me."

For a moment, the woman stared at Longarm as though seeing him for the first time. She saw a man taller and wider than most, with gunmetal-blue eyes in a tanned face, which was clean-shaven except for a bold, sweeping mustache. In the flickering torchlight, those gunmetal eyes reflected controlled anger.

He said curtly, "Now, if you've seen enough of what those four planned for you, let's go back to the fire. I'll drag that body out here later on and cover it up, after I

16

go over it to see if that—Jasper, I recall you said his name was—to see if he had another name or two besides the one he told you."

"And after that?" she asked.

"After that, we'll talk about what comes next. Now, come along."

Chapter 2

Subdued and silent, the woman walked with Longarm back to the clearing. He tossed the torch on the fire and added two or three more pieces of wood from the fast-dwindling pile of chopped tree limbs. Night had arrived now, its blackness crowding the rim of the glade, held at bay only by the dancing firelight.

Longarm was still angry. He made no effort at conversation, but circled the glade at the perimeter of firelight until he found the deadfall log from which the firewood had been cut. An axe was still buried in the log. He used it as a lever to roll the deadfall up close to the fire, and quickly cleared the log of its remaining branches. He motioned to the cleared log.

"Might as well sit down," he told the woman. "We've got to talk a mite. I'll cook up some supper and make coffee after a while. I guess you've got some grub and your bedding on that pack mule tethered over yonder?"

"Yes." She sat down on the log. "I gave those men twenty dollars to buy supplies. They told me they'd buy me a slicker, whatever that is, and a set of blankets. I suppose you'll find them with the supplies."

"Time enough for that," Longarm said.

He hoped there might be a bottle of Maryland rye among the supplies, but he knew the best he could hope for, if there was any whiskey at all, was a bottle of questionable origin, probably the watered-down product of one of the illegal stills in the Indian Nation that supplied half the liquor drunk in the towns along its borders.

"You've got a name, I guess," he told his companion. "Mine's Long. You've already seen my badge, so you know what my business is."

"I'm Maidia Harkness," she replied. Then, somewhat tartly, she went on, "If you'd explained to me what sort of pressures you were under in stopping those men, I wouldn't have been so critical, Marshal. But where I come from, the police don't act as judge and jury. They arrest criminals and take them to jail, and let the courts decide whether they're innocent or guilty."

Longarm decided to let that pass without comment. Instead he asked, "Just where *do* you come from, Miss Harkness? Or is it *Mrs.* Harkness?"

"It's miss. And my home's in Boston."

"I knew it was one of them big towns in the East," Longarm said, nodding. "And this is your first trip to the West?"

"Yes. And I must say, my first impressions of it aren't very favorable."

"They'd have been a lot worse if I hadn't come along when I did," he reminded her. "That is, if you'd stayed alive to get any kind of impression."

Maidia shuddered. "Yes. I'm still having trouble believing all this is happening to me, though. I keep waiting to wake up and find myself at home in bed. It's been something of a nightmare."

"And pretty much your own fault," Longarm couldn't keep himself from replying. "But I can understand why you acted like you did. Back where you come from, there's people underfoot everyplace you turn, all of them living in the pocket of the fellow standing next to them. And a policeman on every corner to look after them and keep them safe."

"It's not quite that simplistic," Maidia said. For the first time since Longarm had seen her, she smiled. Her face changed completely.

She went on, "Perhaps we have come to depend too much on others for protection, though. We've gotten to look on it as automatic, something we buy and take for granted, instead of looking out for ourselves."

"Why'd you come out here, Miss Harkness?"

Longarm was frankly curious. He'd seen all kinds of people during the years he'd been trying to bring civilized behavior to the raw, untamed West, but the Harkness

19

woman didn't fit any of the compartments others had filled.

She seemed surprised. "Why, to help, of course."

"Help who?"

"Those who need help the most. The Indians."

"I see." Longarm made a business of blowing the ash off his cheroot. "Did they ask you to come help them?"

"No, of course not. But other social workers have told me about their needs, and I decided that I'd be of more service to them than to the people I've been trying to help back home."

Longarm was puzzled. "I reckon you lost me around that last bend, Miss Harkness. Is that what you do for a living? Just go around helping people?"

"I suppose you could call it that. I'm a social worker, you see."

"That's just it," he frowned. "I don't see. Now, I guess my business is helping folks by keeping robbers and killers and such behind bars, but from the way you were talking a while ago, you're just as concerned about helping *them* as you are about trying to do something for the folks they take advantage of."

"Everybody has rights in life. Marshal Long, even the ones you call robbers and killers. After all, they're human beings too."

Longarm grinned wryly. "After some of the things I've run into, I might put up a pretty argument that a lot of them ain't what you'd call good examples of human beings."

"Nonsense. Why, you must remember the beautiful words Thomas Jefferson wrote in our Declaration of Independence: '. . . that all men are endowed with certain unalienable rights.' "

"Oh, I know about the Declaration, sure. Only I disremember its saying anything about a body having a right to rob and maim and kill."

"You're evading the issue, Marshal," she said severely. "Take the Indians. We've deprived a great many of them of their lives, and now we're depriving all of them of their liberty, by shutting them up on reservations like the ones here in the Indian Nation."

"Well, now I've been pretty much all over the reservations here in the Nation. I don't recall seeing any Indians shut up, except a few that's turned to thieving from their own people, and killing, and things like that."

"That's an old, feeble argument, Marshal. I've heard it before, many times. And I expect I'll hear it again and again, now that I'm out here in the West. Why, this country belonged to the Indians, and we took it away from them by force."

"I reckon there's something in what you say. We crowded the Indians so close together that we made whole armies where there were only small raiding parties before. George Custer wouldn't have found himself in such a pickle if it hadn't been for that. And there's plenty who have lied to them and stolen from them and sold them guns and whiskey and gotten filthy rich in the process, and ruined such lives as they had in what they're pleased to call the Shining Times. I've traded shots with Indians, white men, Mexicans, and even Chinese, and I've had some of them help me out when I was in a few tight spots, too. There's some Indians just as greedy and ornery as white folks can be, which is how they lost some of what they had. They took a lot of scalps and tortured a lot of their own people, way back when, over sharing what they'd staked out as their territory."

"Oh, I've heard that, too. Why should they share? The land was theirs."

"Land's not worth much to people unless it's used, ma'am."

Maidia was getting angry. "We *spoil* the land! We dig up the soil and cut down the trees and dam up the rivers and kill the animals. The Indians never did things like that!"

Longarm grinned. "You ever see a Comanche buffalo drive? Or a Ponca village after a Pawnee raid?" He hesitated, then added, "I never did see that last myself, but I talked to men who did."

"I'm not saying the Indians are perfect," Maidia retorted angrily. "But they certainly didn't despoil the land and destroy the forests the way we've done in the East, and the way people are beginning to do here in the West."

Longarm sat thoughtfully for a moment, then got up and walked over to the fire. He picked up one of the few remaining long branches that hadn't been reduced to firewood length, and began to pull the burning sticks out of the fire and stamp them under his boots, driving them into the dirt and extinguishing them.

Maidia watched him for a moment, her face showing her perplexity. Then she began to feel the bite of the night wind that the fire had kept her from noticing before.

"What on earth are you doing?" she asked. "You're putting out our fire, and I'm getting cold!"

Longarm said with great seriousness, "Why, seeing as you're so dead set against the trees being cut up for firewood, Miss Harkness, I didn't want you to be embarrassed by sharing any of the heat we been getting from that tree."

"But we need the fire to be comfortable!" she protested. "If we didn't—" She stopped short and smiled. The smile became a laugh.

She said, "All right, Marshal, you've made your point. But I think you exaggerated a little bit, just as I was doing."

Squatting down, Longarm began rebuilding the blaze. Over his shoulder, he said to her as he worked, "The world might be a prettier place if folks were all considerate to each other, but they ain't, and that's why I've got this here job of mine. I can't afford to ponder too much on the way things *ought* to be—I've got to enforce the law, which is about the way things *are*. And I do my best to enforce the hell out of it. Now, I don't know anything about you, except you're a nice-looking young lady, but I'd guess you went to school a lot, and didn't do much rubbing up against real people. And you sure don't know much about Indians. Or men, either."

"I'll admit I deserved the lesson," she replied soberly. "I made a very serious mistake in not going to somebody in Fort Smith and asking about those four men I hired. But the man at the livery stable where I went to find out about getting here to the Cherokee Nation seemed to know them, so I just assumed they were all right."

"Which wasn't a real smart thing to do," Longarm pointed out. He added hastily, "Meaning no offense,

22

ma'am. But I'll see you safe back to Fort Smith, and you can catch a train there to take you back to Boston."

"I have no intention of going back to Boston," Maidia said firmly. "I came out here to work with the Indians, and that's what I intend to do. I appreciate your offer, Marshal Long, but I'll manage quite well on my own, I'm sure."

"You know I can't just ride off and leave you to look out for yourself," Longarm told her sternly. "Now, I'll tell you what. You backtrack with me a little ways tomorrow morning. There's a little place on the river called Webbers Falls, only eight or maybe ten miles from here. I'll find somebody dependable there to ride with you to wherever you're going."

"I have a letter of introduction to a Reverend Miller in some place called Choteau. I found it on the map; it's quite a distance north. There's an Indian school there, and I'm hoping to find a place teaching, to begin with."

"A while back, you said something about being a social worker," Longarm said. "Guess I don't rightly know just what that is."

"Generally, it's just being helpful to poor people and those who don't have an education. I'm qualified as a teacher, though, among other things."

"As long as you got a place waiting, that'll make me feel better. But how about my proposition, Miss Harkness? Will you go along to Webbers Falls with me, and let me pick out somebody to ride with you and see that you get to Choteau safe and sound?"

"Of course I will. I think it's very thoughtful of you to offer to help me." Maidia hesitated for a moment. "I'm afraid I owe you an apology, Marshal. I misjudged your actions earlier—not that I approve of them, you understand—but I'm beginning to see that the standards I've been judging things by can't always be applied to this part of the country."

"You don't need to apologize," Longarm assured her. "And meaning no offense again, you sound a lot smarter now than you did when you were ripping me up one side and down the other for what I done. But that's put behind us, I guess?"

"Yes, I guess it is," she agreed.

23

"Good. Now, if we're going to be comfortable tonight, I've got to look after some camp chores. The first one's to get rid of him—" Longarm nodded at the corpse— "and then I'll see what I can rustle up in the way of some supper."

Keeping her eyes off the body, Maidia said, "You do what's necessary. I don't know much about cooking over a campfire, but I'll help you as much as I can in getting dinner ready."

Longarm dragged the late Jasper to the grave that had been intended for Maidia Harkness. He went through the man's pockets before covering the grave, but found nothing in them that would help identify him, just a few dollars in silver, some crumpled currency, and the usual oddments: a jackknife, a sack of Bull Durham tobacco and cigarette papers, matches, a dollar discount token from a Fort Smith whorehouse, and a gold tooth that he speculated must have come from some past victim. He took off the dead man's gunbelt and carried it back to the fire.

"You generally carry a bandbox or something like that, don't you?" Longarm asked Maidia.

"Of course."

Longarm handed her the pistol. "Here. Put this someplace handy when you get around to it. Later on, you can swap it for something a little more a lady's size."

Maidia pulled back. "A pistol? Oh, no! Why, I couldn't carry a weapon, Marshal. Even if I felt that I could bring myself to carry one, I don't know how to shoot it."

"You can learn. I can teach you all you need to know in ten minutes. The rest is just practicing."

"No, Marshal Long. I'm sure your intentions are good—"

"Now, you listen to me, Miss Harkness. It's like you said yourself a minute ago. What you're used to from back East don't cut the mustard out here. You ain't going to find a policeman on every streetcorner that you can look to for help when you need it. Coming right down to cases, you're apt to be in places where there's not even any streetcorners for a policeman to stand on. Now, you do what I tell you. Take this Colt and learn which end the bullets come out of."

24

Gingerly, Maidia extended her hand and took the weapon. She almost dropped it when Longarm let go of the gunbelt. "My goodness! It's a lot heavier than I thought it would be."

"Part of that's the belt and cartridges. But a gun's going to be heavy, got to be. I'll show you a little bit about it later on. Right now, we better get some grub together before both of us starve."

"I know there's supposed to be some food on the pack mule," Maidia said. "But I'm not sure what kind of food. I told you I'm not very good at camp cooking, but I'll do what I can to help you."

Rummaging in the packsaddle together, they found a large chunk of beef loin, a half-side of bacon, a dozen or so potatoes, and several big white onions. In small cloth bags, they discovered flour, sugar, black-eyed peas, ground coffee, salt and pepper. There were also a few cans of tomatoes and peaches, a battered frying pan, and a large tin coffeepot. A cylinder of tattered rags had at its core an unlabeled bottle. Longarm pulled the cork and sniffed.

"Whiskey," he told Maidia. "Either keg stuff, or out of a still on one of the whiskey ranches hereabout. Might be all right, might not be fit to drink. We'll take it along and find out."

"At least we won't go to bed hungry," Maidia said, looking at the food they'd found. "If we can get it cooked."

"Oh, I can fix it so it's almost fit to eat," Longarm assured her. "Just don't look for anything fancy."

"I'm so hungry I could almost eat it raw," she replied. "But there ought to be some plates and cups."

"I got some tin plates in my saddlebag," he said, "but I only carry one cup. Can't seem to make room for two. But we'll get along all right. And there's water enough for coffee in my canteen. I'd bet there's a spring close by, but I don't aim to go looking for it in the dark. We might as well start supper. While it's cooking, I'll spread our bedrolls and rustle up a little wood for a breakfast fire."

Working together—peeling and slicing potatoes, cutting steaks off the piece of beef loin, fixing them on split branches Longarm cut from a sweet gum tree to broil while the potatoes were fried, passing a casual remark

25

about the food, the amount of coffee and water that would make a drinkable brew—brought a relaxation of the tension that until then had prevailed between Longarm and Maidia Harkness. She proved herself a reasonably adept cook, well able to hold up her end of the work.

In a surprisingly short time, they had the steaks over a bed of glowing coals, with the coffeepot sitting on one side of the coals, and potatoes sizzling in the frying pan on the other side. Longarm picked up the bottle of whiskey and held it to the firelight. The liquor showed a deep reddish brown through the clear glass of the bottle. He shook it hard several times, and nodded with satisfaction when no bubbles formed at the surface of the liquid.

"Whoever made it filtered out the fusel oil," he told Maidia. "At least that's how it looks. But we'll just make sure before we try tasting it."

He pulled the cork and trickled a few drops of liquor into the palm of one hand, set the bottle down, and rubbed the whiskey into the skin of his calloused palm with his fingertips. When he inspected his palm and sniffed at it, he nodded once again.

"It might burn our gullets," he said, "but it won't make us sick."

"How can you tell?"

"Wasn't any oily scum left on my hand," he explained. "These bootleg stills on the whiskey ranches don't always have copper worms. If they don't, and if they don't get the fire hot enough and keep it going steady, the liquor'll come out full of fusel oil, and that stuff just turns your stomach inside out. This ain't what you'd get at a good saloon, but it's safe enough to drink."

He took a small swallow. The liquor was still raw, but it wasn't as bad as he'd been afraid it might be. He held the bottle out to Maidia, and she surprised him by accepting it. She poured a healthy drink into the tin cup they'd taken from Longarm's saddlebags. Maidia could see by Longarm's expression that he'd expected her to refuse. She smiled at him.

"'I'm not a bluenosed reformer, Marshal, even if I am a social worker. I enjoy a drink before dinner at home.

26

There's no reason why one won't taste as good here in the woods."

"I'll take mine right out of the bottle, unless you object," he said. "I ain't too fond of the way corn whiskey smells when I drink it out of a cup. I'm a rye drinker, myself."

"I don't object, Marshal. And I like rye better than bourbon, too." She took a swallow of the liquor and shook her head. "Oh, my! That's very potent!"

"Pretty strong stuff, all right." Longarm looked critically at the steaks, and went on, "It'll be a few minutes before they're done. I'll go get our bedrolls and tend to the animals, if you'll stir the potatoes to keep them from burning."

During supper, the pair of them found a surprising number of things to talk about. Longarm was appalled at Maidia's conception of the way the Indians in the Nation lived, and the relationships between them and the whites. Like most post-Civil War Easterners, she saw the Indians of the Nation as a new kind of slave to be liberated from the white man's yoke.

"You don't really mean the Indians have their own police force?" she asked him at one point, when Longarm mentioned the Indian police.

"Why, sure they do, with uniforms and everything. There just ain't enough of them to cover the whole Nation, that's all. And the Indian police don't let sheriffs or town marshals from Texas or Arkansas or Kansas come into their territory, either."

"But you can, because you're a federal officer," Maidia concluded.

"That's right. U.S. marshals and the army, that's all the outside lawmen allowed by the Indians into the Nation."

"But the army keeps the Indians penned up here!" she objected.

"That ain't quite all the army does, ma'am. Mostly, it keeps the Indian Wars from starting up again. Not against us white folks," he said hastily, as Maidia was about to break in. "Indians have been fighting each other since way back before history began. But it's getting to the point now where the Osages will talk to the Cherokees, and a Kiowa

27

won't try to kill a Cheyenne on sight. Give them a little time, and they'll settle down like us, to a war every ten or fifteen years instead of just one war that goes on all the time."

Maidia studied Longarm's face for a moment, trying to decide whether he was joking or serious. Finally she said, "You really mean that, don't you, Marshal?"

"Why shouldn't I? It's the truth."

"You make the Indians sound so bloodthirsty."

"I wouldn't call them that, Miss Harkness. They just don't put on a lot of false fronts, the way we do."

"But I've always been taught—"

Longarm interrupted her. "I know what you were taught. Most of it was wrong. You'll see that, after you've been in the Nation awhile. No, ma'am, on the whole, there's not any better people than the Indians. Or smarter, or more truthful. An Indian gives you his word, he won't go back on it unless you go back on yours first."

"You're giving me new ideas, Marshal. I'll try to remember what you've said."

"You do that. But I reckon I've just about talked your ear off. If we're going to get started at daybreak, we better turn in."

Longarm busied himself with the fire, banking it for the night, to give Maidia a chance to go off into the bushes without her feeling that he was watching her. He heard her retreating footsteps and heard her returning, and quickly whirled back to the fire, bending to light a cheroot from a twig he picked up from its edge. He held the whiskey bottle out to her.

"I was just about to have my nightcap. You might as well take one, too. You'll sleep better if you do."

Obediently, she took a swallow of the liquor. Longarm smiled inwardly when he saw her drinking from the bottle, as he had, instead of looking for a cup. He drank his own goodnight tot, and proceeded to make his bedtime arrangements: boots laid flat and covered with his folded coat; his Ingersoll watch and chain, with the mean little derringer attached to the other end of the chain, tucked into a boot. He spread his vest flat by his left shoulder, laid his unholstered Colt on it, and covered the pistol with

28

his hat to shield it from the damp night air. He became aware that Maidia, already in her own bedroll, was watching his methodical preparations with a great deal of interest.

She said, "From the way you're arranging your things, Marshal, I get the idea you think those men might come back while we're asleep."

"They won't be coming back," he assured her. "One of them is dead, and two of the others have got bullet holes in them. But if they do show up, or if anybody else does, I'll be ready."

"So I see. That will make me sleep a lot better. Goodnight, Marshal Long."

"Goodnight, Miss Harkness."

Longarm watched through slitted eyes until he saw Maidia give up trying to gaze through the darkness. She looked in one direction, then in another, before she finally settled down to sleep. When her face settled into repose and her breathing became deep and even, Longarm closed his own eyes and relaxed. In no time at all, he was also asleep.

Chapter 3

Longarm might have been sleeping two minutes or two hours when Maidia's stifled, startled cry aroused him. He rolled out of his blankets, to his knees, in one swift motion, sweeping aside the hat that covered his Colt. In an instant, the revolver was in his hand. The banked fire gave off the very faintest glow. There was barely enough light for him to see Maidia. She was sitting up in her bedding. Her head was cocked, swiveling slowly from side to side as she peered into the darkness that surrounded them.

"What's the matter?" Longarm asked her.

"I heard something. A woman screaming somewhere, I think."

"Funny, I didn't hear it. And I count myself a light sleeper.

"Listen!" she said urgently.

He heard the sound then, from far off, a thin wail like the cry of a woman in agony. He said, "That's just a panther calling. It's too far off to smell us out."

"A panther? Isn't that a kind of lion?"

"They're cats," he replied. "Big cats. But they'll mostly let people alone unless they're starving, or unless somebody walks up on one unexpected."

Maidia shuddered. "It sounds so terrible! I've broken out in gooseflesh." She started to stand up, but changed her mind. "Where's the whiskey bottle, Marshal? I think I need some Dutch courage before I can go back to sleep."

"I'll hand it to you," Longarm said. "I'm already out of my bedroll."

He walked gingerly on bare feet to the log where the bottle was sitting, and handed it to Maidia. She drank, gulped, waited a moment, and drank again. Then she handed the bottle to Longarm.

"I'm sorry I woke you up. I guess I'm just nervous," she told him apologetically. "I think I'll be all right now, though."

"Sure you will. You'll drop right off back to sleep."

Longarm went to his own bedroll, rearranged the blankets, replaced the Colt on his vest, and covered it again with his hat. The wind had died as the night deepened. and it was no longer so cold. Just the same, he tossed a few sticks of wood on the fire, thinking the light might add to Maidia's peace of mind. Then he crawled back between the blankets. He'd hardly had time to settle down when Maidia called him again.

"Marshal?"

"I'm right here. What's troubling you?"

"Would you—" she hesitated for a moment— "Would you think I was being terrible if I asked to come over there with you?"

It was the last question Longarm had expected someone like Maidia Harkness to ask. He took his time in answering.

"If you're sure that's what you want to do," he told her.

"I'm sure. I know what I'm saying. I'm not a child."

"Come on over and welcome, then."

Maidia slipped out of her bedroll and pattered across the few feet that separated them. By the light of the freshened fire, Longarm could see that she'd left her skirt in her own blankets. She had on only a blouse that fell to her waist. Her molded thighs gleamed pink-white. She stood briefly beside his bedroll, and Longarm lifted the corner of his blanket. Maidia eased under it beside him.

"I don't need to apologize for asking to join you, do I? You're not the kind of man who'd expect that," she whispered.

"You don't need to apologize or explain or anything else," he told her. "Anybody's likely to feel nerved up the first time or two they try to sleep outdoors."

"I was all right until that panther yowled. I was dreaming—well, I won't tell you what I was dreaming."

"Like I said, you don't have to tell me anything."

31

Longarm was very conscious of the warmth that was reaching him from Maidia's nearly naked body. He wanted to reach out and touch her, but made no move to do so. He didn't want to do or say anything until he was sure what she had in mind.

"Maybe it was the dream as much as the panther that woke me up," she said softly. "But if it hadn't been for the panther, I might not have awakened and realized that I didn't have to be satisfied with just a dream."

Her hand crept out of the covers to caress Longarm's cheek. She ran her palm across his chin, his day-old beard rasping gently as she pressed harder. Then her fingers strayed up to explore the sweep of his mustache.

Not until Maidia's lips replaced her fingers did Longarm move to touch her in return. He brought one of his hands up from her knee, along the satin skin of her thigh and over her hip, and slid it under the edge of her loose blouse. His fingers brushed across her breast and found a nipple, hardening now, unfolding slowly until it stood firm and solid under his gently pinching fingertips.

"Oh, yes," she whispered. "Do that. And then some more." She rolled closer to him, and Longarm felt the weight of her thigh resting on his.

Maidia's tongue was pushing Longarm's lips apart, and he joined his tongue to hers. He was springing erect quickly. Her hand had left his face now, and was stroking his groin, feeling him grow hard under its grasp. Longarm released Maidia's breast long enough to thumb open the buttons of his fly and let her hand find his bare, throbbing flesh. She closed her hand around him, and he felt her body ripple in a small, satisfied shudder.

"I like what I've got in my hand," she said softly. "That's what I was dreaming about, you know."

"And then you woke up."

"Yes. But I know how the dream would have ended. And I'm glad I woke up when I did." Maidia squeezed him, not too gently. "This feels a lot better to me than any dream could."

"There's a way to make it feel better than it does now."

Longarm slid his hand between Maidia's thighs and fingered the warm wetness that was waiting for him there.

32

"Don't hurry me, Marshal. I'm enjoying hefting you right this minute, and the longer I wait, the more I'm going to like it when it gets to where it belongs." She shifted her head a bit and began nibbling on Longarm's earlobe.

"You take your time, Miss Harkness."

Maidia's laughter exploded in Longarm's ear. Between chortles, she said, "That sounds so funny, I can't help myself. Here we are, with me holding onto this beautiful thing for dear life, and you with your fingers in me, and I'm calling you Marshal Long and you're calling me Miss Harkness. Don't you think we ought to be a little bit more informal before we really get serious? You could call me Maidia, you know."

"I was waiting for you to tell me I could—Maidia."

"And you must have a first name?"

Maidia was tonguing Longarm's ear and squeezing him at the same time.

"It's Custis. But I don't answer to it much. Mostly, my friends call me Longarm."

"Not just of the law, either," she whispered. "Long something else, too, or my fingers are lying to me."

"You think you're about ready to find out if they are?"

"Yes." She positioned him. "Go ahead. Show me."

Longarm showed her, deliberately and slowly, pressing into her with neither haste nor hesitation, feeling her breath come faster as he penetrated more deeply until they were fully joined.

"Mmm," Maidia murmured in his ear. "No dream could ever equal what I feel now." She moved her hips from side to side. "Just lie still for a minute or two. I want to do it myself first. You won't get anxious, will you?"

"Not a bit. You do what you feel like doing. I can wait."

"I can't, though. I need to—" Maidia twisted more violently as she spoke— "I need to get my edge off so I can enjoy it more later." She was beginning to work her hips back and forth. "Then, when you get on me, I can— I can—" she shook in a long, shuddering convulsion— "I can hold on longer."

Her voice faded in a sighing murmur, and the tenseness of her muscles melted away. Longarm felt her wetness

33

trickling down his groin. He lay quietly for a few moments until Maidia sighed contendedly and stirred, then he rocked his own hips gently. She shifted her body to let him roll on top of her, and raised her thighs, locking her legs around his hips.

"You read my mind," she said. "Now make the dream I didn't finish come to life."

Longarm was in no hurry. He moved slowly, staying in her deeply, until her inner muscles began throbbing against him. Then he began to thrust, withdrawing slowly and returning fast. Maidia gasped the first time she felt him pounding into her, but as the moments passed and Longarm showed no signs of slowing his pace, her excitement grew. She brought her hips up to meet his thrusts, her body heaving and turning under his, until the pace grew too much for her to maintain. She sank back under his weight and let her legs fall, spreading them wide to receive his strokes, her head pressed hard into the ground, her neck arched, her chin high in the air.

Longarm stopped thrusting. "You want to rest awhile?"

"I'm resting," she said gustily. "You go on. This is the dream I don't want to wake up from, a man on top of me, making love to me like he'll never stop. Oh, I do love it, Longarm! But it's usually over so quickly that I miss the best part, just feeling a man big and hard in me while I lie back and enjoy it. You go on as long as you can. And you'll know when something wonderful's going to happen to me. Don't worry about that."

Longarm went on. As he continued, pounding deeply into her wet, hot depths, the very relaxation of Maidia's unresponsive body began to excite him. He felt himself building, and slowed to hold back. Maidia caught the change in his tempo.

"You're getting tired," she said. "Go on a little longer, if you can. I'm getting ready to come back to life."

Now Longarm no longer tried to keep from letting himself build. He was reaching the stage where he was about to lose control, when Maidia jerked under his pounding as though she had just awakened from a faint. She began to tremble. Her legs tensed and locked around his hips again. She rode with him as the pressure inside him

34

mounted and reached the bursting point. Longarm gave a few last, fierce plunges while Maidia screamed as the panther had screamed earlier. She shook, her hips heaving, her body writhing, as Longarm stiffened and fell forward with a sigh.

Neither Longarm nor Maidia spoke for several moments. Then she said, "I'm glad I spoke up, Longarm. I almost didn't, but I could see you weren't going to make any kind of advance toward me. You wouldn't have, would you?"

"Not after the bad time you had earlier, with that fellow trying to rape you."

"Well, that wasn't very good, of course. I don't like to be treated like a *thing*, and that's what he was doing. And I'm sorry I tore into you the way I did. It was stupid, but I didn't know what had really happened. But you must have forgiven me, or you'd have said no when I asked if I could come into bed with you."

"You're wrong, Maidia. I figured, at the first, you just needed to be with somebody for comforting. After all, a lady like you—"

"There aren't any ladies," Maidia interrupted. "Just women. And we've all got that tickle between our legs, just like you men have. Only most of you are honest about it. Most women aren't." She yawned. "I guess I'm ready to go back to sleep now. It's all right if I stay, isn't it?"

"Why, I ain't about to let go of you," Longarm said with a wide grin. "I want to be where you can reach me easy if that panther wakes you up again."

Maidia went to sleep quickly, her head resting on Longarm's sturdy shoulder. He lay awake for a while, wondering if the panther might scream again, and trying to figure out how he was going to manage to get to Fort Smith on time after promising Maidia he'd see that she found a guide to get her safely to Choteau. He gave that up, deciding to leave it to chance. Then his mind turned to the case he was on.

You got a real pig in a poke here, old son, he told himself for the tenth time since Vail had explained his assignment to him.

Just how in hell Billy expects me to come up with what

him and his Arkansas District friend wants is way past anything I can see. I've got a sneaking hunch that Arkansas chief marshal's just looking for somebody to blame when this business all goes up in smoke.

Vail had been unusually vague when he'd explained to Longarm why it was so important that he go to the Indian Nation. All he'd said was that there was a chance that whoever had been trying to spring Cole Younger from the federal pen in the Indian Nation had to be somebody close to the James gang, and might even be Jesse himself. Then, when Longarm had suggested that the Arkansas chief marshal had plenty of deputies who knew a lot more about the Nation than Longarm did, Vail had pulled rank and snapped, "Damn it, this is a case I'm putting you on, and I expect you to take it without any back-talk, just like any other case! Now, is that plain enough to suit you?"

"It couldn't be much plainer, Billy," Longarm had replied. "I still feel like it's something for the locals to handle, but if you want me to go to the Nation, that's where I'm heading."

"Fine. It's all settled, then," Vail had said curtly.

And that was that, Longarm thought. *Not like the way Billy's been before, when I could talk things out with him friendly. But there's something to this that he ain't told me yet. I'll just have to keep eating the old apple a bite at a time, and maybe I'll find out what it is when I get down to the core.*

He lay awake for a while after that, but the panther didn't scream again. After a while, Longarm went to sleep.

Sunrise found Longarm and Maidia Harkness halfway to Webbers Falls. They'd ridden, for the most part, in silence. Maidia was still tired from the harrowing events of the day before; she hadn't liked getting up in the dark and riding breakfastless except for a few bites of hard jerky. Longarm wasn't too happy, either. He faced losing a half-day of travel time in order to keep his promise to Maidia. That meant he'd have to push hard to make it up in getting on to Fort Smith. There, he knew, the chief marshal had already been notified, by a telegram from Vail, to expect him.

36

If it wasn't for that damn wire, he thought, looking at Maidia's sleepy face as she bobbed along on the horse beside him, *I'd be right tempted to turn around and go up to Choteau with her. Let the Arkansas deputies waste their time nosying around trying to get a smell of Jesse James's trail.*

Even while the thought was passing through his mind, Longarm knew he'd pull no such fool stunt. He'd never turned his back on his duty, and he wasn't about to start now, no matter how much of a fool's errand he figured an assignment to be.

Webbers Falls nestled on the west bank of the Arkansas, but a flat-bottomed ferryboat that plied between the two banks of the river got them safely across. On the ferry, Maidia asked Longarm, "What are you going to do about the mule and the two horses we seem to have acquired? They don't belong to us."

"They didn't, but it looks like they do now. Only not to us, Maidia. To you. You were the one paying the freight for the outlaws that ganged up on you. I'd say you're entitled to keep them, as sort of compensation for what they put you through."

"Would that be honest, Longarm?"

"I don't see why not. If you'd found a silver dollar in the road and there wasn't any way to prove it belonged to anybody, and you didn't know who'd passed that way, wouldn't you keep it?"

"Yes, I suppose I would."

"All right, then. Keep the horses and the mule. If you don't want them after you get where you're going, sell them off, or trade them. If you're real anxious to get shed of them, chances are I can fix up a swap with somebody in the town there to guide you where you're going and take one of the critters for his pay."

"You don't think I ought to turn them in to the police, then?"

"What police? You might see an Indian policeman in Choteau, but chances are that's the only law you'll run into between here and there."

"Go ahead and trade, then. It hadn't occurred to me that I'm going to need a horse for myself. And I suppose

37

the mule wouldn't be much trouble to keep, in this kind of country."

"Not if you're going to be working at an Indian school, it wouldn't. Well, we'll have to see what I can dicker out for you when we get ashore. But I don't suspicion there'll be much trouble."

Longarm's prediction turned out to be correct. Webbers Falls didn't offer much except a general store and a small sawmill powered by a waterwheel; the rest of the town consisted of a couple of dozen houses, mostly those of the families of men working at the sawmill. Longarm showed his badge to the proprietor of the store and described the kind of man he was looking for, and the job that needed to be done. The proprietor scratched his head for a moment.

"Guess Jared Phillips is the man you better talk to before you try anybody else. Jared traps up and down the rivers, so he'd know the land and the trails. And he's old enough so you wouldn't need to worry about him being flighty."

Jared Phillips wasn't just old, Longarm discovered; he was ancient—one of those wizened little men who seems to have an inexhaustible supply of energy, and appears destined to live forever. He was spry enough, though, and interested in taking on the job of guiding Maidia to Choteau in return for the spare horse.

"Yessir, Marshal, I'd be right glad to make a swap like that," he chirruped. "Trapping ain't much right now, and a horse'd sure be a help to me in winter, when I go to set out my lines. And I get along just fine with the Cherokee people. My last wife was Cherokee, which makes me sorta kin to 'em, I guess they figure. So I'll take on the job, if you and the lady agree."

Shortly after noon, having seen Maidia and her new escort safely on their way to Choteau, Longarm was ready to resume his own interrupted trip. He'd planned, when leaving Fort Gibson, on being able to get to Fort Smith in two full days of travel. He was running about a half-day behind. Still, he now thought he might be able to make up most of the lost time. By pushing on a little bit harder

38

than he'd planned, he had a chance of pulling into Fort Smith around midnight.

Unfortunately, his calculations didn't take ferry schedules into consideration. The last boat leaving the slip at Little Juarez on the west side of the Arkansas River pulled out at midnight, and he missed it by a full half-hour. He soon found that his luck wasn't altogether bad, though. There were always a few travelers who got to the slip just a little bit too late to catch the last ferry, and taking care of their needs between midnight and dawn had created a major industry in the settlement called Little Juarez, which had grown up around the landing.

Longarm found a saloon that not only had a good stock of prime Maryland rye, but a passable free lunch. There was a livery stable where he left his horse, and a barbershop that stayed open all night and offered hot baths in addition to the usual tonsorial services. A short stay at the saloon—just long enough to get a snack at the free lunch counter and three healthy shots of biting-good whiskey—prepared Longarm for an hour's soaking in a hot tub, followed by a shave and a trim in the barbershop. Then he had only another couple of hours to kill at the saloon, with all the ingredients at hand to make the killing of time a pleasant occupation.

When he led his horse off the ferryboat the next morning, Longarm felt fairly chipper. He mounted the animal for the short ride up Front Street to the old army headquarters building that had been turned into offices for the Arkansas Federal District. It was too early for Andy Gower, the chief marshal, to be in his office, so Longarm backtracked to a restaurant he'd noticed on the way to the federal building, where he dawdled over a leisurely breakfast and a succession of cups of chicory-laced coffee until he judged the hour was late enough. This time, he found Gower in his office, at a desk piled almost as high with paperwork as Billy Vail's always seemed to be.

Gower was a thin, rangy man with long eyebrows that hung down over chilly gray eyes set in a weatherbeaten face ending in a long lantern jaw. In defiance of the current style, he was clean-shaven. He wore a black-and-white checkered shirt with a puffed-out black cravat in which a diamond stickpin gleamed. A black Prince Albert coat, the mate to Longarm's, hung on a coat tree in one corner of the office, with a pistol belt looped over the hanger that supported the coat.

"You're Long, I suppose," Gower snapped before Longarm could introduce himself. "My clerk said you'd been here earlier, looking for me."

"That's right. It was a little bit early, I guess."

"Early, hell! You were supposed to be here yesterday. I guess you got in during the evening and spent the night tomcatting around the saloons and whorehouses instead of reporting in."

"Matter of fact, I got to the river too late to get on the last ferryboat. And I was too damn tired to report last night, even if I'd made it into town."

"All right, sit down." Gower pushed aside the papers he'd been working on. "Now that you're finally here, I suppose you're ready to go to work?"

Longarm traded stares with his temporary boss. Right at that moment, he'd decided that this case wasn't going to be one he'd enjoy working on. If the greeting he'd gotten from his temporary superior was a fair sample, Gower was a man he was prepared to dislike.

Chapter 4

"I came to work," Longarm replied at last. He kept his voice level and expressionless. "Billy Vail didn't give me a lot to go on. Only thing he said was that the grapevine's put Jesse James at some kind of outlaw hangout over in the Cherokee Nation."

"That's about all we've got," Gower affirmed. "I've been getting reports that there's a lot more activity than usual going on at Belle Starr's place. I guess you've heard about Belle? Calls herself the Bandit Queen?"

"I've heard her name, that's about all," Longarm answered. "And I know she operates in the Nation. But if you've got the time to pass on whatever I'd need to know about her and whoever she runs with, I'd sure like for you to."

Honey, old son, Longarm kept telling himself as he looked at Gower. *Honey catches more flies than vinegar.*

Gower had taken out a pouch of Bull Durham and papers, and was rolling himself a cigarette. He took his time, jogging the flakes of tobacco evenly, wrapping the paper tight, licking the seam, twisting the ends of the completed cylinder. Then he touched a match to the finished smoke. Longarm thought most of the men he'd ever seen smoking cigarettes looked sissified; he noted with mild surprise that Gower did not. Just the opposite, in fact.

Longarm countered by extracting a cheroot from his vest pocket and lighting it. The blue smoke from the cigar and the white, acrid smoke from the cigarette began to fume up the office, and, after a few moments, Gower started talking.

"There's a chance you might have heard about Belle Starr by another name. Belle's had so damn many names

41

since she started out that I don't think she remembers all of them herself. You ever heard of a woman bandit that called herself Belle Reed? Or Belle Shirley? Or maybe even Belle Younger?"

Longarm shook his head. "I must've missed all them names. It's the same Belle, though, I take it?"

"Same Belle," Gower nodded. He took a final drag on the cigarette and exhaled a cloud of thin smoke, then tossed the butt into a cuspidor that stood handy at the corner of his desk. "Since you're new to this district, I suppose the first thing to do is to go back to the beginning."

"Might be, at that." Longarm settled himself back to listen.

"As far as my boys and I have been able to find out," the chief marshal began, "Belle's real name is Myra Belle Shirley. At least, that's how she started life. Her folks were from Missouri, up somewhere around Carthage, which would make them neighbors to the Jameses and the Youngers. Matter of fact, there's some kind of connection between the Shirleys and the Youngers—second cousins twice removed, or something—one of those vague family things that goes back God knows how many years since there was any close kinship. But the Youngers stayed in Missouri when the Shirleys moved to Texas, sometime back in the late sixties or early seventies. Belle's folks still live up in North Texas, somewhere around Fort Worth or Dallas."

"That'd explain how Belle got tied up with Cole Younger, then?" Longarm asked when Gower paused to start rolling another cigarette. "And you and Billy happened onto the connection when you went to talk to Cole Younger in the pen at Stillwater?"

"Damn it, Long, don't start guessing!" Gower snapped. "I knew about the connection before we talked to Cole Younger. Belle claims she was married to Cole when she was just a young girl, and she makes no bones about telling everybody Cole's the daddy of her daughter Pearl. Pearl's about eleven or twelve years old now. I guess you know that Cole was one of Jesse James's bunch before he got caught and landed in the pen."

42

"I don't have to guess about that," Longarm said shortly. "Everybody knows it."

"I suppose so. Well," Gower went on, "Belle had a whole string of husbands—or men she said were her husbands—after Cole pulled out of Texas and went back with the James gang. The thing is, Belle can't seem to get Cole Younger out of her craw. Maybe that's because, as far as we can tell, he's the first man that ever got to her. It happened that time when Cole and Jesse were visiting with the part of the Younger family that had moved to Texas and were living close to Belle's folks."

"Billy Vail told me somebody's been trying real hard to get Cole sprung out of the pen," Longarm said. "I got the idea that's one reason you two went to talk to him. You were afraid he might get out and join up with Jesse again."

"No, damn it, no! We went to offer to let Younger out if he'd lead us to where Jesse and Frank are hiding right now. You know the prison grapevine, Long. I'm dead sure Younger could lead us to the James boys' hideout. But he won't. Said so, flat out. But you are right about one thing. It *is* Belle Starr who's been trying to get Cole sprung. She's been working at that ever since he got locked up. Even while she was married to Jim Reed and Blue Duck and whoever else she was really married to before she hitched up with Sam Starr. And she's still trying, right this minute."

"Blue Duck would be one of Belle's husbands, I guess? Sounds to me like he's an Indian."

"*Was* Indian. Cherokee. So was her first husband—not counting Cole Younger, that is. Right after Cole left Texas, she married this breed, Jim Reed. And Starr's part Cherokee, too."

"I'd say Belle's got a soft spot for Indian studs," Longarm observed with a smile.

"She's got a soft spot—and it's right between her legs—for any man with a hard to poke in it," Gower said.

"You think Jesse James ever poked into it?"

"He probably did, if she got him off alone with her," Gower replied. Then he added, "When you come right down to it, Long, the only time we're sure Belle ever saw Jesse was when Cole Younger took him to Texas on that visit he made to his family. And since it was that time when Cole and Belle first met, I doubt that Jesse had a look-in. There's a rumor that Jesse hid out for a while at Belle's place over in the Nation when she first moved there, but that's the kind of rumor you come to look for when you're dealing with the James boys. Shit! It wouldn't surprise me if somebody started a rumor that Jesse's disguised himself and got a job as one of my deputies!"

"I guess folks are willing to believe almost anything about the Jameses," Longarm commented.

"Looks that way," Gower agreed. "To get back to what I was telling you, Jim Reed got killed in a shootout down in Texas, and Blue Duck married Belle—or the other way around—and a little while after that, Blue Duck got bushwhacked and killed. Then Belle took up with a bad one by the name of Jack Spaniard, but he made some mistakes that put him on the wrong end of a hangman's rope. Her last one before Sam Starr was a burglar, Jim French, but he got shot while he was trying to break into a store. That brings us up to when Belle married Sam Starr."

Longarm's whistle when Gower paused was low and long-drawn. "I'd say the lady really has bad luck with the men she picks out. If she was to wag her butt my way, I'd pass her by."

"If you had any sense, you'd do that after you took one look at her," Gower told him. "Now, Sam Starr's part Cherokee, as I mentioned. He's got a land allotment from the tribe down at the south end of the Cherokee Strip, on the Canadian, close to a little town called Eufaula. That's where he and Belle make their headquarters now. They call it Younger's Bend."

"Named for Cole Younger, I take it?"

"Oh, I'm sure Belle picked out the name. I told you, she's still got a soft spot for Cole. They've built a house there, and a few cabins. Our trouble is, the lay of the land makes it just about impossible for us to watch the place. The river's on one side, with high bluffs running down to the water, the house on top of the bluffs, and a little narrow valley the only way to get to the place. Maybe you'll be better than my boys at figuring out a way to scout the place when you get there."

44

Longarm said mildly, "I didn't know I was going there."

"You do now," Gower retorted.

"It's all the same to me, where I go," Longarm said levelly. "Or who I bring in. What's this Belle Starr wanted for?"

Gower snorted, "Hell! I don't want Belle. She's a nobody, and so is Sam. They're out now on bail on a cattle-rustling charge. If I wanted them, I'd just have them picked up. That's the biggest charge I could hold them on, though. No, Long, it's that bunch of crooks who use the Starr place as a hideout that I'm after. Half the men on my wanted list right now work out of Younger's Bend. About all Belle does is give them a safe place to hide out and help them get rid of what they steal."

"She's a fence, then, instead of a bandit queen?"

"Of course. If I wanted Belle, I could have her picked up any time she rides into Fort Smith on that big black horse she fancies. Oh, Belle puts on a real show! Dolls herself up in a long velvet dress, wears a pair of ivory-handled, silver-plated Smith & Wessons. But it's all blow and no go with Belle, except when it comes to getting rid of the loot her boarders bring in."

"It'd help if I knew what kind of loot she deals in," Longarm suggested.

"Cattle, mostly," Gower replied. "Some jewelry and trinkets from burglaries and stagecoach stickups. Except for the cattle, Belle doesn't handle much but penny-ante stuff. The owlhoots that use Younger's Bend as a hideout —well, that's another matter. They're waist-deep in damn near everything. Bank robberies, train holdups, stagecoach stickups, rustling, you name it. Belle's only dangerous because she provides them with a place to hole up between jobs, and helps them get rid of what they've stolen."

"If the place is as bad as you say, it looks to me like your best bet would be just to go in with a good force and clean it out," Longarm suggested. "After all, it's in your jurisdiction."

"I didn't ask you for advice, Long. Apparently you don't know much about our jurisdictional problem in this district. You ought to, damn it. Billy told me you'd had some assignments in the Nation."

45

"Two or three. Sure, I know the Indian police force has got the primary jurisdiction, and they don't like outside lawmen coming in, even when they're federals, like we are. I've run into that in the cases I've handled there. I know that about the only time we can go into the Indian Nation without being invited is when we're on a chase after some owlhoot who's just committed a crime covered in federal statutes."

"That's the shitty part of it!" Gower growled. "So far, we haven't had a chance to go after any of the Younger's Bend bunch in a hot-pursuit situation. But there's more to the Younger's Bend mess than that. Sam Starr or Belle— and I guess it was Belle's idea, because she's got most of the brains—worked out some kind of deal with the Cherokee Tribal Council. Belle calls it a treaty, which would put Younger's Bend on a level with the U.S. as an independent nation. The treaty says that the Younger's Bend bunch won't pull off anything in the Cherokee Strip if the Indian Police will leave them alone. Hell, Long, I'll never get an invitation from the police over there to come in, as long as that agreement stands!"

For the first time, Longarm felt a flicker of sympathy for Gower. He said thoughtfully, "I see the kind of bind you're in, but I sure hope you're not looking to me to work it out for you."

"If I can't work it out as chief marshal, I don't see how you could as a deputy on temporary assignment here," Gower replied impatiently. "That's not why I asked Billy to send me his top man, Long. I've talked to you enough now so I feel safe in telling you the real reason you're here."

"Thanks. I'd sort of like to hear it."

Gower went to the door of his office, opened it, and looked both ways along the corridor. He came back and sat down. Leaning over his desk, he dropped his voice and said, "That bunch at Younger's Bend is in so many things and gets away with so much that I've got a suspicion a bunch of local marshals and sheriffs are in cahoots with them."

"You mean they're being paid off?"

"That's exactly what I mean. Belle's like any other

46

fence, Long. She's got to have room to work in. The only way a fence can buy that kind of room is by paying off somebody to look the other way when she's making her deals. And once a man on our side of the law begins taking payoffs, it's not long before he's taking money to be out of town when a gang rides in to rob a bank. It starts with the fence, but it's not long in spreading."

"I ain't aiming to embarrass you, Marshal Gower," Longarm said carefully. "But I'd be interested in knowing how far it's spread."

Gower stared at Longarm, his face set grimly. He dropped his voice as he answered. "Yes, you're right, Long. You do need to know how far it's gone. Well, I've got a suspicion, without a damned shred of evidence to back it up, that some of my own deputies have sold out to Belle Starr and her gang."

Longarm studied Gower's face for a moment, trying to find some expression in the chief marshal's pale eyes. There was none, but Gower's face had undergone a subtle change. His long chin was no longer outthrust pugnaciously, and his bushy brows were not pulled together in a scowl now.

Before Longarm could say anything, Gower went on, "That's what I want you to find out, Long. If my suspicions are right, I've got to clean up my own office here before I can do anything about that running sore over in the Nation. And I had to find out whether you could keep yourself in hand when the going gets rough before I was sure you were the man to help me do the job."

"But you've made up your mind now?" Longarm asked.

"Yes. I'm sorry for the bad time I gave you when we first began talking. But you'll understand, I had to know what kind of man you are before I could open up and tell you the whole story."

For several minutes Longarm said nothing. He was digesting the fact that the rough reception he'd gotten had been Gower's way of testing him out, making sure he'd be able to put a curb on his tongue and a rein on his temper when he was taking a rawhiding.

Finally he said, "No offense taken, Marshal Gower. I guess it was about the only way you had to check me out."

"It was the only way I could see. Now the air's cleared between us. How do you feel about it?"

"Better than I did for a while there. I'm just trying to figure out where my starting place is. You don't know if all your men are straight, or who the sell-outs might be, if there are any. So what I've got on my plate is to find out who the rotten apples are."

"I wish I didn't have to agree with you, Long, but I do. I've watched my men for the past four or five months, since things first started going sour. Prisoners escaping, evidence not brought in, witnesses dropping out of sight. It smells, but I can't get down to the source of the stink. You know how easy it is for an honest mistake by a deputy to cause a case to go sour."

Longarm answered. "I guess I ought to. I've made some mistakes like that, now and again."

"Well, that's not what Billy tells me, but we won't go into that. The point is that I can't accuse one of my own deputies of being paid off by Belle unless I've got absolute, ironclad proof. I'm in pretty much the same spot when it comes to accusing a town marshal or a sheriff or sheriff's deputy. If I'm not sure, I can't do anything but keep quiet, no matter what I might suspect."

"Sure. I can see that. It's about the only fair way a man in your position could act. From what Billy's told me, you've got some pretty good men on your force here."

"Of course I have. And it looks like I've got a few bad ones, too," Gower said. He hesitated before adding, "Look here, Long, I know this is a hell of a job for me to ask you to take on. You'll see why I can't turn any of my boys loose on it, though. I've been tempted to, but there's always the chance that I might pick out the wrong one and blow the whole deal to hell."

"That's as good a reason as I can see for holding off," Longarm concurred.

"Billy Vail's the only one I've talked to about it. I used that rumor about Jesse James trying to buy Cole Younger's way out of the pen to give me a reason for meeting Billy in Stillwater, where we could talk without worrying about somebody overhearing," Gower said. "I was surprised, though. Billy took my Jesse James story seriously."

48

"I can tell you why that was," Longarm said. "Billy found out that Jesse and Frank James and three of their men hid out right under his nose, not fifty miles from Denver, over around Leadville, a while back. He never has got over missing that chance to take them."

"Funny," Gower frowned. "I never heard about that."

"Billy damn sure wouldn't mention it," Longarm said. "There wasn't any way he could've known the Jameses were in his territory, of course. They didn't pull any jobs, and nobody'd ever have known who they were if some old friend of theirs from Missouri hadn't spotted them. But he kept quiet until they'd been gone three or four months."

"I'll sure have to josh Billy about that, the next time I see him," Gower said. He smiled for the first time. "I can see how it'd rankle on him, of course, knowing he had Jessse in reach and missing him."

"Hell, it rankles on me a little bit, too," Longarm told Gower. "But I guess anybody on the right side of the law would relish a chance to meet up with James and his gang."

"Well, I don't expect you to find Jesse James at Younger's Bend, Long. Still, if the old story's true and Jesse actually did use Belle's place as a hideout once, there's the outside chance that he might come back there."

"I won't count on it. Fact of the matter is, I don't see that I can count on much of anything. The only thing I'm hoping is that I don't run into some owlhoot I've brought in someplace else, somebody who might recognize me."

"I've thought about that, too. That's one of the things that makes me feel I'm asking you to stick your neck into a noose on my account. And that's why I'm not giving you any orders or instructions, Long. From what Billy's told me, you've got your own way of handling your cases, and I wouldn't want to cramp your style. I don't expect you to report to me until the case is closed, but you know that if you get into a bind, I'll do whatever I can to get you out of it."

Longarm lighted another cheroot before replying. Puffing out a cloud of smoke, he said thoughtfully, "I guess the only way to start eating an apple is to take the first bite, and that's to see how the land lays at Younger's Bend. You say it's right on the Canadian River?"

Gower nodded. "Just to the southeast of a little town called Eufaula. It's a long day's ride from here, but if you get an early start—"

"Now, I sure don't aim to set out today. I had a bellyful of horseback travel getting here from Fort Gibson, and all the sleep I got last night was in a bathtub at that little place by the ferryboat landing across the river."

Gower pulled open a drawer of his desk and took out a drawstring pouch made of buckskin. He tossed it across the desk. The pouch landed in front of Longarm with a metallic clunk.

"I told Billy I'd be responsible for your expenses while you're on this case. Too damn much red tape, routing requisitions through the Denver office, and you can't be running in here every week or so to fill out vouchers. There's five hundred in gold in that bag." Longarm's eyebrows rose as Gower continued, "Bring back what you don't use and write one voucher on what you've spent when the case is closed. I won't argue about how big the voucher is."

"Thanks." Longarm nodded. "I'll make sure you get good value."

"I know you will," Gower replied. "Now, anything else you need?"

"Oh, I picked up an ordnance map before I took off from Fort Gibson. It's old, but it shows the hills and streams, and that's all I need to get me by." Longarm stood up. "I'll be moving, then, Marshal Gower. You'll hear from me when you hear from me, I guess, but don't look for it to be anytime soon."

"Whenever you get a chance to send word," Gower said. "And good luck, Long." Somewhat grimly, he added, "I'm pretty sure you'll need it."

On the boardwalk outside the federal building, Longarm stood for a moment, taking stock. All he really needed was sleep. He mounted and started to look for a hotel. As he headed down Front Street, an idea struck him. His business in Fort Smith was finished, and if he wanted to get an early start for Younger's Bend tomorrow, he'd have to take the last ferry across the Arkansas before midnight, or delay his start until the first boat made the crossing, and that wouldn't be until six the next morning.

There ain't any reason for me to waste the best part of a day, he told himself. *That little town over across the river in the Nation's got all I need, and the saloon there pours as good a Maryland rye as any I'm likely to find here in Arkansas.*

Instead of continuing toward the buildings of Fort Smith, he reined the horse around in the middle of the deserted street and headed back in the direction of the ferry landing.

That river's got to be crossed sooner or later, old son, he thought as his army mount clattered over the brick-paved street, *And it won't be one inch narrower tomorrow morning than it is right now.*

Chapter 5

Longarm's mental alarm clock jerked him into wakefulness. It was still pitch dark, and the room in the small hotel he'd found in Little Juarez was totally silent. There was no sound beyond the door leading to the hallway, no rumbling of wagon wheels or clumping of hooves was audible through the half-open window.

Reaching for his vest, draped over the back of a chair pulled close to the bed, Longarm fingered his watch from its pocket and snapped open the case before lighting one of the matches he'd laid beside the base of the lamp that stood in the seat of the chair. The watch confirmed the message his mind had sent him. It was four o'clock—time to be up and on the trail. By the time he'd dressed, had a quick breakfast, and picked up the horse he'd rented at the livery stable around the corner from the hotel, dawn would be slitting the eastern sky.

He lifted the lamp chimney and touched the match to the wick before the flame got to his fingertips. Light bathed the room. He sat on the edge of the bed, stretching, then reached for the bottle of Maryland rye he'd bought at the saloon before turning in the night before. A full day of sleep the preceding day, and a long, restful night on top of that, had erased the dragged-out feeling he'd had after his talk with Andrew Gower, and the healthy swig of rye he swallowed swept the last vestiges of cobwebs from his brain.

Longarm's gray flannel shirt hung on the right-hand headpost of the bed, his covert-cloth trousers under it. His holstered Colt dangled on the bedpost opposite, where it would be handy if he was forced to reach for it while in bed.

He fastened the top buttons of his balbriggans, slid his arms into his shirt and buttoned it, shoehorned himself into his skintight trousers, then stomped into his stovepipe cavalry boots before standing up.

Before going out to supper last night, Longarm had cleaned his guns—Winchester, Colt, and derringer—and reloaded them with fresh ammunition, but he took a bit of extra time in getting the set of his cross-draw gunbelt completely right. In Longarm's book, a gun was useless baggage if a man had to fumble for it when he needed it in a hurry. Satisfied after a few practice draws, he donned his vest and coat, picked up his Winchester and saddlebags, and went out into the dark morning.

The saloon, restaurant, barber shop, and general store were lighted and taking care of trade. Longarm ignored the saloon. He had the partly finished bottle of rye in his saddlebag, as well as an unopened bottle he'd bought to take along.

A half-dozen vehicles were lined up along the street in front of the cafe: wagons, a buggy, a buckboard, and a surrey. He could see the tarpaulin-covered forms of sleepers in two of the wagon beds, and on one of the surrey's seats, a blanket-wrapped figure wriggled restlessly as Longarm's booted heels thudded on the board sidewalk on his way to the restaurant.

With breakfast behind him, Longarm headed for the livery stable. The attendant recognized him from the day before, and hurried out to the still-dark corral to get the hammerhead bay that Longarm had picked out the day before. The cavalry mount, with its giveaway brand, would be waiting when he got back from Younger's Bend. Having put his saddlebags, bedroll, and rifle in their places, Longarm set his hat a bit more firmly on his head and started west along the riverbank. The first line of dawn brightened the sky just enough to show the well-beaten trail as he set out.

Steadily the light grew brighter as the sky behind Longarm went from gray to baby-pink to sunrise scarlet, and then, in one swift burst, became molten gold. The sunrise warmed his back as the hammerhead bay, fresh from the

53

corral, high-stepped briskly through the dew-wet grasses, not yet turned brown by the first winds of autumn, that bordered the rutted trace. Summer had apparently returned, if only for a brief visit, after the day of gray skies and cold warning winds that he'd ridden through on his way from Fort Gibson. The air warmed steadily as the sun crept up the sky, and when the trail parted from the river an hour after sunrise, Longarm reined in to shed his coat and roll it up in his bedroll.

He took advantage of the stop to study the ordnance map again. It was easy to see where he was at the moment. The dotted line that marked the trace went almost due east, while the Arkansas swept in an arc to the south a few miles from the mouth of the Canadian. There, river and road came together again. The road stayed with the Arkansas for a short distance, then it forked at a ford. The north road followed the Arkansas, and the eastern fork crossed the river and ran on a course roughly parallel to the snakelike bed of the Canadian. Longarm wondered which of the loops in the snake's belly was Younger's Bend.

Shortly before noon he came to the juncture of the rivers. He reined in, wondering if he'd save time by swimming the bay across the river here and picking up the eastern road where it curved along the Canadian, but a long, calculating look at the roiled green surface of the stream convinced him that the risk wasn't worth the little time he'd save.

Besides which, he thought, *there ain't all that much need to hurry. I'll get there when I get there, and Belle Starr sure ain't going to wait supper for me.* He poked the bay with his boot toe, and the animal moved ahead.

A mile or so above the river fork, he came to the ford. It was marked only by the wheel ruts which showed where wagons had pulled off the trace and turned toward the river. When he got to the stream, he saw pairs of stakes driven into the shore on both sides to mark the location of the submerged crossing. Between the stakes on both sides, the ocher earth was cut up by grooves and packed with the half-moons of hooves everywhere he looked between the markers. The hammerhead bay took to the

54

water easily, feeling its way with surprising daintiness through the murky green water along an invisible bottom.

Beyond the ford, the trace bore the signs of fewer wagons and more horses, but was still easy to follow. It meandered through the groves of towering cottonwood and broad-trunked sweet gum, through patches of scrub oak that came barely to Longarm's waist as he sat in the saddle. Here and there, the bright green clumping of crackwillows marked a spring, a brooklet, or a patch of moist ground. A few of the brooks trickled across the road; none of them was wider than a man could step across, or deeper than a few inches, but the soft tinkle of running water making its way to the Canadian River broke the silence of the early afternoon.

Longarm ate in the saddle, chewing bits of jerky shaved off as he rode, moistened with a mouthful of water. He alternated the jerky with a few kernels of parched corn, and topped off his snack with a few dried prunes before lighting a cheroot and settling down for the long afternoon that lay ahead.

On two occasions, he turned off the trace where hooves had beaten a fainter trace toward the Canadian. He had no idea where Younger's Bend was located, except that it bordered the riverbank. The two trails he followed led to fords, not houses. He stopped at each of the crossings to breathe his horse and get the stiffness out of his own thigh muscles by dismounting and walking along the riverbank. He walked with a purpose other than exercise, though. There were so many bends in the Canadian that the high bluffs predominating along its northern bank could be seen far upstream—a series of humps diminishing in size with distance, but visible enough to show signs of settlement where any such signs existed.

He wasn't sure he'd come far enough east to reach Younger's Bend yet, but so far he'd passed no towns or settlements, or even a farm or ranch house where he could stop and ask. There had been a few threads of smoke visible on the south side of the Canadian at each of the two places where he'd ridden from the trace down to the river, but even on the more level, gently rolling land south of the stream, he hadn't gotten a clear view of any houses

55

close enough to justify a visit. Each time, he'd ridden back to the main trace and continued east.

When he reached the third trail that forked south toward the river, Longarm reined in and sat in the saddle, studying the trail for several minutes. This one seemed a bit more distinct than the two he'd explored earlier. The forking was clearer, the ground around it beaten almost bare by hoofprints, the grass beside the trace shorter, as though more horses had grazed on it. Absently, moving his hands by habit rather than consciously, Longarm lighted a cheroot while he studied the trail. It led to a thick stand of scrub oak, and he could not see past the thicket. Still not committed in his mind to following the new trail to the river, Longarm twitched the reins to the left and the hammerhead bay walked slowly along the narrow path.

Beyond the stand of oaks, the trail remained clearly marked. Longarm's interest increased. He rode on, following the hoof-trodden line as it wound between cottonwood and sweet gum, skirted a rock outcrop, crossed an old burn almost bare of vegetation, and plunged again into a thicket of oaks dotted with still more gum trees and cottonwood. He was on rising ground now. The undergrowth thinned to isolated trees as the upward pitch of the slope grew sharper. The trail zigzagged up the rise and dipped on the other side into a narrow valley where it turned to follow its floor.

Here there was barely room for two riders to go abreast, and the trail thinned and became more sharply defined. Longarm reined in at a wide spot and dismounted. To his experienced eyes, the trail had the marks of the kind of approach he'd been looking for, one that was both easy and difficult, a trail that passed through cover for defenders, if the need arose to stand off intruders. Above all, in its passage through the narrow valley, the trail seemed planned to string out any group of men and horses in a way that would allow a relatively small group to bar their passage.

Old son, he told himself, *this is the likeliest spot you've hit. Somebody planned this trail, it didn't just grow up accidental. And even if there ain't no guarantee you're*

56

going to hit pay dirt at the end of it, you better strip down and be ready, just in case you do.

When he'd shed his coat, Longarm had transferred his wallet, with his marshal's badge pinned inside, to his hip pocket. He fished the wallet out now, and dropped his trousers. By letting them down almost to the tops of his closely fitting cavalry boots, he managed to slip the wallet down inside a trouser leg and below the level of the boot top. Pulling up his pants, he inspected the leg. There was no bulge, and the edge of the wallet wouldn't be felt by anybody searching him for a sheath knife or a small-caliber concealed pistol.

He climbed back in the saddle and continued along the trail. It turned south at a cleft in the valley wall. Like the valley through which Longarm had ridden earlier, the opening was wide enough for only a single horseman. When Longarm entered the steep fissure, he saw unmistakable signs on both of its bare dirt sides that bushes and saplings had been uprooted from it in the recent past. The small amount of new growth that struggled to survive on the steep walls was thin and spindly. Nowhere was there enough vegetation to give a man protective cover.

It was planned, all right, Longarm assured himself, noting the barren walls of the defile as he rode deeper into it. *Three or four men posted with rifles up there on the crests could stand off a good-sized army. I don't wonder that Gower's been shying away from bringing in a posse to clean this place up, if it's the place I'm looking for. And it's sure beginning to look like it is.*

The narrow defile ended abruptly. Longarm reined in at its mouth and studied the scene that now lay revealed.

A clearing stretched in front of him. It was roughly oval in shape and something more than a half-mile across at its widest point, which was several hundred yards from the cleft through which Longarm had just passed; the ravine split the low, steep hills that concealed this stretch of level ground. The rise swept in an arc behind him, to both left and right. Somewhere ahead, the level land ended abruptly. Longarm couldn't see the actual ending, but it looked to him as though the flat, clear area stopped at the rim of a

57

sheer cliff, and he guessed that cliff must drop down to the Canadian River.

Trees dotted the clearing; they were widely spaced at its center and more distant edges, thicker as the ground began to rise in the slope that enclosed the place. Among the trees were stumps that had been left when the land was cleared. Centered in the level area, a house stood in the middle of about an acre of ground that had been completely cleared of stumps and trees. The house was neither large nor fancy. It stood on a low fieldstone foundation, and was built from squared timbers chinked with clay. If it had any windows, they were on the other side of the structure. The side facing Longarm was unbroken by windows or a door. A fieldstone chimney rose at one end, and at the other, a pole barn—no more than a roof with widely spaced boards nailed to the supporting posts— nestled close to the house.

Longarm nodded when he saw the arrangement. He told himself, *Old son, you hit the right place. Farmers and ranchers always put their animals away from the house, where the flies won't bother folks inside. Outlaws want their barn close, so they can get to their horses in a hurry in case of trouble.*

Between the house and the slope behind it, stripped saplings had been driven into the ground between the living trees to form two irregular enclosures. One was sizable, and Longarm judged it to be a corral, though it was big enough to pen up a small herd of cattle. The second enclosure, much smaller, held half a dozen hogs. Here and there chickens wandered, scratching the dirt.

Behind one corner of the house he could see the low rise of a well curb. Still farther away stood an outhouse, and at an even greater distance, between the house and the edge where the land dropped away, there were three small cabins. Like the house, they were built from squared timbers and chinked with clay, and, like the house, they appeared to be windowless. All the wood of all the buildings —house, cabins, outhouse, barn—was raw; none of it had ever been painted. All the structures had weathered to a uniform gray, and irregular streaks of red clay chinking glowed in narrow swatches against the gray wood.

There was no one in sight in the clearing, though a plume of gray smoke rose from the chimney of the house. Smaller threads of gray came from the tin stovepipes that protruded from the sides of two of the cabins and dog-legged up above their cedar-shake roofs. As Longarm studied the clearing, his sharp eyes picked up still another line of smoke rising from an area deep in the trees, beyond the staked enclosures, toward the hills. Whatever the source of that smoke might be, it was hidden from Longarm by the trees, which had not been thinned like the stands around the house.

Having fixed locations and directions in his mind, Longarm toed the bay into motion and headed for the house. The horse had taken only a few slow steps when a man came through the trees. He was bent over with the weight of his load; in each hand he carried a large wooden bucket by its bail. He did not see Longarm, but moved at an angle away from him, toward the hogpen. Longarm changed course and started for the same destination. He'd covered half the distance between them before the other looked up and noticed him.

Longarm was close enough now to get a clear view of the stranger. He was an old man, wearing a fringe of grizzled white beard, and now it was obvious that age as much as his load was causing his forward-bending posture. He set the buckets down and waited for Longarm to rein in. Even before Longarm got close enough to pull the bay to a halt, his nose twitched at the sour smell of corn mash coming from the buckets.

Pulling up a yard from the oldster, Longarm said, "I guess I've found the right place. Is this Younger's Bend?"

"Yep." The old man was squinting through bloodshot blue eyes, trying to make out Longarm's features. He swayed as he lifted his head, leaned back, and threw out his arms to keep from falling. It was obvious that he was more than a little bit drunk. He asked, "Looking for somebody, are you?"

"If this is Younger's Bend, I am."

"Told you it is. Now, who you looking for?"

"Depends on who's at home."

"Well, I'm here, for one; you can see that. Ain't expect-

59

ing callers, though. Mind telling me who you come to see?"

"Yes."

When Longarm said no more, the oldtimer continued, "Yes, meaning you mind?"

Again Longarm made no reply.

"Well, then," the man suggested, "tell me who in hell you are and if anybody's expecting you."

"Not now."

Shaking his head as though to clear it, the oldster took a step toward Longarm. One of his feet hit the bucket closest to him and he almost fell down. Only reaching to grab at Longarm's leg saved him. He swayed uncertainly for a moment, then looked up at Longarm.

"Damned if I don't recall your face from someplace," he said, frowning. "Black Hills country, maybe?"

Longarm shook his head.

"Alder Gulch, then."

Again Longarm shook his head.

"Tascosa?" This time the old fellow didn't wait for a negative headshake before asking, "Mariposa?"

"No."

"Damned if you ain't the closest-mouthed son of a bitch I ever run into!" the gaffer exploded in angry frustration. "I guess I was wrong about seeing you afore. I'd sure remember anybody that said nothing at all! Like a fellow I knew up on the Platte. He never talked much, either. We called him Windy. You ain't him, though."

"No. But Windy'll do, for now."

Longarm spoke abstractedly. He didn't remember having seen the old boozehound before, but he'd brought in a lot of men, and this one would probably look different if he was younger, shaved, and sober.

"They call me Yazoo," the old fellow said. "And there's nobody at the house right now but Sam. Steed and McKee have rode into town with Belle, but they oughta be getting back pretty quick. It's close to suppertime. Bobby and Floyd's down in the cabin, if it's one of them you're looking for."

"I'll wait for Belle," Longarm said.

"Figured you would. If you'll wait till I pour this mash in the hog trough, I'll walk over to the house with you."

Longarm swung out of his saddle. "I'll give you a hand. That's a pretty good load."

Slopping hogs wasn't Longarm's idea of a job fit for a grown man, but he wanted to take the closest possible look at Yazoo. He picked up one of the buckets and walked beside the old man to the hogpen. He stood back while Yazoo poured the mash into the trough, though. The smell that had filled his nose while he carried the mash was enough to last him for a while.

"I guess it wouldn't do no good to ask where you rode in from?" Yazoo prodded him as they walked toward the house.

"No." Longarm was leading the bay, but giving Yazoo a good eyeballing in an unobtrusive way.

"Damn it, Windy, you're with friends here. You don't have to be so close-mouthed." When Longarm made no answer, Yazoo shook his head. "I'm still sure I've run across you someplace, only I can't locate you in my mind. Maybe it'll come to me later on. Where-all you been, Windy?"

"Here and there."

"All right, damn it!" Yazoo snorted. "Don't open up! It ain't no skin off my ass. Belle's going to want to know, though. She's right particular about who she lets stay here."

"Then maybe I won't stay."

"You'll stay," Yazoo said positively. "Else you never would've come here."

They reached the house and rounded its corner. There were windows on this side, glassless, but with wooden shutters. A narrow porch with a shed roof extended along the front of the house, and through the open door Longarm could see someone moving around inside. With the sun at his back now, he could also see into the barn, where three or four horses and several mules paced around in the dimness under the high roof. Longarm saw no hitch rail, so he led the bay over to the barn and looped the reins around one of the supporting posts. When he turned back to face the house, there was a man standing on the porch, covering him with a rifle. Longarm noticed that brass-headed tacks had been driven into its stock to form a star.

Longarm spread his arms wide, his hands at shoulder level. "I reckon you'd be Sam Starr," he said mildly.

"I reckon. And just who in hell are you?"

"Aw, this is Windy," Yazoo said. "You don't need to worry about him, Sam. He's all right. I recognize him from someplace, leastwise I think I do. We been chinning it up by the hogpen."

"You didn't ask him here, did you?" Starr asked Yazoo.

"A'course not. He's looking for Belle."

"So are a lot of people." Starr turned to Longarm. "Is Yazoo telling it straight? You know him?"

"He says I do. I'm like him, though. His face looks familiar, but I disremember where I saw him last."

Slowly Starr lowered the gun. "Windy? Is that your name?"

"It's good enough for me to travel under," Longarm replied. He didn't ask Starr's permission to lower his arms, just let them settle down slowly. When Starr made no objection, Longarm asked, "You mind if I wait for Mrs. Starr?"

"What's your business with Belle?"

"I hear you and her take in paying guests now and then."

"Damn it, Sam, Windy's looking for a place to hole up for a while, can't you see that?" Yazoo said.

Starr finally made up his mind. "I guess it's all right," he told Longarm. "Come on in and sit down. Belle ought to be here any minute, she just had some business to do in town."

"That's what Yazoo told me," Longarm said, following Starr into the house.

He looked at the dim interior. It was no more attractive than the outside. A partition had been thrown across one end, and through its door he could see a tousled double bed. In the main room, which took up two-thirds of the dwelling, there were several chairs, a table, and a wood-burning stove that shared the chimney with a fireplace, now standing empty. Pots were on the stove, and the smells of cooking food mingled unidentifiably in the air.

Starr went to the stove, lifted the lid of one of the pots, and stirred the contents. "I told Belle I'd have supper ready when she and the others got back," he explained. "Well, sit down, Windy. You want a drink? I'll guarantee it; we make it right here on the place."

"Pour me one while you're at it, Sam," Yazoo put in.

Longarm said, "I'll join you in a little nip, sure."

Starr pulled a bottle out of a wooden KC Baking Powder box, one of several nailed to the wall at one side of the stove to form a rough sort of kitchen cabinet. He found glasses, put them on the table, and filled them.

Longarm tasted the liquor. It was raw at the edges, and corn whiskey wasn't much to his fancy, but he downed it and said, "Real good stuff, Starr. You do the distilling?"

"Mostly, me and Yazoo. Belle's busy with other things."

Yazoo had finished his drink while Longarm was still tasting. He filled his glass again and held the bottle out to Longarm, who shook his head.

Yazoo urged, "Come on, Windy. One more never hurt a man."

"After while." Longarm said, then turned to Starr. "Quite a place you got here. Good and private."

"That's what everybody says. Good for business, you know."

Longarm was studying Starr as the Bandit Queen's husband moved around the stove, lifting a pot lid, shoving in a fresh stick of wood. Starr was a slight man, and on the short side. Except for his movements, which were swift and sure, and his toed-in walk, he showed no signs of his Cherokee ancestry. Longarm judged that the Indian blood Starr had was pretty well diluted after a hundred years or so of his tribe's intermarriages with whites, blacks, Spaniards—racial discrimination wasn't a Cherokee trait.

Starr's features were regular, his nose a bit broad at the nostrils, his lips full. His face was long rather than square, his chin small and slightly receding. He was clean-shaven, but wore his hair long, brushed straight back to fall just above his shoulders. The hair was not Indian-black, but had a slight auburn tinge. It was perfectly straight, though, and somewhat coarse.

Yazoo was pouring himself another drink. He extended

63

the bottle to Longarm again. "You better keep up, Windy. About all a man—" He stopped short and cocked his head to one side, listening.

Longarm listened too. The thrumming of hooves was coming in through the open door. Three or four horses, as closely as Longarm could tell. The hoofbeats grew steadily louder.

"Must be Belle and the boys coming back," Starr volunteered.

Voices trickled in from outside. Longarm swiveled his chair around to face the door more squarely.

A woman appeared in the doorway. She was tall, her height emphasized by the long green velvet dress she wore; the dress was full-skirted, and its hem swept the floor. She had on a man's Stetson, cream-colored, uncreased; one side of the brim was pulled up and pinned to the crown with a plume of ostrich feathers dyed green to match the dress. What drew Longarm's attention was the pair of silver-plated, pearl-handled pistols that she wore high around her waist.

She looked at Longarm with obsidian-black eyes and asked, "Who in hell are you?"

"It's all right, Belle," Sam said quickly. "His name is Windy, and he's looking for a place to stay. Yazoo knows him, he spoke up for him."

Belle stepped inside the house. She looked at Yazoo. "Is that right, Yazoo? Do you know this dude?"

"From someplace, Belle. He's one of our kind of folks." The old man's speech was growing blurred.

Behind Belle, a young man stood in the doorway, his arms filled with twine-wrapped bundles. He pushed his way past her and moved toward the stove. "Here's the flour and stuff you wanted, Sam," he said, beginning to deposit the packages on the floor.

Another man appeared in the doorway. Belle had come into the house by now, and Longarm had a good view of the newcomer. He recognized him just as the man saw him sitting there. His name was McKee, and Longarm had brought him in for a bank holdup almost two years ago. Now Longarm saw recognition springing into McKee's face.

64

"Why, damn you!" McKee blurted. He was clawing for his gun as he spoke. "You dirty son of a bitch! I told you I'd get—"

Longarm's Colt blasted a split second before McKee had his revolver leveled. A dime-sized hole appeared in the outlaw's forehead. He grimaced as he began crumpling to the floor. He was dead before he finished falling.

Chapter 6

Longarm completed the turn he'd started when he leaped from his chair to draw on McKee. The move brought Belle Starr and Sam under the menace of the Colt's still-smoking muzzle. Belle had her right-hand pistol halfway out of its holster and Sam was starting toward the wall, where his rifle rested on pegs, when Longarm spoke.

"Everybody just stand still. I got no grudges against anybody else around here. Me and McKee had a score to settle, you heard him say so. Turned out it was settled my way. Now it's over and done with, and I don't aim to pull trigger again unless one of you makes me do it."

Silence greeted his announcement. Out of the corner of his eye, Longarm could see Yazoo sitting at the end of the table, his whiskey-glazed eyes not really taking in what had happened. Sam Starr had obeyed the command to freeze, and so had the young man who'd brought in the packages. And so, for that matter, had Belle Starr, but she still had a hand on her revolver's grips. Longarm fixed her with his stony gaze and she opened her hand, letting the pistol slide back into its holster.

Belle said, "Regardless of what your argument was with McKee, I don't like to have strangers showing up here and killing my boarders. Yazoo said your name's Windy. Suppose you tell us the rest of it, and explain what you're doing here."

"Windy's all the name I need, right now," Longarm replied. "It was something personal between McKee and me. Goes back quite a while. You heard what he said and you saw him draw. I was just sitting there, not going for my gun, when he grabbed."

"So I noticed," Belle said dryly. "Whoever you are,

Windy, you've got a quick hand. What was your argument with McKee about?"

"Now that he's dead, I don't see where it matters much," Longarm replied. "Or which one of us was in the right. Looks to me like all that signifies is that I'm standing here and McKee's dead."

"That's one way of looking at it," Belle said. "But just the same, I'd like to know."

"It was private between him and me," Longarm told her in a tone designed to let her see that he wasn't going to say more.

Belle shrugged. "If that's the way you want it." She looked at Longarm narrowly, frowning. "I don't think I've heard your name, but maybe I've seen you before, when I rode with Jesse James."

"Not likely, ma'am. I haven't had the honor of meeting Mr. James. Not that I wouldn't like to reach out and take his hand," Longarm said. Which, he thought, was the truth. Nothing required him to say that if he took Jesse James's hand, it would only be to hold it still while he snapped the cuffs on the outlaw.

Belle's eyes narrowed as she thought aloud. "You're not from the Nation or Texas. I'd have heard about you if you'd been busy in either place. Or Arkansas or Kansas or Missouri. You must come from further west?"

"You could say that without being too far wrong," Longarm agreed.

Yazoo broke in long enough to say, "Save your questions, Belle. I tried 'em all on old Windy, and he ain't answering." His words were slurred, his eyes obviously unfocused.

"You're drunk, Yazoo," Belle said. There was no accusation or anger in her voice; she was simply stating the fact.

"Sure. I try to be, Belle. Mostly I do it, too." He fell forward across the table, his arms dangling down beside his chair.

Belle ignored Yazoo's collapse. She turned to her husband.

"How's supper coming along, Sam? I'm getting hungry."

"It'll be a few minutes, Belle." Sam Starr's voice was

apologetic. "I didn't know exactly when you'd get back, or I'd have had it on the table."

"It's all right. I suppose you can leave the stove for a minute, long enough to carry McKee out to the grove? You can bury him after we eat; there'll be plenty of time before dark."

Starr nodded. "Sure, Belle, plenty of time."

"Get Bobby to give you a hand," Belle went on. "And on the way back, the two of you can unsaddle the horses and put them in the barn."

"All right." Starr turned to the young man. "Come on, Bobby."

Longarm said, "I killed McKee. Only right for me to help you put him away."

"No," Belle said sharply. "You stay right here, Windy. I want to talk to you." She added, "You can holster your gun now. I never did like McKee much, and that's the truth of it. It's no skin off my ass if you two settled a private fuss."

"That's right considerate of you, ma'am," Longarm said as he restored his Colt to its holster.

Sam and Bobby started off on their unpleasant errand. They picked McKee's body up—Sam grabbed the dead man's wrists, Bobby taking hold of the ankles—and disappeared with the slain outlaw swinging between them.

"Sit down, Windy," Belle told Longarm. "I won't press for your name, real or otherwise. Yazoo's word's good enough for me."

"I'm glad you feel that way, ma'am." Longarm settled down in the chair he'd been occupying when McKee came in.

"Call me Belle, for God's sake!" Belle was taking off her hat. She hung it on a peg by the door, unbuckled her gunbelt and hung it on the peg next to the hat. "I told you a minute ago, and I'll say it again for the last time. I don't allow my guests to fight while they're at Younger's Bend. I'm excusing you because you didn't know my rules. McKee did. He broke them, and he's paid. That's over and settled. Just see you don't break them again."

"I'll sure try, Belle."

Belle came and sat down across the table from Longarm, and he got a close look at her for the first time. She looked like anything but the title she'd given herself, he decided. The self-appointed Bandit Queen was a tall woman, beginning to show the spreading hips of middle age. Her waist was still slender, but her hips and buttocks flared out visibly, even under the loose-fitting full skirt of her green velvet dress. Her breasts were small; they made scarcely a bulge under the embroidered bodice of her dress. The flesh of her chin and neck was beginning to sag loosely above the scarf that was tucked into the dress and wrapped high on Belle's throat.

Her chin was small, almost receding, and her lips were a short, straight line. Her nose was an uptilted button between high cheekbones on which a layer of fat was beginning to form.

Belle's eyes were the best thing about her, Longarm decided. Now they were soft and liquid, but he remembered how they'd darkened and snapped with anger during the moments just after McKee's death. Her hair was dark, almost black, and pulled back into a knot at the nape of her neck. Thick bangs, brushed forward at an angle across her forehead, failed to hide the fact that her forehead was unusually high.

She wasn't, Longarm decided, the kind of woman he'd fall all over himself trying to get acquainted with. Remembering Andrew Gower's listing of Belle's husbands and lovers, he wondered what so many men had seen in her.

While Longarm was evaluating Belle, she'd been studying him as closely as he was examining her. She said, "Well, Windy? Like what you're looking at? Because I think I do."

Longarm thought he'd better stretch a point. It was against his nature to lie outright, even to a woman he might be romancing. He didn't have any ideas about romancing Belle Starr, but Longarm thought that, under the circumstances, a little bit of evasion wouldn't do him any harm.

"You look real nice, Belle," he said. "If you didn't have a husband, I'd sure be interested in you."

And that's the straight-line truth, old son, he thought, *even if she don't take what I said exactly like I meant it.*

I'd be interested in her the same as I am in anybody that lives on the wrong side of the law.

"I've got a rule never to let a husband stop me from doing what I feel like doing, when I like a man," she told him. "No man alive owns Belle Starr, the Bandit Queen. You think that over, Windy."

"Oh, I will. I sure will."

"Now that we've got that out of the way, suppose you tell me who showed you how to find Younger's Bend," she said.

"Nobody."

"Don't lie, Windy. Somebody had to tell you."

"Now, Belle, you know how word gets around. Hell, this place is getting as well-known as the Hole in the Wall, Buzzard's Roost, and Brown's Hole." Longarm named only three of the eight or nine places he knew of, from Wyoming and Utah down to the Big Bend of Texas, where men on the run could drop out of sight of the law. It was a regular network of bolt-holes; none of them were actually unknown to lawmen, but most of the hideouts were natural fortresses that would have taken an army with artillery to penetrate.

"Is that the truth?" Belle seemed pleased and flattered.

"Don't have any reason to lie to you. I disremember who it was told me about Younger's Bend, or where I was when I heard about it, but it's a place I've had in the back of my mind for quite a while."

"And you finally got here. Where are you wanted, Windy?"

"Hold on. You've got your rules, Belle, and I got mine. One of them is that I don't talk about myself."

"Yazoo said you were real close-mouthed. I guess he was right."

"He ought to know," Longarm said with a smile.

"Well, I'm going to let you stay," Belle said. "Ten dollars gold a day for your room and meals. If you're short, I'll take a one-third cut of whatever you bring in from the next job you pull. If you haven't got anything planned, I can work out a deal for you with Floyd and Steed, I suppose."

Longarm took time to fish out a cheroot and light it.

When the cigar was drawing well, he asked, "Who are Floyd and Steed?"

"Two of the fellows staying here. They'll be in for supper pretty soon. They've been here quite a while, they'll tell you how easy things are. You know the U.S. law can't touch you here, I guess? Arkansas, Texas, Kansas, Colorado—don't have to worry about any sheriffs from anyplace. Or from the U.S. marshal's office, either."

"That's one of the reasons I'm here," Longarm said truthfully, again letting Belle put her own interpretation on his words.

"I've got a treaty with the Cherokee Nation, you see," Belle went on. Longarm looked up at the word "treaty"; it was the same one that had riled Gower so badly. Belle went on, "The only way the law can come into the Nation is by an invitation from the Indian police, or if they're chasing somebody they've caught on a job."

"So I've heard."

"I was pretty sure you had. But I'm telling you this because I want you to understand how it is here. As long as one of my guests doesn't pull any kind of job in the Nation, my treaty holds. So if you've got any ideas about operating out of here, just be sure it's across one of the state lines."

"I've been moving so fast I ain't had time to look around for any setups for a job," Longarm said.

"Well, when you get ready, you let me know. I can fix up something for you with the fellows I told you about."

"I'll keep it in mind," Longarm promised.

Sam Starr and Bobby came in. "I fed and watered your horse, Windy," Sam said. "Didn't bother your saddle gear, though. Wasn't sure whether you'd be staying or riding on."

"Windy's staying awhile," Belle announced. "Now, you'd better see to supper, Sam. Floyd and Steed will be showing up any minute, yelling how hungry they are. And be sure you set a place for Windy."

Almost before Belle had finished speaking, loud voices outside announced the arrival of the other two outlaws. They burst into the house, still arguing. One of them said to Belle, "Tell this damn fool he's seeing things, Belle.

71

Steed says he seen Sam and Bobby hauling McKee's body up to the grove a few minutes ago."

"He wasn't seeing things, Floyd," Belle replied. "McKee's dead. Sam's going to bury him right after supper."

"See! I was right!" Steed said.

Steed was the blustering type. He was in his mid-twenties, high-colored, husky, broad-shouldered, heavy of leg and thigh. His hands looked like small hams, and his neck was as thick as a steer's. He had a pistol stuck into his belt; Longarm wondered if he made a habit of carrying a gun that way. More than one careless gun-handler who took up the habit of toting an unholstered gun stuck between belly and belt had checked out with a set of bullet-riddled guts.

Floyd was Steed's antithesis. He was pale, his eyes a watery blue, his hair the shade of unbleached tow. His hands were small, almost delicate. His face was thin, and somehow managed to look mournful even when he was smiling. In repose, he appeared to be suffering from either chronic melancholy or a stomachache. Floyd carried his revolver in a cross-draw holster, high on his left side. Longarm marked him as being the one to keep an eye on.

While Belle confirmed McKee's death, Floyd's lips compressed into an even thinner line than they were normally. He asked Belle, "What happened to him?"

"You'll have to ask Windy." Belle pointed to Longarm, who hadn't moved when the two men came in. "There was some sort of old grudge between him and McKee, and he settled it."

Floyd wheeled to face Longarm. "You shot McKee?"

"Yes. He drew on me."

"Why?"

"That was between McKee and me. It's no business of yours." Longarm's voice was level, emotionless.

Floyd frowned. "Maybe I choose to *make* it my business."

"Suit yourself," Longarm said with a laconic shrug.

Belle intervened. "Hold on, Floyd. I saw what happened. So did Sam, so did Bobby and Yazoo, if he could see anything at all, drunk as he was by then."

"Stay out of this, Belle," Floyd told the Bandit Queen.

His voice was a sad whisper. He faced Longarm again. "McKee was a friend of mine."

"Too bad. He was no friend of mine."

"Why'd you kill him?"

"He'd have killed me if I hadn't," Longarm said quietly.

"That's right, Floyd," Sam Starr put in. "All of us saw what happened, Belle, me, Bobby, and Yazoo. McKee saw Windy, started cussing him, and went for his gun. Windy got his out first. That's the way it happened. Windy didn't make the first move."

Floyd appeared not to have heard what Sam said. He was looking Longarm up and down. Finally he snarled, "Windy! That's no name! Who in hell are you?"

"Your eyesight's bad, Floyd. You can see who I am," Longarm replied. He kept his voice even. He didn't want a showdown with Floyd, but he couldn't let the outlaw back him down, either.

"Where'd you come from?" Floyd demanded.

"Outside."

"God damn it, that's no answer!" Floyd was whipping up his anger. When Longarm said nothing, Floyd turned to Belle. "You know him, Belle?"

"No. Yazoo does, though. He said he was all right."

"What the hell does that old whiskeypot know about anything?" Floyd demanded of no one in particular.

Belle said sharply, "You listen to me, Floyd Sharpless! This is my place you're on. I told Windy he was welcome here, just like I've told you. But you won't be welcome if you keep trying to stir up trouble, do you understand me?"

"I understand you," Floyd shot back hotly. "That don't mean I'm going to leave off until I find out about this Windy here."

"Let me tell you something else," Belle said. "McKee had his hand on his gun before Windy went for his. Windy had a bullet through McKee before he could get his gun up and let off a shot. And McKee was quicker than you are."

"Quit trying to scare me, Belle."

"I'm not trying to scare you, I'm just trying to hammer some sense into your head. Now I'll tell you flat out,

Floyd, give up on McKee and why he had a shootout with Windy—it's not your affair. It happened before you and McKee hooked up. And if you're not careful, all those big plans you've been making are going right out to the hogpen, because if you break my rule against fighting here, I'm going to invite you to leave Younger's Bend."

"How the hell is my plan going to work without McKee?" Floyd demanded. "You know I was depending on him, Belle."

"There'll be somebody else along to fill his place," she said.

Steed had been quiet, standing at one side of the room while Floyd and Belle argued. Now he said, "Belle's right, Floyd. We still got Bobby. And Taylor's due to blow in pretty soon."

"That's still only four," Floyd pointed out. "All of us agreed we need at least five, and six would be better."

Longarm's interest had been growing ever since the subject of plans had come up. In Floyd's terms, that could only mean a major job of outlawry, especially if it required a half-dozen men to carry it out. He said nothing, though, letting Belle and Floyd settle the dispute he'd caused between them.

Belle said, "Let's get this settled once and for all, Floyd. I had as much to do with that plan as you did. I want to see you go through with it. Now, take my word, I'll find somebody to fill in for McKee."

Floyd's anger had been deflected from Longarm by his dispute with Belle. He said bitterly, "Sure. Who's it going to be? Yazoo?"

"Who wants me?" Yazoo stirred and sat up. He looked around the room with bleary eyes.

"Nobody wants you, old man," Floyd replied. "Go on back to sleep and sober up."

"Stay awake, Yazoo," Belle commanded.

Yazoo looked from Belle to Floyd and said, "I wisht you two'd make up your mind." He reached for the whiskey bottle on the table.

Belle turned back to Floyd and said, "You'd better have a drink with him, Floyd, and take that edge off your

74

nerves. Sit down now, and don't stir up any more trouble with Windy."

Floyd glared at her angrily, but obeyed. He took a chair and placed it as far from Longarm as the size of the table permitted.

"Sam, get the food dished up," Belle told her husband.

Starr had been standing indecisively at one side of the room, close to Bobby, during the argument between Belle and Floyd. He took a stack of plates out of one of the KC Baking Powder boxes nailed to the wall, and distributed them around the table. Steed and Bobby moved up to sit down. Belle watched them for a moment before joining them, then chose a place next to Longarm.

"Things aren't like this every day," she told him.

"I guess the ruckus is mostly my fault," Longarm said. "Sorry I stirred things up, Belle. But like you told Floyd a minute ago, you saw how it all happened."

"I know it wasn't your fault, Windy. Nobody's blaming you for anything." Belle seemed pleased that Longarm had made the gesture of apologizing. She went on, "I like my guests to get along together, but you men do disagree now and then."

Sam began dishing up. He walked around the table, ladling out stew onto the plates. Longarm looked at his serving. There were chunks of meat and pieces of carrot, onion, and potato in a thin gravy. Next to him, Yazoo was already eating hungrily.

Belle noticed Longarm's hesitation. "Sam's a better cook than you might think, Windy. Eat up. You'll like it."

Longarm said, "I bet I will, at that." He took a sample bite, found the stew edible, and continued to eat.

Sam brought a pan of biscuits from the stove and put it in the middle of the table. Longarm and Floyd reached at the same time, and their hands met over the biscuit pan.

"Help yourself, Floyd," Longarm invited. "I ain't in all that big a hurry."

Floyd grunted and seemed about to speak, but changed his mind. He took a biscuit and went back to his food. Apparently he'd decided to leave matters as they were, at least for the moment.

Sam saw that the biscuit pan was empty, and brought

75

a full one to replace it. Then he went back to the stove, pulled a chair up to it, and began to eat his own meal off the warming shelf. Since no one commented on this, or invited Starr to join the group at the table, Longarm got a pretty clear idea of the status Belle's husband held at Younger's Bend.

Supper was a generally silent meal. Yazoo and Belle were the only ones at the table who had much to say, and when their efforts to start a conversation met with no response from Floyd, Steed, or Longarm, they subsided. Sam Starr kept an eye on the table, and when a plate was emptied, he brought the stew pot from the stove to replenish it. Longarm took a second helping, as did everyone except Belle. The stew was surprisingly tasty, though privately Longarm thought that no stew would ever be a substitute for a good steak served up with a heap of fried potatoes on the platter with it.

"You'd better let the dishes go until later, Sam," Belle said when it was apparent that everyone had finished. "I'd like to see McKee buried before it gets too dark, and you've still got the grave to dig."

Floyd spoke up, "You never mind about burying McKee, Sam. Me and Steed will take care of that."

"I don't recall offering to take on the job," Steed said.

"Shut up, Steed," Floyd snapped. "McKee was our partner. It's only right to see he's put away proper."

Bobby had been as silent as everyone else during the meal; he'd let his eyes follow every move made by Floyd and Steed, and was obviously doing his best to follow whatever example they set. Now the young outlaw asked Floyd, "How come you didn't say anything about me? If I'm in with you and Steed, I guess I can do my share too."

"Of course you can, Bobby," Steed assured him. He stood up and began preparing the dishpan. Yazoo took another drink.

Belle turned to Longarm and said, "There's a cabin vacant, the one on the far end, past Steed and Bobby's and the one where McKee was staying with Floyd. I guess you can have it, provided you don't mind sharing it with Taylor when he gets here."

"I'd be better off there than sharing with Floyd," Longarm said, straight-faced.

"I can fix you up a shakedown here in the house, if you'd rather," Belle suggested. "It'd just be a pallet over against the wall there, though."

"Be glad to have you bunk with me up at the stillhouse, Windy," Yazoo offered. His voice was slurred and he had trouble focusing his eyes. "We could talk about old times."

"Now, Windy doesn't want to stay up there," Belle told Yazoo. "The smell of that mash would keep him from sleeping." She smiled at Longarm as she spoke.

"I'll settle for the cabin," Longarm said. He'd decided it was time to establish the fact that he hadn't come looking for charity. He took out the drawstring pouch Gower had given him, and spilled some of the coins from it to the tabletop. Belle's eyes widened, and so did Yazoo's, at the sight of the gold pieces.

Longarm went on, "You said your going rate's five dollars a day, Belle. I don't know how long I'm going to be around, so suppose I just pay you for two or three days. If I stay longer, I'll pony up with it when this has been used up." He shoved an eagle and a half eagle along the table to Belle, and gathered the remaining coins into the pouch.

"You didn't need to pay anything at all right now, Windy," Belle said. She picked up the gold pieces, however. "Your credit's good here."

Longarm stood up. "I don't reckon you set a night guard, do you?"

"Why should I?" Belle asked. "Oh, if we're looking for trouble, we'll keep watch at night. But there's no reason to, otherwise."

"Good," he said. "Well, I'll mosey on down and settle in, then, before it gets too dark to see."

"There's a lamp in the cabin," Starr volunteered. "And a water bucket. You've seen where the well is, I guess."

"Sure. I'll get along fine, Sam. I'm used to looking out for myself." Longarm started for the door. "I'll see you at breakfast, I guess. Right now, a bed's going to look pretty good. I rode a long ways, these last few days."

He went on outside and started for the barn, where his

horse was still hitched to the pole. Before he'd gotten well off the porch, Belle called to him. She came up to him when he stopped and turned around.

"Don't be too quick with your gun if you hear somebody walking around after dark. I usually take a little stroll before I go to bed, walk down to the bluff and look at the river in the moonlight, or just go around making sure everything's all right."

"I see." Longarm saw only too well. "All right, Belle. I'll be careful."

"You do that. Because if you hear anybody, it'll just be me. I always like to be sure my guests are comfortable." She paused and added in a suggestive whisper, "Comfortable, and well-cared-for, too. I'll see you later, then."

Longarm stood looking at Belle's back as she walked to the house.

Chapter 7

In the fading light that trickled through the paneless window and the open door, Longarm surveyed the interior of the cabin. It was tiny, but its very bareness made it look larger than it was.

A pair of narrow bunks were attached to opposite walls at one end; they were bare except for thin mattresses, and the straw with which the mattresses were stuffed protruded here and there through holes in the ticking. The bunks had no pillows. At the other end of the bleak, uninviting room stood the inevitable monkey stove, a low sheet-iron oval fed through a door in one end, with a single pothole on its top for cooking. A table and two chairs completed the furnishings. An oil lamp stood on the table, and the water bucket Sam Starr had mentioned was behind the stove.

Longarm studied the window. It had no outside shutters, and its location, high in the end wall between the two bunks, made both of them vulnerable. Anybody tall enough to stick a gun through the window could rain bullets on either bunk while the thick timber walls protected him from return fire.

You better sit down and do a little bit of thinking about this mess you walked into, old son, Longarm told himself.

He lighted the lamp, just in case anybody in the house glanced down that way, took the partly full bottle of Maryland rye and his gun-cleaning kit from his saddlebags, and went back into the cabin. As an afterthought, he went back out and fixed in his mind the locations of the cabins occupied by Floyd, Steed, and Bobby. Neither of them was more than a dozen yards away. Back in the cabin, he leaned back in the sturdier of its two straight

79

chairs, lighted a cheroot, and let a swallow of rye trickle down his throat.

If I aim to sleep on one of them bunks tonight, he thought, *chances are I just might not wake up tomorrow morning. Not with Floyd doing everything but coming right out and saying he figures to cut me down first chance he gets.*

He took another conservative sip of the whiskey, and began to clean his Colt. *And then there's Belle,* his thoughts ran on. *She's made it right plain she's got plans to drop in during the night, and that's one lady I got to be one hell of a lot hornier than I am right now to give stud service to. Except, if I aim to stay here until I dig out what Floyd's cooking up, I can't afford to make her mad and have her hand me my walking papers.*

Before considering the alternatives to a night in the cabin, Longarm had another swallow of the rye. After the corn squeezings he'd had before supper, he needed the sharp bite of the rye to clear his throat. Then he carefully reloaded his revolver and holstered it.

Now, I could go sleep up at the stillhouse, but it's a toss-up which smells worse, Yazoo or the barrels of corn mash he's bound to have fermenting up there.

There's the main house, but if Belle's taken a notion to come crawl in with me, she'd be likely to do it there, even with Sam asleep in the next room.

The thing for you to do, old son, is bunk in the barn. Good clean hay's going to smell better than either one of them mattresses. If anybody comes prowling, chances are one of the horses'll nicker. If Belle don't find me here, she'll likely figure I decided to sleep out in case Floyd might take a notion to pay me back during the night for shooting McKee.

Having made up his mind, Longarm saw no need to hurry. He sat quietly until he'd finished his cigar; there'd be no smoking during the night in the barn, with the hay he'd glimpsed piled high along one wall ready to go up in flames if touched by a match or an unextinguished cigar butt. It was fully dark when he blew out the lamp and led his horse back to the barn.

Longarm approached the barn at the end farthest from

80

the house. There was light streaming from the uncurtained, unshuttered windows and the open door. Moving quietly, he led the hammerhead bay into the barn and tethered it, then went to stand at one corner of the house. There was no need to get very close, or strain his ears, to hear the conversation going on inside.

Floyd was saying, "God damn it, Yazoo, think harder! You got to remember where you seen this Windy fellow before!"

"I've tried all I got the power to." Yazoo's voice was tired and his words slurred. "I told you twenty times, it could've been just about anyplace. I tossed the names of a lot of places at him, but he didn't remember, either."

"Now listen, Yazoo," Steed began, but Yazoo had apparently had enough questioning.

"No, Steed. I ain't flogging my brain for you men another minute. Not tonight, at least. I got a batch of mash cooking, and I'm going up and stir it good, and then I'm going to bed."

Longarm stepped back into the shadow of the barn while Yazoo staggered across the narrow porch, managed to navigate the steps without falling down them, and started weaving toward the grove of trees in which the illegal still stood.

Belle's voice broke the silence next. "Why are you so set on finding out about Windy, Floyd? He seems all right to me. And I'm like Yazoo; I've got a feeling I've seen him before. Maybe when I was riding with Jim Reed down in Texas, or somewhere else."

Steed grumbled, "He's with us now, Belle, and if we're his own kind, how come he don't open up more?"

"Because he's careful!" Belle snapped.

"Just the same, he ought to open up a little bit more. Hell, he could be anybody, for all we know!" Floyd grumbled.

"Yeah." This was Bobby's light voice. "How do we know he's all right, Belle?"

"Because I've got a feeling he is!" Belle said curtly.

"That ain't good enough for me," Floyd retorted. "I want him to give us names and tell us about places."

Belle said, "Now, Floyd, if you were on the prod, you

wouldn't be going around telling everybody you're Floyd Sharpless, and there's reward money posted for you in St. Joe and Springville and wherever else you've been tagged with a job."

"I guess not," Floyd admitted reluctantly. "But I knew McKee better than anybody else. We never did hold back a thing from each other, after we commenced traveling together. And I never heard him say a word about having a standing grudge with a man that fits Windy's looks."

Steed's rough voice rumbled, "That don't signify, Floyd. McKee might've kept quiet about something like that, especially if he tangled with Windy and come off sucking a hind tit."

"He might have," Floyd agreed, with doubt in his voice. "Not likely, though, Steed. Well, I'm going to set myself to find out. And maybe I won't even wait to find out before I even my score with him."

"I don't see you've got a score to even with him, Floyd," Sam Starr said. "It was McKee's grudge, not yours."

"I got a right to make it mine if I feel like it," Floyd replied.

"Sure, but I'd watch myself if I was you," Starr said. "Belle and me saw that ruckus, remember. McKee had his gun half out before Windy drew. And then Windy moved faster than any man I ever saw. He shot straight, too; you saw where the slug went."

"I can take care of myself," Floyd retorted. "All of you just remember, stand aside if trouble starts between me and Windy."

"From the way Windy was holding back, anything that starts between you and him will be your idea," Belle said. "Remember, Floyd, I don't allow my guests to fight each other—fists, knives, or guns."

"All right, Belle, I'll try not to push," Floyd promised. "But if anything does get going, I'll damn sure finish it."

There was a scraping of chair legs on the bare wooden floor of the house. Once again, Longarm stepped back into the blackness under the barn's overhanging roof. He couldn't see Floyd, Steed, and Bobby until they'd gotten a few steps from the house, but he could hear them.

Floyd said, "All that digging's made my back ache. I

was sort of figuring we could all set down and figure out how we could handle everything without McKee, but I don't feel like it."

"I just as soon put it off till Taylor gets here," Steed replied. "All I want to do right now is go drop in my bunk."

"Yeah. Me too," Bobby said.

Longarm shook his head at the youth's echoing of Steed. He'd seen the likes of Bobby before—a youngster taken in by the stories of glamorous outlaw lives. He'd seen such youngsters try to capture some of the glamor by joining forces with older, more experienced men, and come up against hard reality. Out of every ten, five gave up and went straight. Out of the other five, one or two survived.

A few more steps took the trio out of earshot. Longarm went into the barn. His eyes had grown accustomed to the darkness now, and he could see what he was doing. The horses and mules were standing quietly. Two or three of the horses nickered, but that was all. He spotted the low loft that filled about a third of the end of the barn farthest from the house. Cleat steps, on one of the posts supporting the rooftree, led up to the loft. Longarm climbed up and found that the loft had just about enough hay in it to make the foundation for a bed. He scraped the hay into a rectangle and spread his bedroll on it. After folding his coat for a pillow and arranging his vest as a pad for his Colt, Longarm stretched out and relaxed as well as he could without taking off his boots. Tonight he thought he'd be better off wearing them than shedding them.

It had been a long day and, in spite of his booted feet, sleep came to him quickly.

Longarm wasn't sure which roused him, the broken rhythm of hooves or the faint call for help. He heard both at the same time and snapped awake, slid his Colt out of its holster, and sat up in bed in the same easy movement.

He listened consciously as soon as he recognized the source of the noises that had awakened him. Neither the irregular hoofbeats nor the cries were close at hand. He stood up and put on his gunbelt, climbed down the cleat steps to the barn floor, and stepped outside. Here the sounds were louder. They seemed to be coming from behind the house.

Longarm walked fast, following the noises to their source. There was no moon, just starglow in a cloudless sky. He strained his vision through the darkness when he'd cleared the corner of the house. Perhaps a hundred yards away he could make out movement. He walked toward the shapeless black form, and slowly it took shape: a horse and rider. There was something wrong with the configuration of the rider, and the horse had gone lame in its off hind-foot.

As the distance between him and the approaching horse diminished, Longarm could understand why he'd been puzzled. There wasn't one rider on the animal, but two. One of them was curled forward in the saddle, and the second rider was holding the limp figure of the first in place. The horse was moving slowly, much slower than Longarm was walking. Several moments passed before the laden beast came close enough for Longarm to see that the rider who was erect was a woman. She must be old, he thought fleetingly; he could see long white hair streaming across her shoulders, and her cries were in the hoarse, high-pitched voice that often comes with age.

She did not see Longarm until he'd gotten to within a few yards of her. Then she croaked in a thin whisper, "Oh, thank God! Help me, please help me! I'm afraid he's hurt real bad!"

"How'd he get hurt?" Longarm asked. He grabbed the reins and pulled the limping horse to a stop. "Horse throw him?"

"No. He—he got shot."

"I see." Longarm decided he'd better stop asking questions and give the woman the help she was pleading for. "You're all right, ma'am? Not hurt or anything?"

"No, I'm not hurt," she whispered, her voice high and rasping. "But my throat. I've called and cried so much . . ."

"You don't have to yell or cry anymore," he told her.

Longarm released the reins, hoping the horse would stand. It did, and he sidled along its neck until he reached the limp figure of the man.

84

"Please, can you hold him up?" the woman grasped. "I've held him so long that I don't have much strength left."

"You can let go. I won't let him fall."

With a relieved sigh, she took her arms away from the slumped waist of the unconscious man. She reeled and almost toppled from the saddle herself, but Longarm held up a hand, which she grasped, steadying herself.

"I'm all right now," she said thinly. "I just lost my balance for a minute. Please, look at Lonnie. I know he's in bad shape, but I think he's still alive."

Longarm pressed a hand to the wounded rider's chest. He felt a heartbeat, slow and irregular, but a beat, just the same.

"He's alive," he told the old woman. "But we got to get him to where he can stretch out, and where there's light so we can see how bad he's hit." He was feeling for the man's wounds as he spoke, but the unconscious rider's shirt was so stiff and thick with dried blood that he could not locate them.

"How long ago was he shot?" he asked.

"Last night. About midnight, I guess. Please, can't you just take care of him now and wait until later for me to tell you how it all happened?"

"I ain't trying to waste time, ma'am. I just need to know how old that wound is, so I can take care of him right."

"Oh. I guess I didn't understand that. But do something for him now, please! I'll help you lift him off the horse."

"No. There ain't enough light even to *see* by out here, let alone to try and bandage up a bullet wound by. Best thing we can do is get him to the Starrs' house. It's just a little ways from here. Then we can tend to him proper."

"All right." The woman swayed again and reached out a hand, seeking support. Longarm reached up and grasped the hand and steadied her.

He asked, "You think you can walk a little piece, ma'am? I can't hold you and your friend in the saddle and walk the horse too."

"Yes. I can walk. If you'll hold him, I'll get off."

Longarm balanced the limp, unwieldly form of the unconscious man while she pulled her skirt free and dis-

85

mounted. She was unsteady on her feet. Longarm put an arm out and she leaned against him. He stifled the exclamation that rose to his throat. What he'd mistaken for an old woman with a creaking voice and long white hair was a young woman with long blonde hair and a voice made hoarse by calling for help and crying. He decided questions could wait.

"You get on the other side," he told the woman. "Just walk by the horse and steady Lonnie as much as you can. I'll hold him up on this side and guide the nag."

Their progress toward the dim shape of the house was painfully slow. The lame horse, with the wounded man balanced precariously on its back, forced them to creep along. They reached the house at last, and Longarm guided the horse around it to the front door.

"Sam! Belle!" he called. "Make a light inside there! I got a man out here who's been hurt real bad. He needs to be looked after right away!"

"Windy?" Sam Starr's sleepy voice called from the blackness of the house. "What's going on?"

"You and Belle get up, Sam!" Longarm called back. "There's a man shot out here, and he needs help!"

A match flickered in the house, then the steadier glow of a lamp replaced it. Sam Starr came out on the porch, carrying the lamp. He was sleepy-eyed and slack-jawed, and wore only his long cotton undersuit. He held up the lamp and peered, blinking, at Longarm, the girl, and the wounded man on the horse.

"Who is he?" Sam asked. "Who shot him?"

"I don't know yet. All I know is he's in real bad shape," Longarm replied.

"Please," the woman said to Starr. "Please, can't you take him inside? Help him? Bandage him up?"

"Sure." Starr came down the steps. He winced when his bare feet met the rough-packed earth, but came on to where Longarm stood beside the horse, supporting the wounded stranger. He looked at the man sagging forward in the saddle, his shirt encrusted with dry blood.

"We better get him inside," Starr said. He handed the lamp to the woman. "Here, you carry this. I'll help Windy."

Between them, Longarm and Sam got the stranger's limp, unwieldy body off the horse. They worked as gently as they could, but, as they started with him into the house, fresh blood began dripping from the unconscious man's back. The drops left a trail, black in the lamplight, up the steps, across the floor, and into the main room.

"Where you want to put him?" Longarm asked.

Starr looked around. "The table's the best place, I guess." He spoke to the girl. "Lady, set that lamp down on a chair and clear that stuff off the table."

There were an almost empty bottle of whiskey and a scattering of dirty glasses on the table. The girl moved quickly, placing the lamp in one of the chairs and setting the glasses and bottle beside it. Longarm and Starr lifted the wounded man to the table. He was too tall for its length, so his legs dangled off one end.

"Put a chair under his feet," Starr told the girl. "We want to get him stretched out as straight as we can."

She'd been hovering around, trying to help. Longarm, seeing her for the first time in the light, wondered how he could have made the mistake of thinking she was old. Her face was smooth and unwrinkled, her lips firm and full, her eyes clear, though their lids were puffed from tears and the night wind. What had fooled him, Longarm decided, was her hair. It was ash-blonde, almost white, and she wore it long and loose, caught up only by a small pin that gathered it at the back of her neck. He squinted at her hairline in the lamplight; there was no telltale sign of dyeing.

Starr tried to move around the table and bumped into the girl. He said, "You get up on one of them chairs and light that ceiling lamp, miss. We're going to need to see what we're doing."

A reflector-type kerosene lamp hung above the table. The girl moved a chair to stand on, and touched the match Starr had given her to the wick. The room grew brighter as she adjusted the flame to stop its smoking.

Longarm got his first good look at the unconscious man. The stranger was young, probably in his mid-twenties, as closely as Longarm could tell through the smudges of grime and trail dust that covered his face. The man was clean-shaven, though now his cheeks and jaws bore the dark stubble of a three or four days' beard. His lips were full but bloodless, so that his face appeared almost to be lacking a mouth. Waxen white lines showed at his nostrils under the coating of dirt. The man was hatless, and a shock of thick brown hair was tousled around his ears.

Looking at the blood that was beginning to pool on the table under the stranger's body and trickle in a slow drip-drip-drip to the floor, Longarm shook his head.

"He's really hurt bad, isn't he?" the girl asked. Her voice was still hoarse, and she spoke in a cracked whisper.

"He don't look very good," Longarm affirmed.

Starr had gone into the bedroom. He came out carrying a handful of white cloth. "One of Belle's old petticoats," he told Longarm, handing him the wadded cloth. "I'll see if I can't find some more in a minute. Looks like we're going to need them."

Longarm frowned. "Where's Belle?"

"I don't know." Sam replied. "She's a restless sleeper, you know. A lot of nights she'll get up and walk down to the river, or up to the groves on the hill. I didn't wake up when she slipped out of bed."

Longarm was busy unbuttoning the man's shirt. He pulled the front open and looked at the raw flesh just below the unconscious stranger's ribcage. It was an exit wound, and the slug had torn out flesh and skin to leave a deep wound almost as big around as the palm of a man's hand. There was a second bullet hole on the other side, but it was a mere scratch compared to the big wound, from which blood seeped steadily.

Longarm ripped pieces of cloth from the petticoat and made a wad to go into the bigger of the two wounds. He tore a wide strip from the hem of the garment and handed it to Starr.

"Slide this under him when I lift up his shoulders," he said.

He lifted the limp form, and Starr slid the bandage under the man's back. Longarm wrapped the improvised bandage as tightly as he could around the man's chest, and tied the ends of the cloth. The man stirred and twitched, and his lips moved for the first time.

"He's trying to say something," the girl whispered. "Do you think he's coming around?"

"Might be," Longarm replied. He handed the girl a piece of the petticoat. "Here. Wet this and sponge off his face."

"There's water in the bucket back of the stove," Starr told her.

High heels beat a tattoo across the porch, and Belle Starr walked into the room. "What's going on here, Sam?" she asked as she came through the door. Inside, she saw the unconscious form of the stranger on the table. "Who is he?" she asked nobody in particular.

"I don't know," Sam replied. "I haven't had time to find out. Windy brought him down to the house." He squinted through the lamplight at his wife. "Where the hell you been, Belle?"

"Down by the river. I couldn't sleep, so I went for a walk." Belle turned to Longarm. "You know who he is, Windy?"

"Nope. I heard a horse and what sounded like a woman's voice, so I went out to look. Found this fellow on a lame nag, with this girl here holding him up. I got them down here and yelled for you and Sam."

"I wondered where you were," Belle said. "I stopped at your cabin—" She saw Sam looking at her and added quickly, "To see if you were comfortable. Then I walked on down to the river."

Booted feet grated over the dirt outside and clumped across the porch. Floyd came in. He had on boots and trousers and his gunbelt, but was shirtless. He blinked in the sudden light.

"What's the trouble, Belle?" he asked. Then, as his eyes adjusted to the brightness, he saw the stranger lying on the table with the girl bathing his face and Longarm adjusting the bandage, which was now stained with blood.

Floyd's eyes slitted and the corners of his mouth pulled down in an angry snarl as he said, "Goddamn! That's Lon Taylor! Me and Steed been looking for him to get here."

"He's the fellow who was going to help you with—" Belle began.

Floyd cut her off. "That's him. Who the hell shot him up? Is this some more of your goddamn work, Windy?"

89

Chapter 8

Before Longarm could say anything, Belle cut Floyd short. "Shut up, Floyd! Windy didn't have anything to do with Taylor being shot. All he's doing is trying to help him."

"That's right," the girl seconded, "if this big man here is the one you call Windy. If it hadn't been for him hearing me calling for help, and if he hadn't come to see what was wrong, I don't know whether we'd have made it to the house."

Floyd was slowly subsiding. He said, "All right, if that's the way of it."

"That's the way of it," Belle assured him. "Now, if you don't want to help, stay out of the way and we'll see what we can do for your friend."

She went to help Longarm. As she bent over Taylor, she asked, "Where were you a while ago, Windy? I went in, but you weren't in the cabin."

"I was like you, Belle—I couldn't sleep, so I moved over to the barn."

"Why the barn? You'd have been welcome here in the house."

"Never mind that now," Longarm said impatiently. "Let's see if we can't stop that blood from coming up through the bandage I put on this poor devil."

Belle looked at the bloodstained bandage. "You need lint under it to stop the blood. Wait a minute, I've got some cloth I can shred up." She hurried into the bedroom.

"Is Lonnie going to be all right?" the girl asked Longarm.

"Too soon to say, ma'am. He's in real bad shape. Lost a lot of blood, I'd judge."

90

Floyd asked the girl, "Who in hell are you, lady? And how'd you get connected up with Lon?"

"I've known Lonnie for years, mister. Ever since we were in school together, back in Kansas." She frowned, her eyes widening. "Why, you must be Floyd. Are you?"

"That's me."

"Lonnie was coming here to meet you. If he hadn't stayed conscious long enough to show me how to go, though, I never would've found this place."

"How'd he get shot?" Floyd asked.

"I—do I have to talk about that now? Can't it all wait until we see how Lonnie's going to do?"

"Sure. I was just asking," Floyd told her. He looked at Taylor on the table. "Old Lon sure don't look too good right now, though. I hope he pulls through."

Belle came in carrying a handful of shredded rags. "Here," she said to Longarm. "We'll untie that bandage enough to get to where he's wounded, and put these over the place. Maybe that'll stop him from bleeding so much."

For the next few minutes, Longarm and Belle worked over Taylor. When the lint had been packed in the gaping wound and the bandage retied, Belle said, "Well, that's all I can see to do for him right now. If he comes to, we'll try to get a little whiskey down him; that'll help his circulation. But all we can do right now is wait and see." She turned to her husband. "Sam, is there any coffee left from supper? I guess we could all use some. Or a drink, or both."

"It's heating, Belle," Sam replied. "And I've got water hottening on the stove, too."

A thudding of boots on the porch announced the arrival of Steed and Bobby. Steed growled, "What's all the fuss up here? Bobby woke up and seen the lights, and we figured something was wrong."

"Taylor just rode in," Floyd said. "He got himself shot up somewhere. I don't know where or how."

"Who done it?" Steed asked.

"How bad is he hurt?" Bobby asked at almost the same moment.

Floyd answered them both at the same time. "I don't know who got him. And we won't know for a while how bad it is." He dropped his voice to a whisper. "The way he looks, he ain't going to make it."

"Goddamn! That blows our job for sure!" Steed exclaimed.

"We'll wait and see," Floyd replied.

"But with McKee dead, and now maybe Taylor, how could we pull it off?" Bobby asked. "You said there had to be five of us at least."

"Shut up, Bobby!" Belle commanded. "Floyd, you and Steed cut it out, too. We'll see what happens to your friend, then we can make a new plan, if we have to. There's others we can bring in besides McKee and Taylor."

Longarm overheard the conversation; they were standing directly behind him. Apparently, in their excitement, they'd forgotten about him. Or, he thought, they might have accepted him as one of their kind by now.

Taylor groaned and his body twitched. His eyes opened, but weren't focused; he shook his head to try to see clearly.

Longarm said over his shoulder, not caring who responded, "Pour a little bit of that whiskey in a glass. Let's try to get a drink down him."

It was the girl who reacted first. She splashed some of the corn liquor into the first glass she picked up from the chair. Longarm raised Taylor's shoulders; the wounded man was still trying to focus his eyes. The girl put the glass to Taylor's lips. He accepted the liquor in his mouth, but gagged when he tried to swallow it. Most of it trickled back out and dripped off his chin onto his bloodstained chest.

"Try again," Longarm urged her.

This time, Taylor managed to get a good swallow of the whiskey down his throat. Holding him by the shoulders, Longarm could feel the muscles of his back beginning to flex.

"Go on," he urged Taylor. "Swallow it on down."

Taylor finally managed to get his vision under control. He looked up at Longarm. "Who're you?" he asked. His voice was thin, almost inaudible.

"He's the man who helped us get here," the girl answered before Longarm could speak.

Taylor turned his eyes to look at her. "Susie. You got me here, didn't you?"

"Yes. But you're hurt real bad, Lonnie. You just lay back now and try to rest. You'll be all right, I know you will!"

"Hey! He's come around!" Floyd exclaimed. He stepped up to the table, followed by Steed and Bobby. They jostled against Longarm, and he stepped away to give them room.

"Said—I'd—be—here," Taylor said in a series of gasping whispers.

"Lonnie! Don't talk now. Save your strength!" the girl urged.

Belle drew Longarm away from the table. "I don't know about him. That bullet took him in a bad place."

"I know," Longarm agreed. "I've seen men hit high in the belly there before. Mostly, they hang on and you think they're going to get over it, but then they just fade off."

"Why'd you decide to sleep in the barn?" Belle asked.

"I didn't like those windows up above the bunks in that cabin. Not with Floyd just a little ways off."

"Don't worry about Floyd. He'll do what I tell him to," she assured him. "Well, we'll just have to wait and see how things turn out."

Sam Starr came up frowning, carrying steaming coffee-cups. "I don't like this a bit, Belle. Somebody might have been trailing that fellow. He could have led a posse right up to our door."

"I'd have heard them, if there was anybody behind him," Longarm told Sam. "There wasn't."

"How in hell do you know, Windy?" Starr asked. His voice was somewhat uncertain, despite the bluster in his words. "They might be tracking him, five or ten miles behind."

"That's the most sensible thing you've said in a long time, Sam," Belle told her husband. She called. "Steed! Bobby! Come here!"

When the two outlaws got to her side, Belle said, "Get your rifles and stand watch up at the gully. We don't know there isn't a posse tracking your friend. It damned sure wasn't any friends of his who shot him."

93

"They'd have got here by now, if they was after him," Steed objected.

"Not if they were waiting for daylight to pick up his tracks," Belle said. She gave Sam no credit for having been the first to come up with the idea. "Now, you stay at the gully until about noon. I'll get Yazoo to bring you some breakfast after while."

Steed looked as though he wanted to object still further, but Belle's black look kept him silent. He shrugged and said, "Come on, Bobby. Belle just might have an idea there."

Longarm went back to the table to look at Taylor. Floyd was still standing there. The girl, too, still stood on the other side of the wounded man. Taylor's eyes were closed, and his chest was rising and falling irregularly.

Floyd asked Longarm, "How's he look to you?"

"I've seen shot men who looked better. He had to wait too long to get those holes plugged up."

"How many holes has he got in him, for Christ's sake?" Floyd asked.

"I saw two, but I didn't go over him too good. I was too busy getting that real bad one stopped up."

"We'd better look him over, then," Belle said. She'd come up to the table, following Longarm.

They searched Taylor's prone form, and did find a third wound, a shallow graze, high on one side, almost in his armpit. It was no more than a scratch, raw but not bleeding now. They agreed that it would be better to leave it alone rather than to disturb Taylor by moving him to get a bandage on it.

"Whoever it was chasing him, they sure did intend to stop him," Floyd commented. He looked at the girl, who hadn't moved while they were making their examination. "You feel like telling us what happened, lady? There's not a hell of a lot we can do for Taylor right now. Not until he gets better—or worse."

"You're right, Floyd," Belle agreed. She raised her voice. "Sam! Come watch Taylor while the rest of us go out on the porch. We need a breath of fresh air. You can start breakfast when we get back."

"Sure, Belle." Sam moved obediently to the table, pulled

94

up a chair, and sat down. "If he comes around again, I'll call you."

"We'd better take care of Taylor's horse," Belle said when she saw the animal still standing in front of the house. "I'll get Sam to take care of it as soon as he has time."

"Never mind, Belle. I'll lead it into the barn and un-saddle it," Longarm told her. "I need to get my vest, any-how. It's got my cigars in the pocket."

He led the animal into the barn, took off its saddlebags and tossed them in a corner, then loosened the cinch and lifted the saddle off. He set it beside the saddlebags, then he went up to the loft, slid his arms into his vest, and ar-ranged his watch chain in its usual style, draped across from the pocket holding his watch to the opposite pocket, in which his derringer nestled, clipped to the other end of the chain. He took enough time to down a swallow of his own Maryland rye, and walked on outside before lighting his cheroot.

In the east, the sky was beginning to show the gray of false dawn, but it was still dark on the porch except for the patch of light from the open house door.

"Well," the girl was saying, "I guess I don't quite know how to start out."

"You might start out by telling us who you are," Belle suggested, "and how you came to hook up with Taylor."

Longarm suddenly realized that things had moved so swiftly since he'd first responded to the girl's cries—that everyone's attention had been focused so completely on Taylor—that nobody had learned the girl's name.

She said, "My name—my name's Dolly Varden."

Belle interrupted her with a laugh, a raucous, sneering chortle. "You'll have to do better than that, missy. I know where that name comes from. You must think we're all ignorant around here, but let me tell you something: I went to the Carthage Female Academy, and I learned how to read books. And that name's right out of a book by an Englishman called Charles Dickens. He made it up a long time ago."

"Really?" the girl asked. Her eyes widened in surprise. "You mean it's just a made-up name?"

95

"That's what it is," Belle told her. "Now, suppose you come down off your high horse and tell us your real name."

"Oh, hell!" the girl sighed. "I didn't know Dolly Varden wasn't real—that is, I didn't know it was made up such a long time back. And I wasn't trying to fool you. I've just called myself that for so long that I'd almost forgotten what my own name is. Until I ran into Lonnie about two weeks ago." She sighed again and went on, "My real name's Susanna. Susanna Mudgett. Everybody just called me Sue, back home. But when Lonnie began calling me Sue, I almost didn't answer him half the time."

Floyd said impatiently, "Come on, Dolly or Sue or whoever you are. We want to hear about Lon Taylor, not about you."

"Appears to me we'll have to hear about both of them, if we want to know what happened to Taylor," Longarm pointed out. He went up the porch steps and sat down on the bench beside Susanna. "You take your time, now. Start wherever you feel like it, and just tell us whatever comes to your mind first. We'll sort it all out."

"All right," she said nodding. "You see, I hadn't seen Lonnie for a long time—five or six years, I guess. Then he stopped in the place where I was working . . ." She hesitated, shook her head angrily, and blurted, "Oh, hell! You'll know sooner or later. I was a saloon girl over in Texarkana, on the Arkansas side of town. Lonnie came in, and I didn't even recognize him right off. He spotted me, though. And then we got to talking. We—we used to be what we called sweethearts, back home. Of course, that was before we really knew what being sweethearts means."

Longarm interrupted, "Back home, you say. That'd be up in Kansas?"

"Yes. Up at Yates Center. Then Lonnie left home, and I . . . well, I did too, later on. And we didn't see each other again until he came into the saloon, there in Texarkana. Lonnie asked me would I come along with him and be his girl, and I said I would."

"All right, Susan or Dolly or whichever you want us to call you—what happened with Lon?" Floyd asked impatiently, after the girl had sat silently for several moments.

"Well, Lonnie said he had to come up here into the Cherokee Nation, to meet some men. I guess you'd be one of them?" she asked Longarm.

He shook his head. "No. He was talking about Floyd and Steed."

"This is Floyd," Belle told her, pointing. "Steed's up watching the gully you came through getting here."

Susanna spoke directly to Floyd now. "He said he was in with you on some kind of job. I didn't understand what it really was until we got to DeQueen. We stayed there awhile—about a week, I guess. It was while we were there that Lonnie told me how he'd—he'd turned outlaw. And he wouldn't tell me what he was going to meet you for, Floyd, but it was some kind of robbery or something. Is that right?"

"Never mind," Floyd said brusquely. "That's not any of your affair. What else did Lon tell you about me?"

She frowned. "Nothing, really. Oh, he talked about you and the others a lot, but he didn't really *say* anything, if you take my meaning. All I ever did know was that he was supposed to meet you at a place called Younger's Bend. I guess that's here, isn't it?"

"It is," Belle said. "Go on. Get on down to where you ran into the law."

"How'd you know it was the law that shot Lonnie?"

"Hmph. Couldn't have been much else," Belle replied. "I could just about tell your story for you. You got to this place where you stopped—DeQueen?" Susanna nodded, and Belle went on, "Taylor told you he was running short of cash and needed some more, so he went out and came back with a bundle. But there was a posse of some kind chasing him, and you two stayed ahead of them for a while, but they caught up with you. Hell, I know what happened, girl. Am I right?"

"Almost, but not exactly," Susanna said. "It was in DeQueen that Lonnie began to run short of money. He'd had to buy me a horse and saddle, you see, when I said I'd go with him. I didn't have those, or any of the kind of clothes I'd need for traveling that way. So when he said he was coming up broke, I gave him what cash I had, which wasn't much. It was enough for us to travel on a ways, though. We cut over into the Indian Nation, and came to a little place called Poteau. We really *did* run out of money there. We had enough to buy some groceries, though, so Lonnie took me to a place he knew about from when he'd been there before, a cave out west from Poteau. He left me there and said he was going to go raise some money. I guess I knew what he meant, but I just didn't let myself think about it."

"Shit!" Floyd snorted. "Nobody could be that innocent! I think you're stringing us a pack of lies, girl! Now, you tell us exactly what happened, or you'll be in trouble!"

"I'm telling you exactly what happened!" Susanna insisted. "I don't remember things like what Lonnie said to me or I said to him, but it's all true, what I've said so far!"

"Let her tell things her own way, Floyd," Longarm told the outlaw. "We can sort it out after we've heard all of it."

"You keep out of this, Windy!" Floyd shot back. "This ain't your affair!"

"Both of you roosters keep quiet and let the girl finish!" Belle commanded.

Longarm patted Susanna's hand. "Go on, tell us what happened next. Tell it just the way it was, though."

"All right, Windy, I'll do the best I can, but everything that started then was—well, it all happened so fast, I might get mixed up." She frowned, trying to remember where she'd left off, then continued, "I stayed in the cave, let's see—the first night, with Lonnie, then he rode off the next morning and said he'd be gone a day, two days at the most. He didn't come back that night, but he rode up the next morning, real early. He said we had to hurry and get out of there, that they were after him."

"Who was after him?" Floyd asked.

"Why, the sheriff and his deputies," Susanna replied. "I didn't find that out until later on, though. Not until they caught up with us late that afternoon. We'd been pushing our horses real hard, riding around whatever towns we saw ahead of us. I guess that slowed us down a little bit. Anyhow, they got close to us and started shooting. They killed my horse, the one Lonnie'd just bought for me. And he took me up in front of him. But then we couldn't go as fast, of course. That's when they shot Lonnie."

Susanna stopped and pressed her hands over her face. Even Floyd stayed quiet until she was able to go on with her story. "It was lucky that Lonnie knew the country better than the posse did. He rode up a little creekbed and over a hill and doubled back and went over two or three more hills, zigzagging all the time. And I didn't see the men who were chasing us again. Lonnie'd been hurt right bad, though. But you know that. So we changed places. I got back of him in the saddle so I could hold him on, and he told me which way to go. He'd told me where we were heading for, right after we shook off the posse. And then I turned in at the place he'd said to look for, and then Windy came up just when the horse was about to give out. And that's really how it all happened."

"Where was this place that Lon went for money?" Floyd asked.

Susanna shook her head. "I don't really know, Floyd. Lonnie didn't tell me where he'd been, or what happened. Oh, I knew he'd done something that was against the law. I knew what was in his mind when he set out from the cave, even if he didn't tell me. And when he came back, I was sure. He never did say where he'd been or what he'd done, though."

"It was likely a stagecoach or a bank job," Belle said thoughtfully. "I know that cave west of Poteau. He could've gone into Poteau, but if he was smart, he'd have gone all the way back to Arkansas. It's not too far, just an hour of hard riding. There are two or three towns there he could've hit—Hartford or Greenwood or Waldon. I don't see that it makes any difference, though. Your job's north of there."

"We'll find out from Lon when he comes around," Floyd said. "He didn't know too much about what we've been figuring to do. All I said when I sent word to him was to get here to Younger's Bend as fast as he could ride. Told him who he'd be riding with, of course. He'd known McKee and Steed from earlier. He didn't know Bobby, but that wouldn't have worried him. Lon trusts me."

99

"He was on his way here, of course. You'd told him how to find the place, judging from what he told Susanna," Belle said thoughtfully.

"You remember, though, Belle, he didn't even tell Susanna until he'd been shot, and he knew she'd need to be able to find her way here," Floyd pointed out.

"Hell, Floyd, I never have made any secret of where Younger's Bend is. There isn't any need to, as long as my treaty with the Cherokees holds good."

Starr called from inside the house, "Belle! Taylor's coming around! He keeps calling for some girl, Sue's her name. Would that be the—"

Susanna hurried inside, followed by the others. Taylor's eyes were open and he was looking around the room. He saw Susanna and tried to sit up, but lacked the strength. She hurried to the table and took his hand.

"I guess you got me here in time," he whispered. His voice was weak and raspy in his throat. "I feel pretty good right now."

"That's fine, Lonnie. You'll be looked after. Everybody's trying to help," she said.

Taylor saw Floyd, who'd come up to the table. "I'll be riding with you on that job, Floyd. Just don't plan on starting it until I feel a little stronger."

"Don't worry, Lon. I'll wait till you heal up," Floyd assured him.

Taylor smiled weakly. "That—that's good."

Floyd saw the whiskey bottle sitting in the chair. He said, "We'll just have a drink on that, by God!" and walked around the table, picked up the bottle, and selected two glasses.

"I'm sure glad you feel better, Lonnie," Susanna said.

Taylor looked at her and smiled. He started to say something, but the words that formed in his mouth failed to come out. His throat pulsed convulsively for a moment, then his eyes rolled upward, the pupils going out of sight even though the eyelids remained wide open. His head fell back and his body seemed to shrink a tiny amount as it went limp.

Susanna stared at him, realization growing in her eyes. "Oh, God!" she gasped. "I—I think Lonnie's dead!"

Chapter 9

"Dead?" Floyd whirled around, still holding the two shots of whiskey he'd poured. "How in hell could he be? He just said he was feeling a lot better!"

"I don't know how he could!" Susanna retorted. "He started to say something, then all of a sudden he died! That's all!"

Longarm came up, took Susanna's arms, and led her away from the table. She was trembling but not crying. He took her outside to the porch and sat her down on the bench. In the house, he heard Floyd say to Belle and Sam, "By God, he's dead, all right."

"Too bad," Belle said. "Damned if you're not having rough luck, Floyd. Maybe we'd just better call off that job we figured on. Seems to me like there's a jinx on it."

"No, by God!" Floyd replied angrily. "We're not calling off anything, Belle! I'm holding you to your word! We'll find somebody to fill in for McKee and Lonnie, even if you and Sam have to take their places."

"Now that's something to think about," Belle said slowly. "I've dressed like a man before; I don't see why I couldn't do it again. Borrow a pair of Bobby's pants and a shirt, paste on a false horsetail mustache. I guess I could still carry it off."

Sam said quietly, "I don't think you could, Belle. You've got pretty big in the ass lately."

"Well, damn you, Sam!"

There was the sound of a slap, and Sam came running out the door, clattered across the porch, and disappeared into the barn. Belle came to the door after him.

"Where'd he go?" she asked Longarm. "No husband of mine is going to make snide remarks about my figure! You

101

think it's all right, don't you, Windy? You don't think my butt's too big?"

"You look just fine to me, Belle," Longarm said. He thought he might divert her from pursuing the luckless Sam. "Of course, I never did see you before just recently, so I don't know what you used to look like."

"Well, I haven't changed all that much," Belle snapped. She pulled skirt tightly around her hips and swayed in front of Longarm. "See?"

"I don't know what you're all thinking about!" Susanna burst out. "Lonnie just died, and everybody's fighting and arguing! Windy, is there somewhere around here that you can take me where I can just be quiet a little while?"

"Sure, Susanna. I'll walk you down to my cabin. You're tuckered out anyhow, and you need to rest up awhile."

Belle said, "Listen, missy. You're new at this game. I'm Belle Starr, the Bandit Queen, and I've seen a lot of men die, including a husband or two. You'll find out, after you've been around awhile, that when something bad happens, you can't waste time mourning over it. You grit you teeth and laugh if you can, and you go on living!"

"Well, it seems real heartless to me!" Susanna said. Her eyes were still dry, but her mouth was drawn down at the corners and her chin was trembling.

"You'll think differently after you've lived a little bit longer," Belle said. Then, turning to Longarm, "Go ahead, Windy. Take her down to your plane and let her sleep a while; that's what she needs. You come back when you get hungry. Sam's going to have breakfast ready pretty soon."

As they walked across the rough, rock-strewn soil of Younger's Bend to the cabin Longarm was supposed to be occupying, the lawman realized that Susanna was suffering from exhaustion as well as from a delayed reaction to Taylor's death. She stumbled several times on pebbles during the short walk from the house, and, halfway there, her legs began to tremble and her body to wobble.

"Help me, Windy!" she pleaded. "I don't think I can walk the rest of the way by myself!"

Longarm put an arm around Susanna and supported her until they got into the cabin. He led her to one of the bunks. She slumped down on it, and he lifted her legs onto the tattered mattress. "Thank you, Windy," she said. "All of a sudden, I'm so . . . soo . . . sleepy . . ."

Her words trailed off with a sigh. Her breathing, which had been ragged, almost spasmodic, settled down into the easy regularity of sleep. Longarm stood for a moment, looking down at her.

Now, in real light, he could see that she must be past her mid-twenties. At the corners of her eyes, fine lines promised crow's-feet soon to show. Delicate lines were also faintly visible running from her nostrils to the corners of her mouth. The mouth itself was almost perfectly circular, with lip-peaks and corners almost imperceptible; her lips were virtually the same width all the way around the small, slightly protruding teeth that showed when her lips were parted with her breathing. Her chin was round, like that of a child whose face is just settling into adulthood. Under her thin dress, the twin globes of firm, round breasts jutted high. Her long ashen hair lay tumbled around her head and shoulders.

Longarm left Susanna sleeping and walked back to the house, where the argument had shifted from the job planned by Floyd to a dispute over who was going to dig Taylor's grave.

"Damned if I'm going to push that shovel into this hard dirt ever again!" Floyd proclaimed. "McKee was my partner a long time. Taylor I don't hardly know."

"You'll have to bury him then, Sam," Belle told Starr, who had apparently returned from the barn. "But if you can get Floyd to help you carry him up to the grove, you can put off digging his grave until Yazoo shows up to help you."

Longarm waited outside until Starr and Floyd came out, carrying Taylor's body between them. He'd learned the army lesson that began somewhere in the dim past, with Attila's hordes or Caesar's legions, never to volunteer. When Floyd and Starr rounded the corner of the house on their way to the grove, he went inside.

Belle sat in a chair at the table, staring at the blood-stained tabletop. "You'll have to wait until Sam gets back and scrubs the table before we can have breakfast," she said. "Unless you want to wash it yourself."

"I'll wait," Longarm told her curtly. "I want a drink before I eat, anyhow."

"There's coffee on the stove and some whiskey left in the bottle," she informed him. "Take your choice."

"Meaning no offense toward your whiskey, Belle, but I've got what's left of a bottle of Maryland rye out in the barn. I'll just step out and get it."

"What's wrong with Younger's Bend whiskey?" she demanded. "Yazoo is as good a whiskey-maker as any you'll find in a regular distillery."

"Oh, there ain't a thing wrong with your liquor, if a man relishes corn whiskey. Just happens I've got a taste for rye."

"Have what you choose," she said curtly. "I don't give a damn."

Not wanting to offend her further by bringing his bottle of rye into the house, Longarm had a sip in the barn, lighted a fresh cheroot, and had a second sip before going back. Yazoo was there, and relatively sober. His eyes were rheumy, but his speech was plain and unslurred by liquor.

The old man nodded. "Morning, Windy. I hear things got sorta roiled up again down here last night."

"A little bit," Longarm agreed. "Maybe that'll be the last of it, though."

"It better be the last of it!" Belle said. Her voice was sharp with anger. "I don't want Younger's Bend getting a reputation as a place where people go to die!" She stamped into the bedroom, slamming the door behind her.

"Belle gets that way now and again," Yazoo chuckled. He saw the whiskey bottle; there was only a half-inch of liquor left in it. "Just what I need to tide me over until breakfast." He tilted the bottle and drained it.

"You make pretty fair moonshine up at your stillhouse, Yazoo," Longarm observed. "Turn out a lot for sale, I guess, besides what Sam and Belle use around the place here—them and Belle's guests?"

"Three barrels a week." Yazoo boasted. "Got customers coming to get it from as far off as Shawnee and Pawhuska and Talequah and Talihini, and a lot from Fort Smith. Yessir! Belle's got a real good business going here!"

"It's a wonder the feds don't come after you," Longarm

104

said. "At your age, I'd hate to face up to going to the pen."

"Shit!" Yazoo spat. "I been turning out moonshine for a long spell, Windy, and I never spent a day in the pen for making it. Closest I come was one time up in Wyoming Territory. Had me a big still up on Horse Creek between Cheyenne and Laramie, and got hauled in. Didn't do time, though. Judge let me go. I figured he'd drank the evidence, from the way he looked."

Something clicked in Longarm's memory. Now he recalled where he'd seen Yazoo before. He'd been waiting in federal court to give evidence in another case when the old man—younger, then, and looking a lot different—had gone on trial.

To get Yazoo's mind off his story, he said quickly, "I looked for you to be drawn down here to the house last night, what with all the ruckus that was being raised."

"I didn't hear a bit of it," Yazoo said. "Slept the night through like a baby." He looked at the empty bottle that he still held. "I guess while I'm waiting for Sam to fix breakfast, I'll go back up and bring down a few more bottles for the house. Walk along with me, if you want a look at my still."

"No. No, thanks, Yazoo. I done all my running around last night."

"Suit yourself." Yazoo shook his head. "Damn me, every time I talk to you, Windy, it almost comes back to me where I run into you afore. I'll recall, one of these days."

Yazoo ambled out the door and headed for the still-house. Longarm felt like sighing with relief. He'd had a nervous moment when he realized that Yazoo's memory of his old arrest might be all that was needed to remind him of the time when his track and Longarm's had crossed before. He was almost glad to see Starr and Floyd come in. Starr went directly to the stove and began clattering pots and pans in preparation for cooking breakfast. Floyd picked up the empty whiskey bottle and stood looking at it for a moment, then he turned to Longarm, scowling.

"Damn you, Windy! You guzzled the last of the moonshine, and I was saving that drink for when I got back from carrying Taylor up the hill!" Floyd drew back the hand holding the bottle, and was just about to throw it into the corner of the room when Belle came in.

"Don't do that, Floyd." Her voice was low, but it had the lash of a whip in it.

Floyd lowered the hand holding the bottle. "Windy got the drink I was saving for myself!" he complained.

"No, he didn't," Belle said. "Windy told me he doesn't especially like corn whiskey. He went out to the barn and had a drink from his own bottle of rye."

"You don't say! I guess you followed him and watched, since you're so damn certain?"

"I didn't have to. I heard Yazoo talking in here a few minutes ago. And I don't want you to sass me anymore, Floyd. Just remember who you're talking to from now on."

Starr paid no attention to the exchange between Belle and Floyd. He brought a pan of water to the table and began scrubbing away the bloodstains left by Taylor.

Longarm said, "Yazoo'll be back in a few minutes. He went up to get some more whiskey. You won't have to wait long for your drink, Floyd."

"Thanks for nothing," Floyd snapped.

Belle stamped her foot. "Another thing, Floyd. I want you to stop trying to pick a fight with Windy. He's been holding back, I can tell that, to keep from arguing with you. Now, I want you two to get along together, Floyd. Remember, you're going to need somebody to take McKee's and Taylor's places if you expect to pull off that job we've been working up."

"Oh, now hold up a minute, Belle! You don't expect me to take Windy in on that! Not after he killed McKee!"

"It was a fair shootout," Belle said. "And I told you right after it happened that it wasn't any of your affair what kind of grudge there was between McKee and Windy."

"It sticks in my craw, just the same," Floyd protested. "Anyhow, I thought it was all settled for you and Sam to fill in for McKee and Taylor."

"We might, and we might not," Belle replied. "I haven't made up my mind yet. But I've seen Windy in action. I know what he can do."

106

"Now let's stop this kind of talk right here," Longarm said firmly. "I feel just about like Floyd does, but maybe not for the same reasons. Belle, before you start including me in any job you and Floyd or anybody else has cooked up, you better find out first if I want to be cut in."

"I just haven't gotten around to it yet, Windy. But it's a big job, and there'll be good money in it for all of us."

"That's as it may be. But I don't know anything about Floyd or Steed or Bobby. Or, come right down to it, about you and Sam, except for what I've heard here and there. I don't say I won't talk about getting in, but I don't let anybody put me up for anything before I say yes."

"Strikes me you're just a mite too damn particular for us to fool with, Windy," Floyd said.

"Maybe I am, but I'm still walking around, and I aim to stay this way. I won't go into anything blind," Longarm said flatly.

Sam Starr interrupted the discussion by dropping plates with a clatter on the tabletop. "Breakfast's ready," he announced. "Sit down and eat before it gets cold."

"We'll talk about things later," Belle said as she moved toward the table. She might have been addressing either Longarm or Floyd. "Let's get breakfast over so Sam can clean things up. He's got a job to get to right away."

Halfway through the silent, strained meal, Yazoo joined them. He came in with two bottles of whiskey under each arm, and set a bottle at each end of the table before depositing the other two in one of the KC Baking Powder boxes.

Floyd drank corn moonshine instead of coffee throughout the meal. The liquor, on his almost empty stomach, made him sleepy. He finished first and stood up unsteadily. "I'm going to get myself forty winks," he announced to the table in general. "You go ahead and have your talk with Windy, Belle. Then you and me will sit down and settle things, once and for all."

When he'd gone, Belle said to Longarm, "We'll have that talk while Sam and Yazoo are up at the grove burying Taylor. And don't worry about Floyd. You can see how he's coming around."

Longarm didn't see, but he wasn't going to tell Belle

107

that he hadn't noticed much of a change in Floyd's attitude. He'd be suspicious if Floyd *did* welcome him in on whatever illegal project Belle had come up with. In fact, the minute Floyd agreed to add him to the group, it would be a signal that the surly outlaw had decided to accept Longarm and use him in carrying out the job, with the idea that there would be a backshooting or a fatal accident when things were over, which would keep Longarm from being on hand to claim a share of the loot. Bandits had been known to kill other bandits for no more reason than that, and in Floyd's case there was the extra motive provided by Longarm's killing of McKee.

All of them had just about finished eating when Floyd left. In a few minutes, Sam Starr stood up and said, "Whenever you're ready, we'll go on up and do our job, Yazoo."

"Guess I'm as ready as I'll ever be." The old man stood up. He picked up one of the bottles from the table and put it under his arm. "I'll just take this along, Sam. Grave-digging gets to be real dry work."

"And don't forget Steed and Bobby," Belle reminded Sam. "I told them you'd bring some breakfast up to them."

"I haven't forgot," Starr replied. "I'll take care of them, Belle. You don't have to worry."

"We've got the place to ourselves until noon," Belle told Longarm after Sam and Yazoo had gone. "Plenty of time for a private talk and a chance to get better acquainted."

"Let's get down to business, then," Longarm said. "You know I'm not looking around for something to do right now. It ain't like I was broke and needed to put a stake together—"

"I know that, Windy," Belle broke in. "I saw that poke you're carrying, remember, when you paid your rent yesterday. You must've pulled off a big job. It's funny, though, I haven't heard about any really big hauls lately. Where were you working?"

"Far enough away so the news wouldn't have reached here yet. And in my regular line, there's a lot of things I do that are kept quiet." Which, Longarm thought, was the real truth.

"That money you've got won't last forever, Windy,"

108

Belle pointed out. "You'd be better off adding to it while you've got the chance than letting this job of mine slip by you. It's big enough to interest you, I know. What I've got planned—"

"Now hold on a minute, Belle." Longarm didn't want to seem too anxious to learn the details of Belle's scheme. He'd maneuvered her into inviting him in, and right now she'd reached the point where nothing in the world was going to stop her from telling him all about it. The less interested he appeared to be, the harder she was going to try to get him in, which meant that she'd spill all the details of her plans, once he let her get started talking.

Longarm went on, "I better tell you first off that I'm not much for partnering. When a man works by himself, he's got nobody to split with. And when the job's finished, there's nobody who can point a finger at him and say he did it."

"Oh, I can understand that. I've only had one really good partner myself, and that was my first husband—" Belle stopped and then added hastily, "First except for Cole Younger, that is. Of course, Cole and me hadn't been married long when he got caught, and he's been in the pen ever since."

"I recall Cole had some bad luck," Longarm told her. "But I never was around the places where the Jameses and the Youngers worked."

Belle was still caught up in her sentimental reminiscences. "I don't guess you ever met my second husband, either. He was the one I meant when I said I'd only had one good partner. Jim Reed." She looked at Longarm and sighed. "Except that Jim was darker, you remind me a lot of Jim."

"I've heard a little bit about him," Longarm said truthfully. "Got cut down while he was getting away from a mail-coach job, didn't he?"

"Yes." Belle stood up and began to pace back and forth across the small room. "Poor Jim would still be alive if I'd been able to go with him to take that mail coach. I was carrying our baby, though, our boy, Ed." She picked up one of the bottles of whiskey and took a swallow from it. "Ed's in a private school back in Missouri right now, you know. So is my other baby, Pearl. That's the beautiful girl I got from Cole. She's dark, like me. Thank God, she didn't turn out to be blonde and look like a floozie."

Belle resumed her nervous pacing. "They're why I've got to keep busy, Windy. You know, it costs a lot of money to keep both of them in the best schools there are."

"Sure. I can see that, Belle," Longarm replied. "And I know you've had bad luck with this job, coming up shorthanded the way you are."

"Now, if Jim Reed was still alive, it wouldn't bother me a bit." Belle took another drink. "You know, Windy, I guess one reason why I want you to be with us on this job is that you remind me so much of Jim. If your hair was just a little bit longer, and you didn't wear your mustache so big . . ."

Longarm cut in, "If Jim Reed was going out on a job, would he have been fool enough to partner up with somebody carrying the sort of grudge against him that Floyd's got against me?"

"No. Jim would get rid of Floyd."

"I draw the line at that, Belle. The only time I throw down on a man is if it's him or me."

"I didn't mean that the way you took it. But you don't have to worry about Floyd, Windy, I keep telling you that. He's not calling the shots, I am."

Longarm frowned thoughtfully. "You said it's a big job. I don't know this country real well, but I can't think of a small town around here where you'd find a whole lot of loose money. Are you sure you're not aiming too high? I wouldn't want to get caught up in a squeeze like the James boys did in Northfield."

"Hell, some dirty skunk tipped off the local law in Northfield." Belle took another swallow from the bottle she was still carrying around as she paced. "That's one thing we don't have to worry about here. Even if somebody did pass on a tip, the local law wouldn't do anything about it."

Longarm studied the smug expression that had crept onto Belle's face. Then he asked, "Are you telling me you've got the marshal or the sheriff paid off, wherever it is your bunch will hit?"

"How do you think I got to be Belle Starr, the Bandit Queen? Listen, Windy, I pay off the law—or enough of it to be safe—in most of the towns just outside this part of the Nation."

"Well, now." Longarm acted as though Belle's boast had impressed him. "That might change my mind about things." Then, as though he still needed more persuasion, he went on, "But I'd still want to know more about it. Outside of Fort Smith, which I hear is a pretty good-sized place, I'd say there's not a bank in any town hereabouts that'd carry enough cash to make a good payoff for five or six men."

"What's wrong with Fort Smith?" Belle asked.

For a moment Longarm was so astonished that he forgot to carry on with his acting. He stared at Belle, surprised. Then he caught himself up and shook his head. "I don't know all that much about the place, but from what I've heard, it's too big for five men to handle. Or fifty, if you come down to cases."

"There are two big banks there," Belle said. "Both of them are big enough to make it worth the trouble."

"I don't know, Belle." Longarm shook his head. "Sounds pretty risky. Hell, there's bound to be too many marshals and deputies in a place like that for you to have all of them bought off."

"You'd be surprised if you knew how many I could make jump if I just said froggy," Belle said with a smirk. She was confident, now, that she was going to succeed in bringing Longarm into her scheme, and she showed it. "Just because I'm a woman doesn't mean I don't know what I'm doing."

"Oh, I won't argue with that, Belle," Longarm told her. "I'll go this far, right now. You let me do a little thinking about it. And while I'm thinking, you do some talking with Floyd. If everything works out, I just might change my mind about throwing in with you on this job."

"I thought you'd come around," she said. "Let's have a drink on it." She held out the bottle.

"I'll drink with you, but I'll go get my own whiskey, if it's all the same to you. Corn liquor just hits my belly in the wrong place."

Belle was miffed, but tried not to show it. She said, "That's your choice, Windy. Go get your bottle." Her voice dropped to a suggestive whisper. "I'll wait until you come back."

Footsteps grated on the hard ground outside and clumped on the porch. Longarm stifled a sigh of relief. It didn't matter to him who was coming in; he wasn't going to be caught by Belle.

Floyd said from the doorway, "Damn it, Belle, I couldn't get to sleep for worrying about that job. McKee, then Taylor. I've got the feeling our luck's gone sour."

Longarm spoke quickly. "You two'll want to talk private, I can see that. Belle, we'll have that drink later. I'll get out of the way now, so you and Floyd can get things straightened out."

Before Belle could object, Longarm was outside the house. He collected his gear from the barn. Tayor's saddlebags caught his eye and he picked them up; there might, he thought, be something in them the girl would need when she awoke. With his bedroll, his Winchester, and the two pairs of saddlebags weighing him down, he walked the short distance to the cabin.

Chapter 10

Susanna was still asleep when Longarm entered the cabin. He moved as quietly as possible to avoid rousing her. He let his saddlebags slide quietly to the floor in the corner beyond the stove and put his bedroll beside them, then leaned his rifle against the wall just inside the door. He thought for a moment of going back up to the house and leaving Susanna to sleep undisturbed, but decided he'd be better off if he stayed clear of Belle, Floyd, Sam, and the rest of the Younger's Bend bunch.

Stepping lightly on the wide floorboards, he pulled the almost empty bottle of rye from his saddlebag and put it on the table, then lighted a cheroot. He settled down in one of the chairs. It creaked when it took his weight. Susanna stirred and woke up. For a moment she stared at the ceiling, then the aroma of Longarm's cigar reached her. She twisted her head on the pillowless bunk, looked at him, and sat up. Her long, tousled blonde hair cascaded over her shoulders, and her eyes were still glazed with sleep.

- "Oh," she said. "Windy. I guess I was a little confused for a minute. I sort of forgot where I am."

"You feel better, now that you've had a good sleep?"

"Yes. At least I think I do." Susanna yawned and stretched. "I guess I'm hungry, though. And I need to . . ." She stopped and looked around the bare little cabin. "I need to go to the outhouse."

"It's not far off. Up the slope a ways. It's toward the house, and if you want me to go with you while you get some breakfast, I'll be glad to."

Her brows drew together in a frown. "I'm hungry, Windy, but I don't think I could stand to sit down and

113

eat off that table where I saw Lonnie die last night. I'd lose my appetite for sure."

"Tell you what. We'll walk up together and I'll go get you some breakfast on a plate, and we'll come back down here while you eat."

"That'd be fine, if you don't mind. I don't mean to be a lot of trouble to you, but—well, even as hungry as I am, I just—I just couldn't stand to eat off that table right now."

"Come on, then, if you're ready."

Before they reached the house, they saw Sam Starr and Yazoo coming back from their unpleasant job in the grove. Longarm told Susanna, "You run on ahead. I want to have a word with those two."

Yazoo greeted Longarm while they were still a dozen paces apart. "You're the damnedest one I ever seen, Windy. Where in hell did you find that blonde-headed woman? Prettiest thing I seen since I been here at Younger's Bend."

"She's Taylor's woman," Longarm told him. "I let her sleep in my cabin. She didn't feel like staying in the house after Taylor died."

"I got to give you credit," Yazoo chuckled. "You sure didn't let no grass grow under your feet."

The oldtimer had obviously been lightening the job of gravedigging with a sip of corn for every shovelful of dirt, so Longarm let Yazoo's remarks pass. He said to Starr. "I hate to put you to extra trouble, but Susanna's hungry, and I don't think there was much left from breakfast except a few biscuits. If you wouldn't mind, could you stir up a bite for her?"

"I don't mind, Windy. I'll get at it right now, before Belle finds some new job for me to do."

Yazoo said, "I want a closer look at that yellow-haired girl. You get to be my age, Windy, you'll find about all you *can* do is look. Now, you go on back down to the cabin with her, and I'll bring her breakfast down there when I start back to the stillhouse."

"I'd take that right kindly, Yazoo. Susanna's still upset about last night, and I'd as soon not leave her by herself."

"Now, I just can't imagine why," Yazoo chortled as he followed Starr toward the house.

Susanna joined Longarm a few moments later. Her face showed her disappointment when she saw he was empty-handed. "Wasn't there anything for breakfast?" she asked.

"Don't worry. We'll just go back to the cabin and wait a few minutes. Your breakfast's going to be coming right along."

Susanna looked puzzled, but she walked with Longarm back to the cabin. She spoke only once, to ask, "Those two men—Mr. Starr and the old one—they were carrying shovels. Had they been . . ."

"They buried him up on the hill there. If you want, we can walk up and look, after while."

"No. I don't think so, Windy. Lonnie's gone, and that's that. It wasn't—" She stopped short, shook her head. "I guess there's not much else to say, is there?"

Susanna was thoughtfully silent while they waited for Yazoo, and maintained her silence while she ate. Longarm didn't try to encourage her to talk. Susanna was young; she hadn't seen enough of life yet to know that death is inevitable and comes in a fashion that seems arbitrary and undiscriminating and always unfair. He sat across the table from her, sipping rye while she ate.

Having cleared her plate, Susanna sighed and stretched. "I guess I was hungrier than I realized. It was—goodness, it seems like a year since I had anything to eat. But it's really only been since yesterday."

"You've been through an awful lot since then," he pointed out.

"Let's don't talk about it, Windy, please. All I want to do is forget everything that's happened since Lonnie first found me, there in Texarkana."

"Maybe that's what you think you want, but I ain't sure it's the best thing," Longarm told her. "I've found out that the things you try to bury have got a mean way of popping up to plague you later on, when they ain't welcome or wanted. Maybe it'd help if you was to get it all out of your system."

Susanna thought this over for a moment. "You might be right, Windy," she said slowly. "I tried to forget about things that had happened to me at home, after I'd left. I never could really put them out of my mind, though."

115

"If you feel like talking, I'm ready to listen." Longarm didn't feel at all ashamed that he had an ulterior motive in making the suggestion. If Susanna began to tell him of her days with Taylor, she might let a few things fall that would help him.

She stood up and walked the length of the little cabin, then came back to the table before she answered him. "It might be too soon to talk about all of it. But there are a few things that keep bothering me."

"Such as what?"

Susanna didn't reply any more quickly this time than she had to his earlier suggestion. She went to the bunk and sat down, crossing her ankles in front of her on the mattress, Indian-style. She closed her eyes and leaned her head back. Her throat was a clean column from chin to shoulders, her long hair a stream of white framing her face. Her low-cut dress exposed the slope of her shoulders, and Longarm could see, in the hollows of her collarbones, the pulsation of her heartbeat.

Longarm didn't try a second time to encourage her to begin talking. He waited patiently until at last she said, "Most of what bothers me is about me and Lonnie. I keep wondering if he might still be alive if he hadn't taken me along with him. You see, if I hadn't been with him, he wouldn't have had to buy me a horse and clothes, and he'd have had enough money to get him to Younger's Bend without his having to stop and steal some. Then the posse wouldn't have been after him, and he'd have gotten here safe and sound."

"You figure you're to blame, some way or other?"

"Well, don't you think I am?"

"Not for a minute, Susanna. It—"

"Windy," she interrupted. "Do me a favor. Please don't call me Susanna anymore. I left that name behind me too long ago. Anyhow, that's what Lonnie called me. Susanna or Susie or Sue."

"Whatever you want. Only I wouldn't know what else to call you."

"I told you last night. Maybe you weren't listening. Dolly. That's the name I've been going by almost from the time I left home."

116

"Sure, I recall what you said now. Belle laughed you down, told you it was a made-up name out of a book. But if it makes you feel better, I'll call you Dolly from here on out."

"Thanks." After a few seconds of thoughtful silence, she asked, "Why don't you think I'm to blame for what happened to Lonnie?"

"Because a man's going to live out his appointed time. It don't matter if it's two years or two hundred, he ain't going to go a day sooner or a day later."

"Do you really believe that, Windy?"

"I sure do. You're too young to remember the War. But I saw men hit on one side of me and on the other, in front of me and in back of me. And there's only one way I can see that explains why one of the bullets that took their lives didn't hit me. It just plain wasn't my time to go."

"I never did think of it that way," she said softly.

"You think about it, then. It's a mighty comforting way to look at things. If it hadn't been you that your old sweetheart ran into, he'd have come across somebody else."

"Lonnie and I weren't really sweethearts, you know," she said. "Why, we weren't more than about twelve or thirteen when we thought we'd just been made for one another. And then . . ."

Longarm waited until he saw that Susanna—Dolly, rather—wasn't going to go on without encouragement. He said, "Go on, Dolly. Talk it all out of your system."

"We grew up in the same little town, you know, Lonnie and me. But all we ever did was kiss a few times. Not even real kisses, either. I guess you know what I mean?" Longarm nodded and she went on, "Oh, I liked Lonnie all right, I guess, but it was somebody else that I fell for. Fell real hard. And I thought he fell as hard for me. I guess he did, but not the way I was thinking. He just had a hard-on for me. And all of a sudden I was pregnant. Fifteen years old, Windy. And Phil was already married."

"So you had to run away."

"Just about. I was lucky, even if I didn't understand it at the time. He was well-to-do. When my family turned me away after they found out I was pregnant, he gave me

117

enough money so I didn't have a bad time while I waited for the baby. And then the baby didn't live but a week. The thing was, I couldn't go back home."

"You said last night that you were working in a saloon when Lonnie bumped into you," Longarm said.

"Yes. Phil's money ran out, of course. I found a job, but I found that keeping the job depended on taking care of the boss. It didn't take me long to figure out that I'd be better off just taking care of men, instead of working behind the counter ten hours and then taking care of one boss who was only paying me for my ten hours behind the counter. So that's how Lonnie came to find me in a saloon in Texarkana."

"Somewhere along the way, you'd picked up Dolly Varden for your name," Longarm said.

"Yes. Damn Belle Starr and her education! She almost ruined that nice name for me. It's not important, though, Windy. You know, for a while, up until last night, I almost went back to being Susanna Mudgett. That was because of Lonnie. But I intend to go on being Dolly Varden. Do you blame me?"

"Not if it's what you want to do. I'd say Belle's a mite jealous of you. You're a lot younger and prettier than she is. It's up to you whether you want to be Dolly or Susanna."

"Right now, I feel like Dolly. I'll tell you something I didn't intend to. I don't think I'd have stayed with Lonnie, even if nothing had happened to him. He made me remember how I was when I was Susanna, and I think I like Dolly better."

"I'd say you've made up your mind, then. As long as you're sure you won't regret it."

"I won't. And now that I've decided to be Dolly, pour me a drink out of that bottle of rye, if you will, Windy. Dolly enjoys a drink. Susanna was always just a little bit of a namby-pamby."

Longarm handed Dolly the bottle and she tipped it to her mouth. He said, "I don't suppose you'll be staying here at Younger's Bend any longer than you can help."

"No. For one thing, I don't like Belle Starr. She's a

118

nasty old woman who's pretending to be something she's not."

Longarm chuckled, and his respect for Dolly's good sense rose several notches. Then he grew serious. "When Taylor told you about this job he was coming up here for, did he give you any idea where it was going to be pulled off?"

"No. I—I don't think Lonnie really trusted me to keep my mouth shut about things like that. He didn't even tell me where we were going until after he got shot. Then he knew I had to know how to find Younger's Bend, in case he might not be able to tell me later."

"And he didn't tell you anything about Floyd or Steed, either?"

"Just their names. Except that he didn't mention the young one—Bobby, isn't that his name?"

"Yes. I don't reckon Floyd would put a whole lot in a letter. Letters have got a way of getting lost, or going to somebody they weren't supposed to."

"Why, Windy? Why are you asking me all these things?"

"Just curious, Dolly. But I'll tell you what I'll do; I'll make a dicker with you, if you're interested."

"What kind of dicker?"

"You already said you want to get away from Younger's Bend. I'll see that you do that, tomorrow or the next day, and see you on a train with enough money to pay your way to Texarkana or wherever you want to go, and a little bit extra."

"And what do you want me to do in return?"

"For one thing, I want you to keep Belle Starr off me."

"How am I supposed to do that?"

"Act like you're getting a case on me, falling for me. If I got Belle judged right, she's not going to be so hot after me if there's somebody younger and prettier than her giving her competition."

"You said that's one part of the deal. What's the rest of it?"

"Pester me to take you to Fort Smith, to buy you some new clothes and pretties."

"Why?"

Longarm shook his head. "If we're going to deal, you've got to take my part of it on trust. I won't say why."

Dolly thought about Longarm's offer for a moment. Then she nodded. "All right, Windy. I'll hang onto your arm and make sheep-eyes at you whenever we're around Belle. That won't be hard to do, but I'll enjoy it all the more because Belle's the kind of woman she is. And I'll certainly keep telling you that I want to go to Fort Smith, because I'd go just about anywhere to get away from Younger's Bend, and the sooner the better."

"We got a deal, then, you and me," Longarm said. "Oh. One more thing. If you'll take special note of any names you might hear Belle or Sam or Floyd or—well, any of them—any names they might let drop when I'm not around, try to remember and pass them on to me."

"Just any kind of names?"

"That's right, Dolly. People or places or whatever."

The request plainly puzzled her, but she nodded. "All right. I guess that's not too hard to do."

"Good." Longarm glanced out the door. The sun was already dropping down the sky toward late afternoon. "Now, I'll tell you what. I don't want to spend any time up at the house before supper. If you'd like to, we could walk down to the river and take a look at it, or throw rocks in the water, or whatever. Or we can stay here in the cabin and talk till supper, whichever you'd rather do."

"Why can't we talk while we watch the river?"

"No reason I can see why we shouldn't."

"Then let's walk down to the river."

They spent two pleasant hours talking of nothing much, just letting time flow by, sitting on the bluff above the Canadian, tossing in a rock and now and then a twig, just to see what the river's uncertain currents did with it. When the sun dipped below the trees around them and began to shoot horizontal rays through the spaces between the trunks, Longarm said, "We better go on back. I didn't eat anything at noon, and my belly's telling me about it."

"You missed eating on my account, Windy," Dolly said self-accusingly. "I was telling you all my troubles when you should have been up at the house getting your meal."

"You were feeling right low about that time," Longarm

said. "It looked to me like you needed somebody to listen to you a lot more than I needed vittles."

"I was still being Susanna Mudgett then. I was feeling sorry for myself. I couldn't quite make up my mind whether I'd stay Susanna or go back to being Dolly."

"I didn't look at it quite that way," Longarm said thoughtfully. "But I sure noticed how you changed when you decided to be Dolly."

"It's made me feel so good, I can even stand going up to the Starrs' house to eat, even with Belle buzzing around. And I'm getting hungry, thinking about supper, so let's go."

As they reached the cluster of cabins, the door to Floyd's cabin opened, and Floyd came out and walked toward them. Longarm was just about to tell Dolly to be ready to get out of the way if she saw Floyd going for his gun, when the outlaw stopped and spread his arms wide, his hands at mid-thigh. He was not wearing a gun.

Floyd raised his voice and called, "I want to talk to you a minute, Windy."

Longarm waited until there was only a gap of five or six feet between them before he asked, "You mean, talk private?"

"Yeah. Just you and me."

Longarm said to Dolly, "You go ahead up to the house. I'll follow along as soon as Floyd and me get through talking." As the girl moved away, he asked Floyd, "You want to go inside, or just stay here and gab?"

"It won't take long for me to say what's on my mind."

"All right, fire away."

Floyd had trouble getting out the first words. "I—damn it, I don't feel right yet about you gunning down McKee, you might as well know that from the start."

"I wasn't looking for you to change your mind, Floyd, even if you know what was behind that as well as I do. McKee wasn't a man to forget taking a whipping."

"He never told me anybody'd wiped him up in a fight."

"You and McKee partnered a long time, so I guess you'd know him pretty well. Would he be likely to tell you something like that?"

"No," Floyd said slowly. "No, I guess not. Well, anyhow, I've cooled down about you and him. You and Belle both told me it wasn't my affair, and I got to admit you're right."

"Glad to hear that. I wasn't looking to have a run-in with you."

"That ain't what I wanted to say, though. If you're of a mind to join me and Steed and Bobby in this job we've got set up, we'll let you come in."

"That your idea?" Longarm asked. "Or Belle's?"

"It was Belle's idea at the start. You know that damned well. Now that I've come to see things her way, I guess you can say it's my idea, too."

"I don't know, Floyd. I'd just about made up my mind to move on," Longarm said. "I still think I might."

"This is about as safe a place as you'll find, if you're on the prod, Windy. If it was me, I'd stay."

"Well, I ain't decided yet. And I don't know anything about this job of yours, so I can't say yes or no to you about coming in."

"It's a big one. There's going to be a lot of money to split. You might as well have a share of it."

"*If* it comes off," Longarm put in.

"It'll come off," Floyd said confidently.

"How many ways are you figuring to split?"

"If you come in, five. Me, Steed, Bobby, and you will take a full share each. Belle and Sam get one between 'em."

"How much are you figuring the take will come to? Because splitting nothing five ways leaves all of us with zero."

"Belle says—"

Longarm broke in emphatically, "I don't give a pile of hot cow shit for what Belle says. I'm asking *you*, man to man."

"Seven thousand, at least. Maybe more."

Longarm squinted as he did a quick calculation. "Which'd make the split fifteen, sixteen hundred. That don't hardly seem enough to make it worth my trouble, Floyd."

"Belle says it could go as high as ten thousand. Anyhow, we'll all be taking the same risk."

"Belle talks like shit out of a goose that's been fed green corn—hot and slick and plenty of it."

Floyd said earnestly, "Look here, Windy, I know Belle's the biggest liar, but in this part of the country she's money in our pockets."

"I don't see how you figure that."

"Listen, I know as much as anybody does about Belle. I was with Jim Reed when we robbed the Austin mail coach outside of San Antonio. Belle did go out on a job or two with Reed. Then, after she settled down here with Sam, she done some rustling, mostly just buying up the rustled stock and switching brands and selling it up in Kansas or down in Texas. And she does some fencing too, for owlhoots who've picked up watches and rings and jewelry and whatnot, and need to turn it into cash. That's how she got started paying off the marshals and deputies in the little towns just outside of the Nation. She's got a lot of strings that keep the law tied up, that's why Belle's worth something to us."

Longarm studied Floyd's face for a moment, then nodded. "I see what you're getting at, Floyd. Maybe I misjudged Belle. I had her down as a blowhard, all show and no go, riding around with those silver-plated pistols, calling herself the Bandit Queen. And you and me both know Belle nor no other woman ever rode on a job with Frank and Jesse James, like she claims to have done."

"Sure, Belle talks too much," Floyd agreed. "But most of her and Sam's split is going to pay for information and for having the marshal and deputies look the other way when we go out on this job."

"Well, that puts another light on it. I might just change my mind about moving on."

Floyd studied Longarm's face for a moment, then he said, "Tell me something straight, Windy. What's your real handle? The one the law knows you by?"

Longarm shook his head. "Not now, Floyd. It ain't that I don't trust you, but if I tell you that, you'll have an ace on me and I won't have a damn thing on you until after we've pulled a job together."

Floyd didn't like Longarm's answer, and showed his displeasure in his expression. Then he grinned wolfishly and said, "I guess that's a reasonable way to look at it. And you sure as hell know your way around. Well, how about it? Are you coming in?"

"Maybe, after I've heard a little more than I know now."

"More, meaning what?"

"If you don't see that, Floyd, you're not as smart as I took you to be. Tell you what. Right now, I'm as hungry as a bitch wolf right after cubbing. Let's you and Steed and the boy and me set down and jaw with Belle after supper. If I like what I hear, I'll tell you then whether I'm in or out."

Chapter 11

There were too many at supper for the table to accommodate. Belle put Longarm, Dolly, Floyd, Steed, and Bobby at the table, and held a place for herself. Sam and Yazoo ate, bending forward uncomfortably in their chairs, over one of the benches that had been brought in from the porch and placed near the stove. Sam pieced out 'a meal in quick gulps between jumping up in response to Belle's frequent calls for him to replenish the dishes on the table.

Longarm was sure that Belle knew of the talk he'd had with Floyd; the outlaw had held a whispered session with her in one corner of the room before they'd sat down. He'd looked for the air to be cleared by his grudging half-decision to join the gang in their job, wherever and whatever it was, but the atmosphere still stayed taut.

There was very little conversation during the meal, in spite of the tongue-loosening that might have been expected from the drinks poured by Floyd and Steed from the fresh bottles of corn liquor Yazoo had brought with him from the stillhouse. Longarm filled a glass out of politeness, but took only the smallest sips possible. Despite the whiskey they consumed, though, Floyd and Steed were unusually silent.

What talk did pass around the table was dominated by Belle. She had been cheerful until she saw Dolly doing as Longarm had requested, clinging to him and lifting her face to him with admiring glances, then she had frozen up. She chattered at length about her children, Ed and Pearl, and their problems with the schools they were attending in Missouri. As though by mutual consent, unhappy subjects such as the deaths of McKee and Taylor weren't mentioned. There was no discussion—not even the barest mention—of the job that was soon to take place. Bobby tried to talk about it once, but was commanded gruffly by Steed to shut up and eat.

Longarm grew more and more disgusted as the meal progressed. He'd thought that, with Floyd's unexpected thawing-out, there would be enough table talk to give him a pretty good idea of the kind of outlawry that was in the offing.

"We'll go out on the porch," Belle announced when she saw that everyone had finished eating. "Sam's going to need to clean up in here and wash the dishes. Yazoo, you'd better help him, since there's such a pile of them."

Outside, the air was cool in the early, moonless night. Lamplight from the door spilled out as they found places. Belle and Floyd took the remaining bench; Longarm, with Dolly doing her duty by clinging to him, stood in a corner of the porch, where he could see the other four in the best light. He wasn't looking for trouble, but knew by instinct that getting a good position in a chancy situation could be the difference between winning and losing. Steed and Bobby settled down on the step; their faces were the only ones that caught the lamplight. Those of the others were vague, whitish blurs in the dark.

Belle said, "I'm glad you finally made up your mind, Windy. Of course, if you hadn't decided to come in, Sam and I would have gone along. But now that—"

"Wait a minute," Steed broke in. "If we're going to talk about the job, what about the girl there?"

"What about her?" Longarm asked. "She's with me."

"I'm sure all of us noticed that," Belle said acidly.

"You know what we decided," Steed went on. "No talking except amongst us, Belle. No outsiders."

"I'm not an outsider," Dolly said. "Lonnie was coming here to join up with you, and he wouldn't have brought me if he hadn't thought it was all right."

"Taylor's one thing," Steed insisted. "Me and Floyd knew him. We don't know a damn thing about Windy."

Longarm didn't see much point in setting everybody's temper on edge with an argument at the very beginning. He said, "All right. She's not going to be here long, any-

126

how, but if you don't want her around while we're talking, I guess she won't mind going back to the cabin."

"I'll go if you say so, Windy." There was sugar in Dolly's voice, and she leaned back to look sweetly at Longarm.

"If Floyd and Steed don't want her around, she'd better go," Belle said. "What we've got to talk about won't take long."

"Go on, then, Dolly," Longarm nodded. "I'll be along after while."

"Now, then," Belle began when Dolly had flounced off, "I guess we're all glad that Windy's going to ride with us—"

"He is?" Bobby asked. "I didn't know that."

"I just hadn't had time to pass the word to you," Floyd told him. "Go on, Belle. Windy still ain't sure. Says he wants to know more about how much we figure the take's going to be and where we're expecting to get it."

Longarm said curtly, "I don't buy a pig in a poke, Belle. I made that plain to Floyd when we talked before supper."

"Don't worry," Belle replied confidently. "There'll be a good split. Crops are coming in at this time of the year, you know, and all the banks keep a lot of cash on hand. Farmers pay back what they've borrowed, and the factors that buy the big crops need money to operate with. There's not a bank across the Arkansas line that won't be good for ten to fifteen thousand if it's hit inside of the next month."

"Sounds reasonable," Longarm said, "provided you know which bank to pick out. And if you're damn sure which one's going to be the easiest to take."

"I told you not to worry," Belle retorted. "I know which of the banks in Fort Smith—"

"Fort Smith?" Longarm interrupted. "That sounds awful damned risky. A lot of town marshals there. Sheriff's deputies too, and a whole big bunch of federal marshals. At least that's the way I heard it."

"I explained to him how you've got strings out on a lot of the law, Belle," Floyd said quickly. "But Windy still ain't satisfied. Maybe you can tell him more than I could."

"I'm sure I could, but I don't intend to," Belle said tartly. She swiveled on the bench to face Longarm. "I just

127

wanted to see what you'd say when I mentioned Fort Smith, Windy, but I'm like you—I wouldn't look at that place twice. No, we won't be taking one of the banks there, not with just four men. We'll go to one of the little places. There's three or four towns a little way over the Arkansas line where there's only one bank, but it'll have close to twenty thousand in the safe for the next month. And it's in the little towns where I've got the marshals hogtied."

"I like that better," Longarm told her. "Now, when will we be riding?"

"Not for a few days." Belle frowned. "Maybe a week. I've got to hear from my friends across the line before I'll know when the right time will be."

Longarm nodded. "That suits me fine. I've got a little business of my own that I need to take care of. I can tend to it and get back in plenty of time."

"What kind of business?" Floyd asked; suspicion dripped from his words.

"Not anything real important. I promised Dolly I'd take her to the train so she can go home." He dropped into a deprecating tone and added, "She's getting to bother me. I can't afford to have a woman like her hanging on me, you men know that."

"Yeah," Floyd replied. He seemed relieved. "Well, I don't see anything wrong with that. Do you, Belle?"

"No. I'll be as glad as Windy will be to get her away from here. Taylor made a mistake in bringing her along with him in the first place."

Steed asked Longarm, "It's all settled, then?"

"If you men and Belle are satisfied, so am I." He turned to Belle. "We'll be coming back here to Younger's Bend to hole up after the job, I expect? I don't feel like I want to go back on the prod right away."

"That's something else you won't have to worry about, Windy," Belle said. "You make a clean getaway without any federal marshals chasing you into the Nation, and you'll be safe from the law here as long as you feel like staying."

"All right. It's settled as far as I'm concerned, then." Longarm stood up. "Now I'll go down to the cabin and tell the girl to get ready to ride into Fort Smith tomorrow.

128

And as soon as I get her on the train to Kansas, I'll be back."

"You guarantee we can count on that?" Floyd asked.

"You damn sure can, Floyd," Longarm said feelingly. "This is one job I don't intend to miss out on!"

An excited, sparkling-eyed Dolly greeted Longarm at the door of the cabin. She said, her words tumbling out all over each other, "Come look what I've found, Windy!"

She took Longarm's hand and led him to the table. A pile of currency rose from its center. Around the edges were a half-dozen items: a sheath knife, a pile of pistol cartridges, two pairs of socks, several bandannas, a tin cup, three battered cigars with split wrappers, a block of matches, a bag of ground coffee, and some scraggy scraps of jerky. The heap of greenbacks dominated everything, however.

"Looks like there's quite a wad there," Longarm said.

"Nearly a thousand dollars. I counted it."

"It's out of Taylor's saddlebags, ain't it?" Longarm asked.

"Yes. I wanted to bathe, and looked in them for some soap. And there it was, all that money."

"Must be what he got when he left you in that cave."

"Of course. I'm sure it is. He held up a bank, I guess. I don't know where, or anything about it. Lonnie didn't tell me. But that doesn't matter, Windy. I want you to have it. You've been so good to me."

Longarm looked at the money thoughtfully. If he took it, he'd see that it got back somehow to the place Taylor had stolen it from. He'd just hand it over to Gower and let him see to returning it. But he couldn't tell Dolly that, and felt he ought to press her to keep it. A false step now might endanger the image he'd created with Belle and the outlaws.

He said, "I don't need a dead man's money, Dolly. You're entitled to it. You'll need it. We're going out tomorrow to Fort Smith, and I'll see you on a train for wherever you feel like heading."

"No. It'd remind me of Lonnie and Susanna Mudgett. I want to forget both of them."

"All right. If you're sure you don't want it, I'll keep it, and I thank you most kindly."

"You said we were going out tomorrow? That's something else I have to thank you for."

Dolly threw her arms around Longarm and raised herself on tiptoe to kiss him. He bent to meet her, expecting the kiss to be only a friendly one. It turned into something more. Dolly's tongue pushed his lips apart, and Longarm responded as any man would. He caught Dolly up in his arms and pulled her to him. Her hips pushed against his groin and he felt himself getting hard.

Dolly broke the kiss to whisper, "It's getting late, and if we're going to start traveling tomorrow, we'll need to rest tonight, Windy. Don't you think it's about time you blew out the lamp so we can go to bed?"

"If you want to," Longarm replied. Then, as an afterthought, he asked, "This ain't something more like the money, is it? You ain't asking me just because you feel like you owe me something?"

"No. I wanted you to come to bed with me when I woke up this morning and saw you looking at me. I've wanted all day for you to grab me up and hold me and kiss me, but you never did make a move to."

Longarm blew out the lamp before he said, "I guess I figured it was too soon after—"

"After Lonnie?" she finished for him. "I guess it would be, for Susanna. But I'm Dolly now, remember?"

Side by side in the sudden darkness, they groped along the cabin wall until they reached one of the bunks. Longarm heard the soft rustling of cloth as Dolly drew her dress over her head. She pushed against him and the delicate fragrance of freshly soaped woman-skin wafted to his nostrils. He felt her fingers find his as he unbuckled his gunbelt and laid it beside the bunk, then she was working at the buttons of his trousers as he undid his shirt. He stepped out of his pants and stripped off his balbriggans. Then Dolly's flesh pressed against his.

The hard nipples of her round, soft breasts brushed across his chest, and her hands ran down his lean hips and found his growing erection. She guided it between her thighs and closed her legs. Pulling his head down, Dolly found Longarm's lips while she moved her hips gently back and forth.

Longarm was hard now, but Dolly seemed in no hurry, and he was contented to let her set the timing. He cupped his hand around her breast. His calloused fingers moved back and forth between their close-pressed bodies, rubbing a nipple almost as hard, now, as his fingertips.

Dolly changed the motion and rhythm of her hips. She began rotating them while still rocking back and forth. Longarm lifted her and eased her to the narrow bunk, lowering himself on top of her.

"No. Not yet," Dolly said. She squeezed her thighs tightly together and whispered, "Here. Let me show you."

Longarm felt her hands at his hips, raising them. He let her guide him, and she pulled his hips forward. He crawled on his knees until his spread legs straddled her waist. Dolly's hands moved from his hips to grasp his erection, and she arched her back, settling herself below him. Soft warmth surrounded him and he realized that she'd tucked his hard length between her breasts and was pushing them together. Her knee came up and prodded his back. Longarm began to move back and forth in the valley between her breasts.

"I like to feel a man on me for a while, first," Dolly said huskily. She bent her head forward, and each time Longarm reached the end of one of his strokes, her tongue darted out in a gently rasping caress. As Longarm continued his steady stroking, he came to expect the moist, wet contact on his tender, distended tip. He tried to speed up, to experience it more often, but Dolly turned her head aside and squeezed her breasts harder together to narrow the passage between them and slow him down.

"Slow," she told him. "Don't hurry things."

"If that's how you want it," he replied.

There was a hypnotic effect to the measured rhythm he was keeping. Longarm lost track of time, but it seemed to him that he'd been straddling Dolly for hours when she suddenly released the pressure on her breasts and turned beneath him to lie on her side. Longarm felt abandoned without the caresses he'd been enjoying. He put a hand on her shoulder to turn her on her back again.

"Lie down behind me," she told him. "We'll rest awhile."

Longarm was more than ready to move on to more conventional caresses, but he did as she told him. Dolly raised her leg and trapped him between her thighs once more. For a long while she did not move, and as the cool air touched his shaft, he felt his erection beginning to fade. Dolly must have felt him softening too, for she began to caress him with her fingers, softly circling him at first, then suddenly curling her fingertip to bring a fingernail into play. The sensation mingled pain and pleasure. Longarm wasn't sure he enjoyed it, but his erection returned very quickly, and with it, his desire to go into Dolly deeply and fully.

"Let's stop playing games, Dolly," he said. "I know you're doing your best to pleasure me, but I'm ready for the real thing now."

Wordlessly, Dolly spread her thighs and pushed him inside her. Longarm lunged, intending to bury himself in her with a single, hard thrust. But to his surprise, Dolly was not moist, and her fingernail caresses had made him so tender that he was forced to stop. He refused to give up. He pushed slowly and patiently, and, little by little, felt her growing moist and opening to accept him.

Now Longarm could thrust. He drew his hips back and plunged full-length, and Dolly quivered and sighed. Again and again he drove in, feeling her respond with quick backward jerks of her hips as he reached the greatest depth of his pentration. The long preliminaries had their effect. Longarm felt himself building sooner than usual, but the narrow bunk bothered him; he felt as though he was going to tumble to the floor each time he drew back to make a full penetration.

Buried as deeply within her as he could push, Longarm stopped. Dolly stirred and half-turned her head inquiringly, but said nothing. Longarm worked a hand under her hips, picked her up, and pulled her into an all-fours position. He brought his own body erect, grasped Dolly with a firm hand on each of her hips, and started stroking again. This time there was no feeling of falling off the narrow bunk to inhibit his long lunges. Dolly was wet and hot now, and she was beginning to squirm in his grasp. Long-arm increased the speed of his thrusts until his time ran out and he let himself go.

"Only a little bit longer," Dolly cried. "Just a little bit, Windy?"

He held himself rigid, plunging in full-stroke again and again and yet again, until Dolly cried out in a thin scream that faded into soft sighs, and her hips, under his hands, gyrated for a few mad moments, then stopped as she went limp and folded up in a heap on the tattered mattress. To give both her and himself room, Longarm withdrew, and went and sat down on the bunk against the opposite wall. The cabin was so small that he was only an out-stretched arm's length from her.

Dolly unfolded her body and lay straight, on her side, facing him. They could see one another dimly in the faint skyglow that the tiny, high window allowed to trickle into the cabin.

"Do you think I'm pretty bad?" she asked him.

"Now, that's a Susanna Mudgett question," he answered.

"I don't mean bad, like a bad woman. I mean bad as a woman to make love to."

"No. Sort of unusual, though. You waste a hell of a long time before you get down to the real part of it."

"I have to, Windy. If I don't, it doesn't do a thing for me except hurt because I'm so dry inside. But if I fondle a man and feel him a long time—longer than I did with you, Windy—then I moisten up, and it doesn't hurt me."

"I've known women who liked to feel me up. But none of them ever took as long as you, or handled me the way you did."

"In one of the places I worked, there was a girl who taught me that trick."

"You ought to tell a man why you're doing it. If he's any kind of man, he won't mind."

"It makes most men mad when I try to tell them. They start to droop, and I lose a customer." She shook her head; Longarm could just see the movement in the gloom. "You know, Windy, you're the first man in more than a year who's brought me on?"

"How about your old hometown sweetheart?"

133

"Lonnie? I wasn't sweet on him. When he ran into me there in Texarkana, I thought for a while I could go back to being Susanna Mudgett. But I couldn't. And he didn't do anything at all for me. All I felt was him prodding around in me." Dolly sighed. "I guess it's really my fault."

"Maybe. But maybe you just never started right."

She frowned. "I guess I don't know what you mean."

"Come over here, Dolly."

Dolly didn't question his invitation. She got off the bunk and took the half-step necessary to reach Longarm. He took her hand and pulled her gently down onto his lap. Dolly relaxed with a contented sigh, and tried to curl up when his arms went around her, but he ran one hand down over her breasts and stomach in a long, sweeping, soft caress that ended when he reached her thighs and pressed on them with just enough force to keep her body straight.

Bending his head down, Longarm began to kiss Dolly's breasts, circling their nipples in turn with his lips and, between kisses, brushing over them with his chin and mustache. Her skin erupted in gooseflesh when the sharp hairs of his beard rasped across her nipples. Longarm slipped a hand between her thighs, buried his fingers in her silken pubic hair, and started to rub gently within her soft and still-moist folds. Dolly's body, so relaxed when she'd first settled down on his lap, began to grow stiff.

So did Longarm, but he waited until he was completely hard before lifting her around. He stretched his legs and brought them up between hers as he moved her. Then he lowered Dolly until he could feel her dewy fur against his erection. He held her suspended for a moment, her hips swaying, and lowered her even more slowly while sliding into her. He let her body descend by fractions of an inch, each movement putting him in her deeper and deeper.

Even while Longarm was only half-buried inside her, Dolly began to breathe irregularly. His hands, in her armpits, could feel the expansion and contraction of her ribs. When he'd gone in almost all the way, Longarm released Dolly's body. As she slid down the final few inches of his erection, he brought his own hips up with a sharp, quick snap to stop her descent. The shock of this final penetra-

134

tion brought from Dolly's lips an involuntary gasp of surprised pleasure.

She fell forward against him, her head lolling on his shoulder, and whispered, "Oh, that was wonderful. I've never had a man go into me so deep, or fill me up the way you do."

Longarm stood up. He let Dolly ride him as he shuffled his feet, turning around. He held her to him while they dropped to the bunk, and when their bodies met the thin, tattered mattress, he thrust hard. Dolly whimpered, a jagged little cry, as his weight drove in. Involuntarily she raised her legs and locked her ankles around his waist.

"I'm starting to build up already," she told him in a low voice. "Just stay with me as long as you can. I think this is going to be something I've never had happen to me before."

Longarm began easing himself in and out with slow, deliberate strokes. When he felt himself beginning to build, he stopped and pressed hard against Dolly. She squirmed with impatience while she waited for him to begin thrusting again, but Longarm took his time. He let her build with him until, at last, she began to gasp deep in her throat while her body shivered in rolling spasms and her upward thrusts grew frantic. Then he let himself go, pounding hard and fast, driving into her relentlessly.

Only after she'd begun to fall back and lie limp, accepting his thrusts but unable to respond to them any longer, did Longarm speed, with a few quick jabs, to his own orgasm. Then he let himself down on her gently while her body continued to quiver, and now and then to shake in a little convulsive spasm. He lay on her, still buried in her depths but flaccid now, almost as drained as she was.

At last Dolly said, "I'm half asleep, but I still want to feel you in me, even if you're not still hard."

"Go to sleep, if you want to," he told her. "I'll stay here until you do."

He kept his promise, waiting until Dolly's breasts rose and fell beneath his chest in deep, regular breathing. Then Longarm left her, moving softly so that he wouldn't wake her. He stepped over to the other bunk and stretched out.

He lay there for a short while, listening to the soft rhythm of Dolly's breathing. He was too relaxed and pleasantly exhausted to think about the long ride they'd be making the next day, and the problems he'd be facing during the days that would follow. Soon he fell asleep too.

Chapter 12

Longarm noticed Dolly studying him over the rim of her raised coffee cup as he lighted a cheroot. He'd looked up before she had expected him to, before she could blink the sadness from her eyes. Through the swirl of blue smoke that shimmered between them, he asked her, "You sure you're doing what you really want to, Dolly?"

"I'm doing what I think best, Windy. I never will go back to Yates Center. My family turned me out once, and I don't intend to give them a chance to do it again."

"And you'd sooner go back to . . ." he hesitated.

Dolly finished the thought. "To whoring in a saloon? I'm used to it, and it's not a bad life. Oh, sure, I'd like to stay with you, at least right this minute, but I know I can't. I'd always be afraid I'd slow you down at some time when you couldn't afford it, like I did Lonnie. Or I might turn out to get like Belle Starr. So I'll go back to Texarkana for a while. Sooner or later, I'll move on. Who knows? We might run into one another again sometime."

"We might at that," Longarm agreed.

They were sitting in the dining room of the Union Depot in Fort Smith. The day before, they'd left Younger's Bend before daylight and ridden steadily. At Little Juarez, they'd been in time to stop at the general store and buy Dolly a cloak to cover the somewhat battered dress that was the only garment she'd had left after losing her horse and saddlebags while escaping from the posse that had been chasing her and Taylor. Longarm tried to persuade her to get a new dress too, but she'd refused. She was wearing the cloak now, of a light blue that brought out the almost white sheen of her long hair, which fell down her back in rippling waves.

After getting off the ferryboat that had taken them across the Arkansas to Fort Smith, they'd learned that the first train Dolly could take to her chosen destination wouldn't pull out until midafternoon of the following day, so Longarm had taken a room for them at the Fenolio Hotel. It had been a long night and, predictably, neither of them had gotten much sleep. Dolly had been insatiable, and Longarm had kept responding to her urging for just one more time. Now, with only a few minutes left before the southbound train was due, they faced the inevitable parting that always convinces casual lovers they haven't had enough time together.

Longarm saw Dolly's eyes shift past him and her eyebrows pull together in a frown. He asked, "What's the matter?"

"Windy, is the law here in Fort Smith looking for you?"

"Not that I know of. Why should they be?" Then, realizing his mistake as soon as he'd asked the question, he added quickly, "There hasn't been time for me to get on the wanted list here in Arkansas, and I never have pulled any kind of job close to Fort Smith. Why?"

"There's a man over by the wall there who's been watching us. I thought once or twice he was going to come over to our table, but he never did."

Longarm swiveled in his chair to look where Dolly's eyes had been fixed. He saw nobody who seemed especially interested in them.

Dolly shook her head. "He's not there now. When I looked away from him to talk to you, he just disappeared."

"I don't reckon it amounts to anything. Could be he mistook one of us for somebody he knew."

"I guess that was it. And he left when he saw he was wrong."

"Something like that."

Outside the depot, the whistle of an approaching train sounded. Longarm said, "That'd be the Frisco southbound coming in; it's the only train that's due. Maybe we better get out on the platform. It only stops here for about ten minutes, just long enough for the baggage to be unloaded and the passengers to get on."

"I'd like to stay with you, Windy. You know that."

"Sure. I'd like for you to. But both of us know it just ain't in the cards, Dolly."

"No. Well . . ."

Dolly stood up. Longarm dropped fifteen cents on the table and they walked through the depot and out onto the platform. The train was just coming into sight. The engine passed them with a loud whoosh of steam from its cylinders as it slowed for the stop. The baggage cars slid by, and the porters and handlers began dragging their high, four-wheeled carts along, keeping abreast of the cars they'd be working. Passengers waiting to get aboard started shifting their positions to be where the day coaches and Pullmans would stop. From the coach windows, as the train finally halted, faces pressed against the windowpanes as those traveling beyond Fort Smith gazed out to scan the boarding passengers.

"Let's walk back to the observation car," Longarm suggested. "There's not usually anybody on the last car when a train makes a stop. It'll be a little bit more private than saying goodbye with all those people gawking at us."

Dolly slipped her arm through Longarm's as they walked slowly toward the back of the train. She said, "I don't know how long I'll be in Texarkana, but if you're ever down that way—"

"Don't worry, I'll stop in."

She smiled. "You don't even know which saloon I'll be at."

"Won't make any difference. Texarkana ain't all that big a town. I'll find you, if I come that way."

Dolly suddenly became serious. "I'll never see you again, will I, Windy?"

"It's hard to say. A man in my line of work don't know where he's apt to turn up from one day to the next."

"I don't know how I'll ever be able to thank you for everything you've done for me."

"You don't need to thank me for anything. You already have."

A pair of short blasts sounded from the locomotive's whistle, and the voice of the conductor called from the center of the train, "Boa-ard! All aboard!"

Longarm assisted Dolly up the steps of the observation

139

platform, then followed her and stood on the bottom step. Dolly bent forward to kiss him goodbye. Their lips were still pressed together when the train began to inch forward. Longarm held his place until the observation car reached the middle of the station platform, then stepped off. Dolly lifted her arm to wave at him, and her expression changed from one of almost tearful sadness into a look of alarm.

"Windy!" she called. "Behind you! The man who was in the cafe!"

Longarm whirled. A burly man stood a dozen paces away, half-hidden by one of the latticed ironwork pillars that supported the roof over the platform. He was drawing a pistol from a shoulder holster.

Longarm drew as he dropped off the platform. The burly man had not yet cleared his revolver from its holster when he saw Longarm's lightning-fast move. He stepped behind the pillar. Longarm had anticipated the move. He held his fire, and when his booted feet hit the cinder roadbed a foot or more below the level of the platform, he curled his legs under him and leaned to one side. The edge of the wooden platform now hid him from the stranger.

Down the track, the train was rounding a curve. Longarm was vaguely aware of Dolly, who still stood on the observation platform, a blur of blue cloak and white face, as the train moved on out of sight.

On his hands and knees, Longarm scuttled along the tracks, keeping his body low so that his movements would be invisible to his assailant. The stranger was thinking fast too. A shot cracked, and a slug plowed through the thick planking of the station platform, a foot or two behind Longarm.

Longarm stopped. A second shot rang out and lead ripped into the platform behind him, beyond the point where he'd been when the unknown shooter had first seen him. The stranger was bracketing shots at Longarm's cover, trying to pin him down. Longarm looked at the platform. There wasn't room enough under it for him to squeeze through; heavy supporting timbers came down to within a few inches of the roadbed. On the other side, four sets of tracks ran parallel to the depot, creating a wide, bare swath that was totally without any protection.

From the platform above his head, Longarm heard a man's voice shouting. "All you people get in the depot! I'm a railroad detective and there's a dangerous outlaw over there by the tracks! There'll probably be more shooting! All of you get out of the way! Clear the platform!"

Taking a chance that the man who'd identified himself as a railroad detective was more occupied with getting the spectators out of the way than with watching for him, Longarm raised his head above the edge of his protective bulwark and looked at the scene. People were scurrying toward the depot doors and toward the ends of the station. The gun-wielding yard dick was still standing close to the latticework pillar behind which he'd taken shelter when Longarm first saw him. Longarm dropped back below the edge of his shield and reversed his direction, crawling back toward where he'd started from.

As he edged along, he tried to plan a way out of his precarious situation. His wallet, with his badge in it, was still in his boot top, where'd been carrying it since he'd gotten close to Younger's Bend. He didn't want to show the badge unless he was forced to. For all he knew, the man on the platform might be one of those being paid off by Belle Starr. At the same time, he didn't want to get into a shootout with a yard bull.

Crawling on his hands and knees, still holding his Colt in one hand, Longarm wondered how the detective had come to single him out for attention. The reason came to him in a flash. It had been Dolly, of course. She'd been seen by the posse that had been chasing Lonnie Taylor after Taylor had carried out whatever robbery he'd staged to get the cash he needed. There would have been no very accurate description of Taylor circulated, but Dolly, with her long ash-blonde hair, had almost certainly been described, and there weren't all that many natural ash-blondes along the Arkansas border.

It all holds together, old son, Longarm told himself as he continued his crawl behind the cover of the platform. *That fellow must've been prowling around the depot and seen Dolly with me. Just because we were together, he figured I was Taylor. Then why the hell didn't he make his play there in the restaurant?*

141

He puzzled over that while covering the next few feet in the direction of the platform's end, and the answer came logically.

Damn! He must've ducked out of the restaurant to send somebody after help. Didn't want to run the risk of trying to take me by himself. He waited till the last minute, figured I was going on the train with her, and threw down on me when he saw me step off the car. Which means this place is going to be mighty uncomfortable in a few minutes, as soon as the real law gets here.

Instinct or habit had kept Longarm looking back occasionally as he crawled. He saw the end of the platform a few yards ahead, and glanced back over his shoulder just in time to catch a flicker of motion along the area he'd just passed. He dropped flat and rolled to bring his Colt into action. The flicker turned into the gun hand of the railroad detective as he extended it over the edge of the boards. Longarm tossed off a shot, aiming short of the pistol. A chunk of the platform's edge exploded in a shower of splinters and the hand holding the gun disappeared.

Longarm couldn't be sure that his pursuer hadn't peered along the platform while he wasn't looking back. He speeded up his crawl, but it was slow at best. A pillar rose to the awning's edge at the corner just ahead of him, where the platform ended. Longarm reached it and rose behind it. It didn't shield him completely. He hadn't quite gotten his feet under him when a bullet clanged on the ironwork and ricocheted off toward the tracks.

Longarm didn't want to fire, but he had no other choice. He broke cover long enough to spot the pursuing yard bull, and sent a slug into the platform at the man's feet. The detective dived for the protection of the closest pillar. It didn't shield him fully, any more than the one Longarm was behind shielded him, but as long as the man stayed behind the iron support, he wouldn't be able to shoot accurately, if at all.

A baggage cart loaded with wooden barrels stood at the platform's edge. Longarm measured the distance to the cart. He didn't give the fellow who was after him very high grades for marksmanship, but he wasn't going to underestimate the man, either. He'd used up only two of the five rounds his Colt carried in its cylinder. The yard bull had also shot twice, so they were neck-and-neck on ammunition. Longarm debated reloading before he moved, concluded that speed was worth more than two shots, and dived for the baggage cart.

He hit the ground midway between the pillar and the cart. He landed rolling, and the shot triggered by the detective skittered off the brickwork that extended from the platform's edge to some fifteen or twenty feet beyond it, to the end of the Railway Express office that stood at one side of the depot.

The sliding door of the office was open. A man stood in it, peering curiously toward the area where he'd heard shooting. Longarm reached the baggage cart and stood behind it long enough to lift its yoke from the supporting arm and turn the cart in the direction of the open door. With any luck, he'd find a back door that he could get out of before the yard bull caught up with him.

As Longarm pulled the cart, walking backward, depending on the stacked barrels and iron-spoked wheels to protect him from his assailant's fire, the railroad detective snapped off three fast shots. They slammed into the barrels. Liquid began spurting from them, and the acrid scent of spoiled cottonseed oil filled the air.

Longarm stopped long enough to pull a match out of his pocket and flick it into flame with his thumbnail. He tossed the match on the ground and, to buy time, leaned out from behind the barrels and triggered a shot in the general direction of the pillar that shielded his pursuer.

When he pulled the cart forward, the oil from the leaking barrels splashed on the burning match. A sheet of flame rippled slowly toward the depot, and a cloud of dense smoke billowed up. The smoke shielded Longarm while he abandoned the baggage cart and ran flat-out for the open door of the Railway Express agency. The agent was still standing in the doorway, staring goggle-eyed at the flames that were rising from the oil.

"Hey, you can't come in here!" he called when he saw Longarm heading for the door.

143

"Like hell I can't!" Longarm replied, brushing past the man into the building.

He looked around. The place was more a shed than anything else. A waist-high counter ran half of its length, and a scale stood at the end of the counter. Bundles, bags, bales, boxes, and barrels were scattered and piled around the floor. There were windows, but they were set high in the walls, just below the eaves. They were long and narrow and fitted with iron bars. He spotted the back door and saw that it was not only closed tightly, but barred with a thick iron strap held by a swivel-bolt at one end and a massive padlock through a shackle at the other.

"Open that door!" he ordered the agent.

"Not on your life!" the man retorted. He ran out the door and disappeared.

Longarm covered the distance to the barred door in two long strides. He stood aside, aimed carefully, and shattered the padlock with a bullet. The staple through which the lock passed was torn out of the wall, and the bar swung down with a clatter.

For a moment the door resisted Longarm's tugging. Then it slowly started moving on the rollers that ran in a track above it. Longarm stopped when he'd cracked it wide enough for him to slip out. He peered around the edge. The railroad detective was just coming up to the back of the express office; apparently he'd detoured through the depot to avoid the flames.

Longarm pulled his head back quickly, hoping the man hadn't seen him. He'd glimpsed the gun his pursuer was carrying in his hand. Shielded by the door, he saw the yard bull go past the slitted opening and head for one corner of the express office. He gave the man a minute or so to get around the corner, then slid through the cracked-open door and started across the open ell between the agency office and the depot. He'd taken only three steps when a harsh command stopped him.

"Hold it! You take another step and I'll cut you down!"

Longarm stopped. He didn't want a bullet in the back.

"Now," the railroad detective commanded. "Keep your hands right where they are and turn around so I can look at you."

144

Shuffling his feet, Longarm turned. He faced the railroad detective and didn't like what he saw. The man was only a dozen feet distant, standing at the corner of the express office. His fingers were wrapped so tightly around the butt of his Remington-Beals .44 single-action that the knuckles were white. His forefinger twitched on the trigger. Longarm felt better when he saw that the gun's hammer wasn't drawn back.

Still, Longarm didn't feel easy about his position. Yard bulls normally did little more police work than chasing hoboes off freights and keeping the railroad yards clear of sneak-thieves and drifters. A few of them were former sheriffs' deputies or town marshals or one-time Pinkerton men who could no longer pull their weight in regular law-enforcement jobs.

A lot of them were bullies who enjoyed beating up the helpless bums they dragged off freight cars, and some of them had been forced out of regular jobs because they were habitual drunks. The more Longarm thought about railroad detectives, the less inclined he was to surrender to the one holding him at gunpoint and then clear things up by showing his badge.

There were a lot of yard bulls who cooperated with crooks. They got more money than their jobs paid them by tipping off outlaws and boxcar thieves to special shipments that made a robbery profitable. Belle Starr, Longarm thought, would have to be paying off a lot of railroad workers in order to carry out her felonious specialty of selling rustled cattle.

By now the railroad detective had scrutinized Longarm from hatbrim to boot toes. He nodded with satisfaction. "Yep. You're the one, all right."

There was only one thing Longarm could see to do: play for time. He suggested, "Suppose you tell me which one you're talking about, friend, because I damn sure don't know."

"Like hell you don't! You're the son of a bitch who stuck up the bank in Midland four or five days ago."

"You're dead wrong. I've never been to Midland." Longarm moved his left hand a hair's breadth, and the yard bull drew back the hammer of his pistol. Longarm

145

froze instantly. He hoped the weapon didn't have a hair trigger.

"I told you not to move!" the man barked. "I'd as soon shoot you as look at you! The reward notice said dead or alive, so you're worth five hundred dollars to me whether you walk in or I drag you in."

"You're making a mistake," Longarm protested. He was careful to keep his voice to a level, conversational tone. "Four or five days ago I was over in the Cherokee Nation. I don't even know where that town you mentioned is located."

"That's about what I'd expect you to say," the yard bull said with a nervous nod. "You sound real convincing too, I'll credit you with that. I might even believe you if I hadn't seen you with that blonde woman in the depot restaurant. The reward notice described her a lot better than it did you. A man'd have to be blind not to spot her."

Longarm weighed his alternatives. The cocked revolver held by the yard bull reduced them drastically. He was very sure the railroad dick had sent for help as he detoured through the depot, and even if he hadn't, somebody must have reported the gunfire out on the station platform. Unless the yard bull had reloaded, which Longarm didn't think was very likely, he had one round left in his pistol. That was just what remained in Longarm's Colt.

"Looks like you've got me dead to rights," he told the railroad detective. "But there's not any reason for you to settle for a little chicken-shit five hundred dollars for taking me in. I've got a thousand in my inside coat pocket. It's worth every dime of it to me if you'll say I got away from you."

"A thousand?" the yard bull's eyes narrowed covetously.

Longarm could almost read the man's mind. There wasn't any reason to settle for five hundred or a thousand either. If he shot now, he'd take the thousand off Longarm's body and then claim another five hundred as his reward.

"A thousand," Longarm repeated. "Here, if you think I'm lying, I'll show it to you."

Longarm raised his left hand as though to reach inside his breast pocket. The yard bull's eyes followed the move-

146

ment. Longarm brought his Colt up and fired. The railroad dick's dying reflex triggered his own gun, but Longarm was flat on the ground by the time the hammer fell, and the slug whistled through the air over his head.

Longarm had started to scramble to his feet when a fresh voice barked commandingly, "Stay right there on the ground, mister. You move a finger and you're a dead man!"

By rolling his eyes, Longarm could see who'd spoken. This time it wasn't an inexperienced, greedy railroad detective. The man standing at the corner of the depot wore the uniform of the Fort Smith city constable's force. And the gun he held, with its muzzle pointed at Longarm, wasn't a revolver, but a sawed-off shotgun.

Chapter 13

Even if there'd been another live round in his Colt, Longarm wouldn't have argued with the scattergun. He said, "You've got me, mister. Just don't get an itch in your trigger finger."

"Let go of your gun and move your hand away from it," the uniformed constable ordered.

Longarm obeyed. The command itself, and the tone in which it was delivered, told him the man knew what he was doing.

"That's fine," the constable said. His voice was cool. "Now roll over, away from the gun, and lay quiet until I tell you different."

Once again, Longarm did as he was told. He rolled, stopping on his back so that he could see what the Fort Smith officer was doing.

At the moment, the policeman was still standing where he'd been covering Longarm with the shotgun. It was a hammerless double, and Longarm couldn't see from his position whether the safety was off or on.

Not that it would make much difference, he thought ruefully. *Only a damned fool makes a move when he's in the kind of fix I'm in right now.*

Moving deliberately, without taking his eyes off Longarm, the constable picked up Longarm's Colt. He dropped it into the capacious side pocket of his uniform coat, then he said, "All right. You can stand up now."

Longarm got to his feet. He was once again faced with the same problem that had stopped him from surrendering to the railroad detective. For all he knew, and based on what Andrew Gower had told him, half of the Fort Smith constables might be on Belle Starr's payoff list. He'd gotten

148

by this far without the risk of revealing his identity to anybody except Gower, and with the end of his job in sight, he didn't propose to waste the effort he'd already put in on the case.

Though he hadn't quite decided just how he was going to handle things in this new situation, Longarm still stalled for time. He said, "If you'll just listen to me a minute, officer, I'll explain what this was all about."

"I don't need any explanation from you," the constable said curtly. "I got here just as Castell was dropping. That's all I need. You can give your explanation to the judge when you stand up to face a murder charge."

"Castell? That'd be the fellow who was trying to hold me up?" Longarm asked.

"If you mean the man you just killed, his name's Castell and he was a railroad bull for the Frisco. And if he was holding a gun on you, he must've had a reason to."

"Sure he did. He wanted the money I've got in my coat pocket."

"How'd he find out you're carrying enough money to make him draw his gun on you?" the officer asked suspiciously. "That won't wash worth a damn, mister. We got a report there was a gunfight going on here at the depot. That was quite a while ago. You and Castell must've been swapping shots for some time."

"He mistook me for somebody else," Longarm said. "That's how the trouble started."

"I think you're lying. Castell can't tell his side, and I'm damned if I'm going to let you get away with killing somebody, even a half-assed yard bull." The constable shifted the shotgun in order to get to his handcuffs, which were dangling from a strap on his wide uniform belt.

Longarm took the only chance he was likely to get. With the speed of a striking snake, he whisked his hand along his watch chain to get the derringer that nestled in his vest pocket. Before the Fort Smith officer could bring his shotgun around, Longarm's derringer was jammed into his throat.

Longarm said, "Now it's your turn to keep quiet and follow orders, mister. First off, I'll take that scattergun you're holding."

He took the shotgun and slid the breechlock aside with his thumb. The action opened and he held the gun up to drop its shells on the ground. "Now hand over your pistol," he ordered. He gave the Smith & Wesson revolver the same treatment, breaking its breech to let the ejector ring lift out the shells, then upending the weapon to let the shells fall out. He handed the revolver back to the constable. "Here. Put it in your holster."

"You mind telling me what you're going to do?" the officer asked.

"I was just about to. If this depot's like most I've seen, there's likely a hack or two outside. We're going to walk around the station to the sidewalk, and you're going to tell the hackman to drive us along to Front Street. And that's all you need to know right now."

For a moment the constable seemed on the verge of refusing, but Longarm applied a bit of extra pressure with the derringer's muzzle, and the man shrugged.

"All right," he said. "If that's what you want, I guess you're the boss right now."

As they walked around the back of the depot, Longarm moved the derringer from his captive's throat to his ribs. The constable didn't make any effort to escape or to slow their progress. As Longarm had anticipated, there were several livery rigs standing beside the sidewalk in front of the depot. He poked the man's ribs with the derringer. The constable called to the hackman on the seat of the last carriage in line, "Police business! Take us down Front Street until I tell you to turn off."

"You paying the hire?" the hackie asked suspiciously.

"I told you it's police business," the constable growled impatiently. "Now do what I said. Drive us along Front Street."

Inside the hack, Longarm told the constable, "I'll just take your handcuffs and keys now."

Under the threat of the mean-looking little derringer, the officer passed the cuffs and keys to Longarm. He made no objection when Longarm handcuffed his hands behind his back and put the key into his own pocket. Then Longarm felt in the constable's hip pocket and found the bandanna handkerchief he'd been pretty sure would be there.

150

The bandana went around the constable's mouth, silencing him. The hack had been moving slowly up Front Street. Longarm looked out just in time to see the federal office building as they passed it. He retrieved his Colt from the constable's pocket and cracked open the sliding panel behind the hackman's head.

"You can pull up here long enough for me to get out," he told the driver. "Then the officer wants to go on out Front to—what's that big street, quite a ways on east?"

"You must mean Division Street," the hackie said. "It's about a mile further on up Front Street."

"That's the one," Longarm agreed. "You just go right along, and then go out Division Street."

"What about my fare?" the driver asked, reining up.

"You heard what the officer said. This is police business."

Longarm closed the panel and jumped out of the hack, then started back to the federal building in a brisk walk. Before he turned off the sidewalk into the building where Andrew Gower's office was located, he looked over his shoulder. The hack was moving on along Front Street at a good clip. Longarm hoped the constable wouldn't succeed in attracting the hackman's attention too soon. He closed the door of the federal building behind him and started down the short corridor to Gower's office.

From the anteroom of the chief marshal's office, Longarm could see Gower at his desk, absorbed in reading a letter. He pushed past the protesting clerk and went in, closing the door behind him.

Gower looked up from the letter. "Long! What in the hell are you doing in Fort Smith?"

"I figured you'd better know what's in the wind, so you can get ready to move when the time comes."

"Damn it, you're supposed to be at Younger's Bend, getting the evidence I need to clean things up around here."

"I was, until yesterday."

"You sure didn't spend a lot of time there. Let's see—was it just a week ago you left Fort Smith?"

"More or less. I'll be going back right away, if you can

fix things up with the constable's force so I can get out of town without them throwing me in jail."

"Jail? Why would they want to do that?"

"Well, it's sort of a long story."

Gower sighed. "I guess I've got time to listen to it. Sit down, Long." He took out his sack of Bull Durham and began rolling a cigarette. Longarm fished out a cheroot and lighted it, waiting until Gower was ready for him to start. The chief marshal touched a match to the twisted tip of his cigarette and said, "All right. Billy Vail warned me you'd be into one thing right after another. What did you do to get crossways with the local constables?"

"Well, for one thing, I took a pistol and a scattergun away from one of them, down at the Union Depot a little while ago. I don't imagine they'll let that pass by without taking notice."

"Maybe I can get the chief constable to smooth things down. What's the name of this man you disarmed?"

"We didn't exactly trade introductions. If you want me to ask him, I'll have to chase down the hack that's taking him out of town."

Gower found the patience to ask, "Why did you have to take his weapons away?"

"Well, I didn't want him to toss me in jail for murder, and put you to all the trouble of getting me out. Figured it'd be better to stay out in the first place."

"Murder!" Gower exploded. "Who got killed?"

"One of the Frisco's yard bulls. The constable mentioned that his name was Castell."

Gower stared at Longarm. Then, in a voice that he was obviously keeping calm with a great deal of effort, said, "Long, I think you'd better start at the beginning and tell me everything that happened."

Longarm gave the chief marshal a condensed version of what had taken place from the time of his arrival at Younger's Bend. When he'd finished, Gower was staring at him across the desk, wordless and wide-eyed.

"Billy Vail said you had your own ways of doing things," the chief marshal said thoughtfully. "It seems to me you've pretty well crippled Floyd Sharpless and his bunch. I remember him, we've had fliers on him. He's wanted for a dozen different jobs. I can't quite place Steed, and the boy seems like a greenhorn doing his best to get started the wrong way."

"I'd say it's Bobby's first big job," Longarm agreed. "He's the only one of the three I don't feel right about."

"Don't waste any sympathy on him, Long. He's bad to begin with, or he wouldn't be running with Sharpless and Steed."

"I guess. There's a lot left for me to do, though. I got to dig out the names you want, the lawmen on Belle Starr's payoff list. So, as soon as you can square up things with the constables here, I'll be riding back out to Younger's Bend."

"I suppose you'll have to," Gower said after a moment's consideration. "And you'll have to find a way to get word to me about this bank holdup they're planning. Where and when, and anything else."

Longarm shook his head. "I can't tell you what I don't know myself. Belle's cagey. She was talking about Fort Smith, but I let her see that didn't take me in. Then she went on to tell about big banks in little towns close to the border."

"I don't suppose she mentioned any names?"

"Not Belle. And if I got her figured right, she won't say where the job's going to be until we set out to do it."

"She'd take no chance of the word leaking out," Gower said. "You'll have to narrow it down, then, Long. I sure can't put men in every town within striking distance."

"All right, I'll do the best I can. Now let's see how I'm going to get back there and do some more prodding."

Gower made another cigarette and lighted it before he answered. Then he said, "Well, Castell's no great loss to anybody. He came to me when he first got here, asking for a deputy's badge. I sent a wire back to the Pinkertons, where he'd been working, and found out they'd thrown him out for taking payoffs. I can see to it that the railroad doesn't raise too much fuss. Too bad, though. If you hadn't been so quick on the trigger, he might have told us something."

"He was all ready to finish me off, to get the money I told him I was carrying," Longarm reminded the chief marshal. He reached into his breast pocket and took out the cash Dolly had found in Taylor's saddlebags. "Here. There's not anywhere near the whole bundle, of course. Not quite a thousand. But it oughta go back to that bank in Midland."

"I'll see that it's returned, and get the reward offer on Taylor pulled down. Now, you go find a place to stay tonight. I'll have a talk with the chief constable and see if I can't get you out of town without any more gunplay."

"I stayed at the Fenolio Hotel last night," Longarm told Gower. "I didn't check out, because I had more than half a hunch that I wouldn't want to start back to Younger's Bend until tomorrow, seeing as how the train left as late as it did. I suppose it'd be smart of me to go right on over to the hotel now, and keep out of sight till you get things fixed up."

"If you hadn't offered to, that's what I was getting ready to tell you to do," Gower said. "Just don't let the Fort Smith constable get hold of you until I've had a talk with their chief. Murphy's a pretty good man. He's as worried about these payoffs as I am. Go on over to the Fenolio and stay out of trouble. I'll stop in after I've talked to Murphy."

Longarm slept until Gower knocked at his door; it was a bit after ten. Gower saw the bottle of Maryland rye on the bureau and looked at it yearningly.

"Help yourself," Longarm invited.

"Thanks." The chief marshal poured himself a sizeable slug, took a sip, and sat down. He rolled and lighted a cigarette before picking up the glass again. "Well, I've got your problem solved, Long."

"Sort of figured you would."

"But it was damn dry work, arguing with Murphy. First Irish cop I ever knew who won't take a drink." Gower sipped appreciatively. "Now. After I explained to him what happened, he agreed to keep Milford quiet."

"Who's Milford?"

"He's the constable you kidnapped."

"Hell, if he's smart, he wouldn't want anybody to know about that, anyway."

"That's how Murphy looked at it. He didn't want one of his men to be laughed off the force."

Longarm looked at Gower speculatively. "You might as well trot it out. What's Murphy want me to do?"

"Help him get one of his men in at Younger's Bend. He's had the same suspicion I have about payoffs to some of his fellows by Belle Starr. There's been a rash of house burglaries here in Fort Smith lately, and you know as well as Murphy and I that sneak thieves can't operate unless they've got a place to get rid of the stuff they pick up. Jewelry, watches, things of that kind. And a fence can't operate without protection from somebody inside the law."

"Damn it, Gower, I'm not in solid enough with Belle Starr to bring in somebody else in with me."

"That's what I told Murphy you'd say. He gave me another choice, but I told him that'd be up to you."

"What's the other choice?" Longarm asked suspiciously. He had a pretty good idea what Gower was leading up to.

"Get the information he wants yourself."

"Now hold up, damn it! I got enough on my plate, just finding out what you're after. Let your friend Murphy do his own job."

"No. I can't do that, Long. I've already made a trade with him."

"What'd you trade him?"

"A way to set you in solid with the bunch at Younger's Bend."

Longarm looked narrowly at Gower. He needed a minute to think this one over, so he got up and poured himself a fresh drink and topped off the glass the chief marshal was holding.

"Go on," he said, after he'd returned to his chair. "I'd like to know just how he figures to do that."

"You mentioned that Sharpless and Steed were still suspicious of you."

"Not what you'd call suspicious. Floyd's still mad at me because I had to gun down one of his old sidekicks. And Steed just plain don't like anybody."

"Murphy's scheme might ease things for you," Gower suggested.

"Go ahead. Lay it out where I can look at it."

"Murphy's in very solid with the newspaper here in Fort Smith. He's got the idea—and I think it's a pretty good one—that if he makes a big fuss, the editor will write a story that'll make Castell's killing compare with the assassination of Abe Lincoln. And he'll see that the story says the man who shot Castell got away. That'll clean your skirts completely with the bunch of Younger's Bend."

Longarm took a swallow of rye while he considered Gower's suggestion. He could see that it might ease the strain that existed between him and Floyd. Finally he nodded.

"I won't guarantee to get your friend Murphy what he's after," he said carefully. "But I'll make a stab at it. That's about the best I can do."

"That's all he can expect," Gower agreed. "I made it plain to him that as long as you're wearing a federal badge, our case comes first."

"Let's leave it that way, then," Longarm said. "When's this newspaper piece coming out? It'll have to be soon, if it's going to do me any good."

"It'll be in tomorrow morning's paper," Gower promised. "And I sure as hell hope it works!"

"So do I," Longarm agreed. "But we won't be no further behind than we are now, if it don't."

A stack of newspapers stood on the hotel's registration desk when Longarm went by the next morning on his way to breakfast in the dining room. He picked one up. It still smelled of printer's ink. He glanced at the glaring headlines. The editor of the Fort Smith *Elevator* had pulled out all the stops.

RAILROAD POLICEMAN FOULLY MURDERED! the top headline proclaimed. In only slightly smaller type, the line below read, *FLEEING DESPERADO SOUGHT BY OFFICERS!*

Chuckling inwardly, but keeping his face impassive, Longarm folded the paper under his arm and read the story while waiting for his breakfast to be cooked and served.

Fort Smith's good citizenry is appalled by the latest

156

outrage perpetrated by the desperadoes who slink into our fair and law-abiding community from their privileged sanctuaries in the Cherokee and Choctaw Nations. The latest victim of their foul misdeeds is the heroic Junius Castell, a policeman employed by the St. Louis & San Francisco Railway Co. Officer Castell was shot to death behind the Union Station yesterday just before the supper hour by a vicious killer who is even now being pursued in the direction of Van Buren by the dedicated men of our proud constabulary.

It is not known how Officer Castell allowed the desperado to "get the drop" on him. Officer Castell was known to be of an utterly fearless nature and an excellent shot with the pistol, having been formerly an investigator for the famous Pinkerton Detective Agency. The murdered victim's revolver was found beside him, with all of its six shells fired, when his body was discovered by Officer Milford of the Fort Smith force. Chief Constable Murphy is of the opinion that there was an exchange of gunfire in which the heartless miscreant who slew Officer Castell was wounded. A large force has gone in search of the killer, who is reported to have been witnessed slinking from the scene of the crime in a northerly direction. The good Chief has sworn that no stone will be left unturned, no nook or cranny in which the desperate outlaw murderer might hide will be overlooked, until the bloodthirsty fiend who perpetrated the foul misdeed has been brought before the Bar of Justice, where he is expected to be sentenced to a well-deserved hanging.

Well, old son, Longarm chuckled to himself, *That chief sure did deliver what he said he was going to. Why, hell, if I didn't know what really happened, I'd be right tempted to jump right up and start chasing myself.*

Folding the paper, Longarm tucked it into his coat pocket and gave his attention to the platter of steak and eggs the waiter set before him. An hour later, when he'd claimed his horse and gear from Hare's Livery Stable on

157

the Texas Road and started for the ferry, he transferred the newspaper to his saddlebag. As he rode toward Younger's Bend after crossing on the ferry, he felt less like he was going naked to stir up a hornet's nest.

Chapter 14

Because Longarm didn't relish the idea of being mistaken for someone else and getting potshot at in the dark, he slept beside the trail after his late start, and arrived at Younger's Bend in broad daylight. Sam Starr was carrying a bucket of water from the well to the house when Longarm rode up.

"Hello, Windy. What'd you do, ride all night last night, getting here at this time of day?" Starr asked.

"No. Slept along the trail. Got a late start out of Fort Smith." Longarm dismounted and led his hammerhead bay to the barn.

Starr put the bucket of water on the steps and followed him into the barn. He said, "We looked for you yesterday."

"And figured when I didn't show up that I might not be coming back? That ain't my way of doing business, Sam."

"Well, there was a lot of conversation. Floyd's still a little bit upset about McKee, you know."

"Damned if that man don't let a thing stick in his craw worse than anybody I ever met." Longarm took the saddle off the bay and tossed it across one of the stall partitions to air out. He threw his saddlebags over one shoulder, his bedroll over the other, and picked up his Winchester.

"I guess nobody's moved into my cabin while I was gone?"

"Of course not. Listen, Windy, if you're hungry, I can fix you a bite. It won't be a bit of trouble."

"Oh, I had breakfast when I got up this morning, Sam. Thanks all the same, but I can hold out till noon."

"I guess the girl got off on the train all right?"

159

"Yep. She's on her way. Hell, she's probably already back in Texarkana by this time."

"Belle was thinking—" Starr stopped abruptly. "Well, it ain't important."

"What you started to say was, Belle was thinking I might decide to go along with the girl, and not come back?"

"Something like that," Starr replied. He added quickly, "She'll be glad to know you're back, though."

Longarm looked around questioningly. "Where is Belle, anyhow?"

"She's gone with Yazoo to deliver a load of whiskey. I generally go too, when we're making a delivery, but this time Floyd said he'd enjoy a little boat ride. And Steed and Bobby rode into Eufaula; they said they wanted to look the town over."

"Boat ride?" Longarm's brow creased. "Hell, Sam, I didn't even know you *had* a boat around the place."

He hadn't paid much attention to Belle's moonshining operations. Even though she was breaking a federal law by making untaxed liquor, the Cherokee Nation was still only marginally under direct Federal jurisdiction. It was a matter of common consent that the Indian police would take care of controlling the hundreds of illicit stills that operated on what the local residents called "whiskey ranches." Longarm hadn't given much thought to the manner in which Belle delivered the whiskey Yazoo produced; he'd just assumed that the customers came after the liquor and hauled it away themselves.

Sam said, "Well, Belle don't like for the whiskey-buyers to come here to the place. We got a boat down at the foot of the bluff, and Yazoo poles it across the river, drifts downstream a couple of miles, and there's the customer, waiting at his regular place with his wagon, on the other side of the Canadian."

Longarm nodded his understanding. From a moonshiner's standpoint, making delivery at some anonymous spot along a riverbank made more sense than having wagons beat a well-defined track to the still.

"Well, then," he said, "I guess I'll go on down to the cabin and settle back in."

160

"You're sure you don't want me to fix you a bite to eat?" Sam asked. "Dinner's going to be late, because Belle and Floyd and Yazoo likely won't be back by noon."

"No, thanks. I'll hold out all right. No need for you to take extra trouble."

"Oh, I don't mind doing something a little extra for you, Windy. Which is more than I'd say for most of Belle's guests. There's times when—" Starr stopped abruptly. "Well, never mind. You just come on back when you get hungry."

"I'll do that," Longarm promised as he started for the cabin.

Apparently no one had been inside the place during his absence. There was dust on everything, and the bottle of Maryland rye that he'd left standing on the table still had a drink or two left in it. Longarm had part of the whiskey while he undid his bedroll and took a few of his possibles—including a supply of cheroots and a fresh bottle of rye—from his saddlebags. The folded newspaper came to hand, and he put it on the table to take up to the house with him when Belle and the others returned. Since he had nothing else to do, he stretched out on the bedroll and devoted himself to thinking while he rested. The job he'd promised to take on for Murphy required a little bit of planning.

Noon came and passed with no solution having presented itself. Longarm was beginning to get hungry. He stood up and stretched, finished off the almost empty bottle, and led the hammerhead bay up to the house. Starr was sitting on the porch, cleaning his guns. Longarm noticed that the quiet, browbeaten husband of the ebullient Bandit Queen handled his weapons with professional skill, and gave them the sort of care that any sensible man who depended on guns for his livelihood, if not for actual survival, might be expected to give them.

"Getting hungry?" Starr asked.

"A mite. But you go on with what you're doing. My belly's telling me it's there, but it ain't yelling at me yet."

Starr gave the barrel of his Spencer carbine a final rub with an oil rag, and propped the weapon up beside the bench he was sitting on. "I haven't started dinner yet,

161

because Yazoo usually puts out a line when he takes the boat to make a delivery, and brings back a mess of fish." He looked at Longarm curiously. "You ever remember where you ran into Yazoo before, Windy?"

Longarm shook his head. "Hell, Sam, you know how it is. A man gets around a lot, pretty much moving fast and not staying anyplace too long. He sees a lot of faces. And it ain't likely Yazoo looks like he did, wherever it was we bumped into each other."

"Sure. Not unless it's somebody he's partnered with, or had trouble with." Starr looked obliquely at Longarm. "You didn't have much trouble remembering McKee."

"McKee looked just like he did when me and him had our run-in. And when you've got a grudge between you and somebody, you ain't as likely to forget him as you would a man you just had a drink with, or sat in a poker game with somewhere."

"I guess you know Floyd and Steed are still edgy because you won't give them your real handle."

"I can't say I blame them," Longarm replied. "But I told Floyd I wasn't about to give him anything on me until I had something on him. He ought to understand that."

"Oh, I guess he does. Up to a point. But he's still edgy."

"He'll get over it. I didn't ask him and Steed to take me in on whatever job it is they're cooking up. It was their idea—or Belle's, I disremember which."

"Sounds like Belle's. I don't recall being around when it first come up." He stared challengingly at Longarm and added, "Belle's got a lot on her mind, you know. She's always figuring something out ahead of time, and now and then she'll forget to tell me things."

"How'd you and Belle happen to meet up, Sam?" Longarm asked.

"Jim Reed was a good friend of mine. Cherokee blood in both of us, you know. We were on few jobs together before Jim and Belle got married. Then, after Jim got killed, it was a while before I saw Belle. And when I did, we hit it off right well, so we married up. You know, while Jim and Belle was married, they stayed on the run most of the time. Down in Texas, here in the

Nation, up in Missouri for a while, then to Arkansas, and back to Texas. That's not good for a woman trying to bring up a couple of kids."

Longarm had difficulty picturing the soft-spoken, mild-mannered Sam Starr riding with an outlaw who'd gotten the kind of reputation Jim Reed had for ingenuity, daring, and cold-bloodedness. Sam seemed to be the kind of man who fitted best into the role he now filled, as the subservient husband of a domineering wife. And he had more than a hunch that it had been Belle who'd done most of the wooing in their romance. He wondered just how big a part Sam's land at Younger's Bend had played in her decision to marry him.

"So you settled down here."

"Well, I had the land from my tribe's allotment. And even if Belle did send the children back to Missouri to get a good education, it'll be here for them to come back to when they're older. And it's a nice place to live. Convenient and private."

"That's sure the truth," Longarm agreed. He was tempted to ask about the naming of Sam's land for Belle's first lover, but he'd begun to feel sorry for Starr. As long as Sam was contented to walk in the shadow of his wife, that wasn't Longarm's affair.

Beyond the cabins, Longarm saw Belle, Floyd, and Yazoo coming across the level area between the house and the bluff. Yazoo was carrying a string of fish.

"Oh-oh," Starr said, his eyes following Longarm's. "Time for me to put on the skillet. I hope you like catfish rolled in cornmeal and fried in bacon grease till they're nice and crusty on the outside."

"To tell you the truth, Sam, it's been such a while since I've had anything much but steak that I sort of disremember what fresh catfish tastes like."

"If I had the time, I'd cook up a stew the Cherokee way, with some gobo root and ramp and dowali in with the fish. But that'd take too long, and I'd have to go pick the other things I need. Frying's faster."

Starr stood up. "I'll go poke up the fire and get the grease heating up. Belle's going to be hungry. She won't feel like waiting long."

"Well, Windy, I'm glad you got back all right," Belle greeted Longarm when the trio got close to the house.

"Me too," Yazoo chimed in. "If you and Sam ain't et already, I got a right good string of fish here for dinner."

"We waited for you," Longarm said. "Sam's inside now, getting ready to cook."

"See, Floyd?" Yazoo said. "Told you I better stop there at the river and gut out these fish. I knew Sam'd expect me to bring in a mess. Now we won't have to wait; they're all ready to go in the pan. I'll take 'em in and they'll be ready afore you know it."

Floyd's only acknowledgement was a nod. He was studying Longarm. "You get the girl sent off all right?" he asked.

"Sure, why? Didn't you expect me to?"

"I thought you took a damn fool chance, going into a place as big as Fort Smith, with a fresh want out on you."

"Well, I did have a mite of trouble," Longarm admitted straight-facedly, his voice casual.

"Somebody spotted you?" Belle asked anxiously.

"In a way."

Floyd snorted. "What the hell kind of answer is that? Either they spotted you or they didn't."

"It wasn't me they spotted," Longarm explained. "It was the girl. Then, because I happened to be with her, they figured I was Taylor. There was a reward out on him for that bank he robbed on the way up."

"You just told us the girl got on the train all right," Floyd said suspiciously. "How could they spot you with her, if you wasn't on the train too?"

Longarm said patiently, "It happened at the depot, Floyd. I'd just put Dolly on the train. I was standing there watching it pull out when she yelled at me to look out."

"Well, what happened?" Belle demanded.

"We had a little set-to." Longarm knew that Belle and Floyd wouldn't be satisfied with that. They'd want a complete explanation, but he had cultivated a reputation for being close-mouthed, and didn't intend to volunteer anything they failed to drag out of him.

"Damn it, Windy, you're the tightest-lipped man I've

164

ever run into!" Belle complained. "I guess you deserve your name. Go ahead and tell us what happened!"

"Yeah," Floyd seconded. "Whoever seen you must've been fixing to throw down on you, for the girl to tell you to watch out."

"Oh, he was. Had his gun out."

"And you outdrew him?" Floyd's tone, if not his words, as much as called Longarm a liar.

"I was right at the edge of the platform. I jumped off it before he shot."

"And then you got him?" Belle frowned.

"Not right away. We waltzed around a little bit first."

"But you *did* get the son of a bitch?" Floyd insisted.

"Oh, sure. He's deader than hell right now," Longarm replied.

"Who was it thought they recognized you?" Belle asked.

"Railroad bull."

"Well, that's not as bad as the real law," Belle said. "At least you won't have every little tin-badge town marshal and deputy sheriff along the border on the look-out for you."

"Why, Belle, there's not anybody going to be on the lookout for me," Longarm told her. "At least, not any more than there has been before now."

"How do you figure that?" she asked.

"Because nobody saw me."

"Oh, shit!" Floyd blurted. "In a place like a depot, in a town as big as Fort Smith? There's people around depots all the time, day and night!"

"I'm of the same mind Floyd is," Belle said slowly. She frowned and went on, "Somebody must've seen you."

"I guess so. But nobody noticed me that much."

"You'll have one hell of a job convincing me of that," Floyd said.

"Oh, I can prove it, Floyd," Longarm told him in a quiet voice, almost a whisper.

"I don't see how."

"Just keep a curb-rein on your curiosity until I've had a chance to go down to my cabin. I've got all the proof you could ask for," Longarm said confidently.

"I can't wait to see that," Floyd said. He was almost sneering.

Longarm didn't have to respond, because at that moment Sam Starr stepped out onto the porch and called, "Dinner's ready! Come on and eat before it gets cold!"

Although fried catfish wasn't something he'd have ordered at his favorite steak house in Denver, Longarm had to admit that Starr's version of it was very tasty indeed. Under a thin, crisp crust, the tender white flesh of the virtually boneless fish flaked off, moist and toothsome. The fluffy brown biscuits that went with the meal did double duty; after the fish had all been eaten, biscuits and warm honey provided an ample dessert.

After they'd eaten, Floyd said, "Well, Belle, maybe you and Sam and Windy and me better sit right here and finish up planning that bank job."

"What about Steed and Bobby?" Longarm asked.

"They'll do what I tell 'em to," Floyd replied. "Me and Steed's worked together before. We won't have any trouble. But with two or three new ones coming in—"

"Not now,- Floyd," Belle broke in decisively. "We'll talk about the job after supper. Steed and Bobby will be back from Eufaula then, and we can get it all settled without having to go over everything two or three times. Besides, Sam and I have to spend the afternoon up at the stillhouse with Yazoo. He's got to start a fresh batch of mash cooking in a day or so, and we'll need more sugar for it. We need bottles too. We'll be going to Eufaula tomorrow to pick up what we'll have to have."

"That's right," Yazoo piped up. "I got every barrel and keg filled plumb to the brim up there right now. I can't keep making moonshine unless I got what I need to work with."

"After supper suits me," Longarm said. "We better get things settled pretty soon, though. I can't hang around here forever."

"You better hang around long enough to do what you've said you will," Floyd snapped. "And another thing—you said you could prove that yarn you were spinning us a while ago, about what happened in Fort

166

Smith. I'd like to see you do that, before we start planning a job you'll be in with us on."

"I'll bring along my proof when I come up for supper," Longarm promised. "Now, if everybody's going to be busy, I'm going down to the cabin and get some shut-eye."

Steed and Bobby had returned when Longarm came up to join the group for supper. He brought along the copy of the Fort Smith *Elevator*, keeping it folded so the headlines wouldn't show. Floyd challenged him as soon as he walked into the house.

"Well, Windy? I told Steed and Bobby about that crazy yarn you handed me and Belle today. They want to see how you figure to prove it, too."

"Sure." Longarm unfolded the paper and held it up. "Read it yourself."

There was silence for several minutes, while everyone in the room bent over the newspaper. Belle was the first to finish. She looked up at Longarm and started laughing.

"Well, by God, Windy, you're as good as your word! You really did cut down that railroad bull! And got away with it!"

Steed asked, "Did the son of a bitch get off five shots at you before you knocked him over?"

"I couldn't help that, Steed," Longarm explained. "He kept jumping behind one of those iron posts, there outside the depot. Wasn't much way I could get a clean shot at him until I worked him around out in back."

"I guess it happened just about like you said it did," Floyd finally admitted. "Windy, the way that newspaper write-up reads, you'll fit in with us just like gravy goes with potatoes."

Bobby stared at Longarm goggle-eyed. "You really did kill a policeman, Windy? Shot it out with him, right there in the depot?"

"You read what the paper says, Bobby," Longarm replied.

"Well, I got no more reason to hang back," Steed announced. "If Windy's notched himself up a cop, even just a railroad bull, he's with us all the way."

"That's how I've felt all along," Belle told them. "Now,

we can get down to business after supper and finish up our plans."

Supper was the first really cheerful meal that Longarm remembered having eaten at Younger's Bend. Before, there had always been Floyd's suspicion, or Belle's badly hidden jealousy, or some kind of strain or pall hanging over the table. Two or three times, Floyd tried to bring up the impending job, but Belle put him off with a reminder that there'd be time to talk and plan later on. When they'd finished, Belle told Yazoo to go up to the stillhouse and bring back two or three fresh bottles of whiskey, and as soon as Sam had cleared the table, she indicated that she was ready at last for them to get down to business.

"We'll have to make up our minds tonight which day we're going to take the bank," she began.

"What's the hurry?" Floyd asked.

"I've found out that the bank's going to get a shipment of gold and currency from the New Orleans mint in the next three or four days," she replied. "If we go in on the fifth or sixth day, we'll get most of it. We don't want to be there before the shipment gets in, and we don't want to wait too long, or a lot of it will have been handed out to the factors buying up the farm crops."

"Just how'd you get the news of that mint shipment, Belle? If you don't mind telling me, that is," Longarm asked.

"My whiskey customers pay me in more ways than with money, Windy. They carry messages, too." Belle smiled wisely. "I can't be riding into Eufaula every day just to pick up mail. Besides, I don't trust the mail. How do I know the federal marshals and the post office don't work in cahoots?"

Longarm could have told her that nothing could be further from the truth. He remembered a half-dozen times when a look at a piece of suspected mail might have saved a case for him, but Billy Vail had never been able to get the cooperation of the postal officials in allowing mail going through their hands to be opened. He said nothing, of course, just nodded understandingly.

Floyd said, "So that's why you went along with Yazoo

168

today! Damn it, Belle, you might've said something before now. Me and Steed have been wondering all along just how you was going to find out when this job ought to be pulled."

"I don't tell everybody my business," Belle said tartly. "If everybody knew what I know, or how I work things out, I'd lose my edge."

"All right, never mind that now," Floyd told her. "If the bank's going to have all that money on hand in three or four days, we'd better get cracking."

"We're still going to be short a man, even with Windy joining in," Steed pointed out.

"No. Sam's going with you," Belle said. "We've known all along the job needs five men. There'll be one at the end of the block on each side of the bank, and three to do the inside work. What you and Floyd and Windy have got to work out is who's going to go in and who's going to be the outside guards."

"That's easy enough," Floyd said. "It's just good sense for me and Steed and Windy to handle the bank. Now that my mind's at rest about Windy, I figure he's the equal of me and Steed any day. He'll keep cool and move fast, and if there's shooting, he'll handle it quick and straight."

"Oh, now wait a minute, Floyd!" Bobby protested. "I was in with you and Steed before Windy come along. It seems to me it's only right that I'd go inside. That's where the fun will be."

"Hold up there, Bobby," Longarm told the youth. "This ain't no play-party we're going on. It's business."

"You think I don't know that, Windy?" Bobby shot back. "And I can do anything you can, as good as you can. Sure, Floyd and Steed think you're right big of a much now, because you killed that officer in Fort Smith. Well, that don't make you one bit better than me!"

"That's enough, Bobby!" Floyd commanded. "You and Steed both agreed when we started out on this job that I was going to have the last word. All right, I'm giving you the last word now. You and Sam will be the outside guards. Me and Steed and Windy will take care of the inside work."

Bobby didn't look happy, but he subsided. Longarm

169

turned to Belle. "I still don't know where this bank is we're going to take."

"You don't, do you, Windy? Well, neither does Floyd or Steed or Bobby. Or Sam, either, for that matter. The only one who knows that is me, and I'm not going to tell anybody until the very last minute."

"Now wait a minute, Belle!" Floyd flared. "You never said that before. That's no goddamn way to work! I'm with Windy. I want to know where we're going, how long it's going to take us to get there, what we can look for, and how we'll get away."

"I'll give you part of it, Floyd," she answered. "But not everything."

"You better tell us the whole layout, Belle," Longarm said. "I told you once before, I don't buy a pig in a poke."

Longarm was anxious to get the whole picture. He still had a few days during which he could manage to find a way to get word to Gower where the gang planned to strike, and set up the trap that would catch the entire bunch. With Sam in custody, he was pretty sure that either Belle or Sam would talk.

"This is one pig you'll buy without seeing it," Belle said. The emphasis she gave her words left no doubt in Longarm's mind that she couldn't be argued around. She went on, "Now, you don't need to know where the bank is, not yet. The fewer people who know that, the less chance there is of word getting out about the job."

"You might be right about that part of it, Belle," Longarm began.

Belle cut him off short. "I know damn well I'm right about the whole plan, Windy. Now shut up, all of you, and I'll tell you what you need to know. You can find out the rest later on."

All of them listened intently while Belle explained the layout. There would be no marshals or sheriff's deputies around to interfere, she guaranteed. There were only three in town, one deputy sheriff and two marshals, and she had two of the three in her pocket. They could be counted on to get the third man out of the way.

As for the bank, it was in the middle of the block. The

two men outside could guard the street in both directions and keep anybody from getting close while the holdup was taking place. The outside men would hold the reins of the horses ridden by the three who'd go in. There might be a private guard inside the bank; some of them hired a man when there was a lot of extra money on hand. Handling him would be up to the men who went in. They'd also have to get the tellers and bank officers away from their desks, because all of them had weapons close at hand.

At ten o'clock, the time set for the holdup, the bank would have been open two hours, so the vault was sure to be open. The inside men would divide the loot among themselves; she'd see that they had sacks to put it in. The whole job shouldn't take more than four or five minutes, and then they'd all be riding out.

Their approach and escape routes would be mapped out for them by Sam, the night before. They'd be stopping at a place she and Sam knew well. At that time, they'd also work out what to do in the event they had to separate during their getaway.

"So that's the way it's going to work," Belle said firmly as she concluded her explanation. "Now, what day do you want to move, Floyd? I'll have to send a letter to the man who's handling things for me, when I go to Eufaula tomorrow."

"No use putting it off." Floyd didn't speak with quite as much authority as he had earlier. Belle's dominance of their discussion had somehow diminished his stature. "If it's all the same to everybody, we'll give the money shipment three days to get to the bank. We'll pull the job on the fourth."

"Sounds all right to me," Steed agreed.

"I guess so," Bobby said, when Floyd looked at him. "Whatever you say, Floyd."

"Windy?" Floyd asked Longarm.

Longarm nodded.

"All right," Belle said succinctly. "It's settled, then."

Longarm told Belle, "I reckon I'll ride into Eufaula with you and Sam tomorrow, if you've got no objections to my company. I need cigars, and I'd sort of like to look the place over, since I've never been there."

"If you want to," Belle said. "We could use somebody to give us a hand with the mules." She looked at the others. "You can see there's not one thing for you to worry about. When Belle Starr plans a job, it's done right. I don't leave anything to chance. You just handle things the way I've told you to, and it'll come off as smooth as silk!"

Chapter 15

Although the sky was clear when Longarm, Sam, and Belle
started from the house shortly after daylight, a line of low,
black clouds showed to the northeast when they came out
of the ravine and started along the trail leading to Eufaula.
Each of them led a pack mule, which clopped behind them
on a lead-rope and slowed the progress of the longer-
legged horses. By the time they'd covered half the distance
to the little town, the clouds had crept closer and there
was a smell of rain in the air.

Belle scanned the sky anxiously. She'd put on what
Longarm supposed was her regular going-to-town costume;
at least it was what she'd been wearing the first time he'd
seen her, when she and Sam had just returned from a visit
to Eufaula. For this trip, Belle wore the same long green
velvet dress with a full, flowing ankle-length skirt and a
white scarf tucked in and drawn high around her neck.

Her hat was the same one, a wide-brimmed white
Stetson with one side of the brim caught up by a pin that
held a streaming plume. Around her waist, Belle had
strapped on her polished gunbelt with its twin holsters
carrying pearl-handled, silver-plated Smith & Wesson .32s.
She wore the belt high on her waist. Belle rode in a
silver-trimmed sidesaddle, as though to underscore the
fact that, while she might be the Bandit Queen, she was
still a perfect lady.

"I hope you remembered to put my slicker in your
saddle roll," she said to Sam as the trail widened so the
three of them could ride abreast. "And brought enough
tarps, too. If a rain comes up, half the sugar will be melted
away by the time we get back, unless the bags are
covered."

"I smelled the rain coming last night before I went to bed," Sam replied patiently. "Your slicker and all the tarps we'll need are lashed across the packsaddles."

Longarm said, "Maybe it won't rain hard. It don't look to me like those clouds are moving very fast."

"It'll rain," Sam told him. "Maybe not until late, and maybe not very hard. It's early in the season for a real downpour, but we'll get at least a drizzle before we get back."

"If we hurry, maybe we can get back before the rain starts," Belle fretted. "I just hate to think of my nice dress and all that sugar getting wet."

"Stop worrying, Belle," Sam said. "If it rains, there's not a damned thing we can do to stop it. It'll just have to rain, won't it?"

Signs of settlement increased as they drew closer to Eufaula. For the first five or six miles of the ride, the trail had curved along a northern crook of the Canadian River. Then the trace became more clearly defined and the first houses began to appear. The houses were small when the trail swung northeast and left the river, and the land had been only partly cleared. The transition from a wooded path with cottonwood and blackjack oak growing thickly along its sides had been sudden when they changed direction. The first small fields and shacks dotted the roadside for a short distance, then gave way to wider cornfields and bigger houses. The fields were stubble-dotted from the recent harvest, and the narrow trace turned quickly into a wheel-rutted road beaten in the red soil.

Eufaula appeared ahead. It was a straggling town, stretched out in a single line of stores widely spaced along the road, which curved into the settlement. Even at a distance, the false fronts that rose above most of the awnings failed to hide the fact that except for two or three of the bigger buildings, the structures had only a single story. Red was the dominant color. Barn-red paint covered all but a few of the stores, and in most cases, the painting had been confined to their fronts. The sides had only the dark patina laid on them by sun and rain to distinguish their raw wood from the shining yellow pine boards of the newer buildings.

Even Longarm's sharp eyes couldn't make out the wording on the signs above the stores until they got within pistol-shot of the community. Most of the signs were small, their lettering straggly and thin. The stores were concentrated on one side of the main street—a continuation of the road—and on the less closely built side, there was an unusually large area vacant except for the big barn and corral of a livery stable. In the bare space, a number of unhitched wagons, buggies, and sulkies stood, their tongues slanting to the ground. Eufaula's residences were scattered, without the regularity imposed by streets, in ill-defined half-circles on both sides of the main road. Longarm was surprised at their number; there must have been a hundred houses.

"It sure ain't such a much of a town," he remarked as they got close enough for him to read the signs. "But I guess it's a lot better for you that it ain't."

"We like it the way it is," Belle replied curtly. "But even if it grows, it still won't be big enough for any law to move in and bother us at the Bend for a long time to come."

They reined in at the hitch rail in front of the general store. A few doors farther on, another sign proclaimed the presence of yet another general store; it was in a newer building, still unpainted.

Belle said to Sam, "I guess you'd better take a mule and start rounding up bottles. I'll do the trading while you're taking care of that."

"If you ain't got anything you need for me to help you with, I'll just find me a nice quiet saloon and sit down with a sip of Maryland rye until you've done your business," Longarm said. "I can get my cigars before we ride out; I've got enough in my pocket to tide me over for a while."

Belle laughed mockingly. "Your memory's too short, Windy. I guess you haven't been in the Nation long enough to remember that saloons are against the law here."

Longarm frowned. "Now wait just a minute. That little town on this side of the Arkansas across from Fort Smith, the place they call Little Juarez. There's plenty of saloons there."

175

"And they pay plenty to stay open, too," Belle retorted. "So do the saloons you'll find in the Nation right on the Missouri border up north, and on this side of the Red River, down on the Texas line, where there's a town on the other side."

"Belle's right, Windy," Sam said. Bitterness crept into his tone as he went on, "Our Great White Father back in the East doesn't think us Indians can hold our liquor. You know, we go crazy wild when we take a drink, and start killing all you white people."

Belle added, "So the only liquor you're going to find here in Eufaula is what we make out at the place, or what comes from one of the little whiskey ranches in the brush farther east. And it's none of it as good as the whiskey Yazoo turns out."

Longarm turned to Sam. "But you're going to buy bottles. Where from?"

"Jugs," Sam told him. "We've got to save all the bottles we can get our hands on to send over into Arkansas. We deliver the whiskey here in jugs, and the customers bring their own bottles."

"I'll be damned," Longarm said, shaking his head. "I never heard of such a damn fool thing."

"Oh, we like it that way," Belle told him. "The moonshine we make at the Bend pays the freight and a lot more. The jobs we pull off are all gravy."

Longarm saw his plan to get away from Belle and Sam going up in smoke. He'd intended to work things out so that he'd have a few minutes by himself, enough time to mail to Gower the note he'd written last night, telling him that the bank job had been set and advising him that as yet he hadn't been able to learn which bank in which town would be the target.

He said, "Well, if that's the way of it, I guess I'll just walk around and stretch my legs while you two tend to your business."

"You can help me, if you've a mind to," Belle suggested. "Two of those mules have to be loaded with hundred-pound sacks of sugar. It'll hurry things along if you'll give the storekeeper a hand, and we might get started back to the Bend in time to miss getting caught in the rain."

There wasn't any way Longarm could see of avoiding Belle's request. "Why, sure, Belle," he said. "I'll be glad to."

Sam said, "I'll be on my way, then. It'll take me an hour or more to make the rounds. I'll meet you here at the store, and we can get some cheese and crackers and eat them before we start back." He looked questioningly at Longarm and added, "If that'll tide you over until supper, Windy. It's about the best we can do here. There isn't any restaurant."

"That'll suit me fine," Longarm replied.

Starr untied the mule from his saddle-strings and set off on foot, leading the animal. Longarm watched him until he turned between two of the buildings and was out of sight, then he followed Belle into the store.

Longarm found the general store no different from a hundred others he'd seen in towns like Eufaula. Its interior was a wild jumble of goods arranged with little logic. Calico dresses crowded farming tools such as rakes and hoes. Shoes and bolts of cloth shared the same table. Patent medicines jostled cans of peaches on shelves behind the counter. Harness straps and horse collars hung on the walls beside slabs of bacon. Hams dangled by their curing-cords from the rafters, next to heavy work shoes suspended by their knotted laces. There was the inevitable wheel of cheese standing on the counter next to the tobacco cutter.

A short, bald man in a soiled, striped apron made of mattress ticking came from somewhere in the dimness at the back of the store. He said, "Well, Belle, I was wondering when you'd be coming for that sugar you ordered. It's been here for almost a week."

"I'm ready for it now, Eleazar," Belle said. "And I've even brought somebody to help you load it on the mules."

"Good, good. Now that the boy's back in school again, I'm a little shorthanded." He looked at Longarm. "Well, I'd say you ought to be able to lift a sack of sugar without too much trouble."

Longarm grinned but made no reply. The thought flashed through his mind that he might be able to entrust his note to the storekeeper to mail, but, judging from the gossipy exchange between the man and Belle, he'd be

177

a fool to take a chance. His note to Gower might wind up in Belle's hands if he risked giving it to the storekeeper to mail.

Belle said, "There are some other things I need besides the sugar, Eleazar. A sack of scratch-feed—the eggs haven't been very good since I ran out a few days ago— and matches, we're running low. If you've got a fresh comb of the red clover honey, put it in a bucket for me to take back. Sam might want something else, I don't know. Flour, or something like that. He'll tell you when he comes back from picking up the bottles. And I guess we'd better load the sugar on right away. It looks like it might be getting ready to rain."

"Be a shame if it spoiled the blowout for the newly-weds," the storekeeper said. "You'll be going, I guess?"

"What blowout?" Belle asked, frowning. "And who's getting married? I haven't heard anything about a wedding."

"Why, Sam's Aunt Lucy's girl, Sairey. She's marrying young Fred Mayes. Thought sure you'd heard."

"Sam's kin don't pay much attention to us out at the Bend," Belle said shortly. "But I don't guess we'll go to the wedding, since we didn't get invited."

"You'd be too late for it, anyhow," Eleazar told her. "They had that this morning early. But the shindy's just about getting started good right now, and it'll probably go on most of the night."

"Well, you and Windy go ahead and load the sugar," Belle said. "Be sure it's covered good, Windy. Sugar's too dear to let the rain get to it and melt it away."

"I'll look after it, Belle," Longarm assured her. He watched Belle go out the door, one hand holding her velvet skirt above her ankles to keep it from dragging on the dusty floor. Then he turned back to the storekeeper.

"I'll make sure the saddles on the mules are clear, then we can start toting the sugar out."

There were five one-hundred-pound sacks of sugar to be loaded, and Longarm lashed three to one mule, two to the other. He covered the sacks carefully with the tarpaulins that were tied to the packsaddles. It was easier to do the job right than to have Belle jawing at him, he thought

178

as he tied off the last crosshitch on the heaviest load. The other load wouldn't be lashed down until the rest of the supplies had been added to it.

Belle came up just as he was finishing. She inspected the completed load carefully before nodding her satisfaction.

Longarm said, "Think I'll walk around and stretch my legs. I'll be back before you're ready to leave."

"If you run into Sam, don't tell him about his cousin's wedding," Belle cautioned. "We don't get along with that side of Sam's family, but if he hears about the shindy, Sam's going to want to look in on it."

"I'll keep quiet about it," Longarm promised.

He walked quickly down to the post office and mailed his note to Gower. A barbershop across the street caught his eye as he came out. He crossed over after fingering his stubbled chin, deciding that a good shave would improve his spirits. He didn't think Belle and Sam would have any trouble locating him if Sam showed up and they got ready to start back.

While the barber was rubbing in the last drops of bay rum on Longarm's now-smooth face, he saw Sam leading the third mule, loaded now with bulging tow sacks, in the direction of the store. He got out of the barbershop as fast as possible, and walked into the store just in time to hear Belle exclaim, "Get some sense into your head, Sam Starr! We'd be just about as welcome at Aunt Lucy Suratt's as a case of smallpox!"

"Not when there's a party going on to celebrate a wedding," Sam retorted. "They'd get madder if they found out we was in town and didn't come to it than they would if we was to show up."

Longarm left them to argue it out, and walked over to the counter where cigars were displayed. To his surprise, a partly emptied box of his favorite cheroots stood among three or four other kinds on the shelf. Pointing to the cigars, he told the storekeeper, "If you got a full box of that kind, I'll buy it off you. Or if you ain't, I'll take what's left in this box."

"Take what's there and welcome," Elezear said. "I've

only got two customers buys that kind, I just keep 'em on hand to oblige."

"I'll leave a few, if it's going to put your customers out," Longarm offered.

"If you want all of 'em, take 'em. I can't sell something but once." Eleazar counted the number of cheroots left in the box and handed it over to Longarm. "Does this go on Belle's bill?"

"No." Longarm tossed a half eagle on the counter. "Take the price out of that." He saw that Belle and Sam were winding up their argument. "Well?" he asked. "We going to the shindy or back to the Bend?"

"We'll go say our hellos to Aunt Lucy and the rest," Belle replied. She made no effort to keep the anger from her voice. "I can't make Sam see he's just poking his head into a hornet's nest. You don't have to come unless you want to."

"I've got nothing better to do. And I'll be right there handy when you get set to go back."

"All right. We'll load the rest of the order and go stay at the shindy a half-hour or so, then head for home. We'll get wet before we get home, but Sam's got his head set."

"If we get wet, we get wet," Sam said curtly. "Come on. If we're going, we might as well finish up here and get to Aunt Lucy's before the food runs out."

They could hear the music a quarter of a mile before they got to the festivities. The twanging of a guitar, the scratchy high notes of a violin or two, and the thumping of a drum accompanied them as they wound along a dirt road well past the town itself to a house that stood isolated in a grove of mixed sycamore and sweet gum.

When the road straightened out enough for them to look down it, they saw that a board platform, only inches above ground level, had been raised for the dancers who stamped and spun to the music. At one side, long tables were heaped with food. Longarm judged that there must be thirty or more people there, counting those at the tables and on the dance floor and the few who sat on the porch of the house where it was shady.

Off the road, there were wagons, buggies, and saddle

horses, as well as a few saddle mules, tethered in a glade far enough from the house to keep the flies from swarming over the entertainment area. Sam had been leading the way, with Belle riding just behind him and Longarm bringing up the rear. Sam reined in and surveyed the crowd.

"Looks like the whole damn family's here," he told Belle over his shoulder.

"Not including your cousin Henry, I hope," she snapped. "If that renegade shows his face at one of your family parties, and I'm there too, I intend to shoot his head off."

"Now, Belle," Sam said. "You just leave it to me to settle with Henry."

Longarm had drawn abreast of the Starrs. He asked Sam, "You sure I'm going to be welcome here? Because from the way you and Belle have been talking, I got the idea your family's sort of split up, and don't get along any too well together."

"Oh, you know how families are," Starr said. "There was a big split long years back, between the ones who were for and against John Ross, the Cherokee chief who signed the removal treaty. But that was fifty years ago, and Ross has been dead for a long time."

"That doesn't seem to make any difference to the Starrs and the Wests and the Suratts," Belle said. Her voice was sharp. "And that's got nothing to do with Henry West. He's the son of a bitch who turned Sam and me in to the federals on a cattle-stealing charge."

"Just the same, my family's big enough to forget fusses when one branch or another's throwing a shindy," Sam said confidently. "Come on. We'll pull in and leave our animals here with the others, and walk up to the house."

As far as Longarm could tell, Sam and Belle weren't openly snubbed by anybody as they circulated around the edge of the dance floor. There were some who returned short, stern-faced replies when Belle and Sam greeted them, but there were about as many others who seemed glad enough to see the Starrs of Younger's Bend.

Longarm tried his best to do the impossible: make himself inconspicuous and still act as though he felt at home. He was introduced to a number of Starrs and Wests and Suratts and others whose names he didn't catch, young and old, male and female, and all of them seemed to accept his presence there as normal.

It was difficult for Longarm to realize that all, or almost all, of those at the gathering were from the same family. As far as he could see, there was no common trait among the three clans. He met a variety of Starrs and Wests and Suratts who might have been pure Anglo-Saxon, full-blood Cherokee, or part Spanish or part black. The more of the family he saw, the more confused he got.

He stubbed his toe with Belle just after they'd completed the circuit of the porch, where the elder members of the group had gathered. She said, "All right, we've done what you wanted to, Sam. Now let's go home."

"Home? Damn it, Belle, this place right here's home for the time being. We just got here. We can't up and leave like we think we're too good to mix with 'em."

"You mix, then." She turned to Longarm. "Come on, Windy. Dance with me. I might not look it, but I'm one hell of a fine dancer. Used to dance professionally, you know, over in Dallas and out in California."

"I'd be real proud to lead you out on the floor there, Belle," he replied. "But all I'd do is make you look like a fool. I got two left feet when it comes to dancing."

"Oh, hell, you're just bashful!"

"No. I'm telling you the truth. Seems like the music goes to my head and gets my feet all mixed up. I end up falling on my face and making my partner mad. After that happened a time or two, I swore I never was going to try to dance anymore."

"Oh, you're just no good for a woman at all, Windy!" Belle snapped. "Well, if Sam's so dead set on staying, I intend to have as much fun as I can." She looked around, and saw a young man close by. "Jim! Jim July! Come on and dance with your old Aunt Belle!"

For a moment the youth seemed on the verge of refusing, but then he smiled, showing big, yellowed teeth, and took Belle by the arm, and then they were stamping and whirling with the others on the dance floor.

Sam said to Longarm, "Well, Belle's taken care of, so I'm going to do some dancing myself. Go help yourself to vittles, Windy. There's whiskey under the tables. Just lift up any of the tablecloths and pick up a jug."

Left to himself, Longarm sampled the food. There were ham and chicken and spareribs and beef, cornbread and biscuits and a variety of vegetables, few of which he recognized, not being much of a vegetable fancier. There were fried squirrel and rabbit and possum, beans of several kinds, pickled crabapples, and tiny orange persimmons wrinkled into sweetness. There were some pots of stew that smelled appetizing, but which Longarm left alone because he wasn't sure what might have gone into them.

While he ate, he studied the shifting crowd. Fresh faces were constantly appearing, but Longarm couldn't tell whether they belonged to new arrivals or people he hadn't noticed before. He saw that Sam had gone onto the dance floor, but wasn't dancing with Belle. She was still twirling around with the young Cherokee she'd called Jim, and Sam had taken a short, chubby, middle-aged woman for his partner. A young couple, their faces flushed and perspiring, pushed past him, heading for the tables. Longarm stepped aside and bumped into someone behind him.

"Beg pardon," he said, swiveling around.

He glanced at the woman he'd jostled, and then opened his eyes wide for a better look. She was strikingly attractive in a regal sort of way, even with her face twisted into a grimace of dismay as she juggled the bowl of stew she was carrying. Longarm grabbed her by the shoulders and steadied her in time to keep the stew from slopping over the side of the bowl.

"Thank you," she said, flashing him a smile.

"Maybe I better walk in front of you to keep somebody else from bumping into you like I did," he suggested.

"That's not necessary. I'm just taking this to my aunt, over there on the porch."

"Mrs. Lucy Suratt?" Longarm fished up the name of the only aunt he'd heard mentioned.

183

"No. My Aunt Sarah. Aunt Lucy's my aunt once removed, if I remember the family tree correctly."

She started toward the porch, and Longarm walked ahead of her, clearing a path. They rounded the corner of the dance floor just as Belle came rushing up.

"Windy!" Belle panted. "Have you seen Sam?"

"Not since a few minutes ago. He was out dancing, then."

"He's not on the dance floor. I've looked."

"You trying to find him and talk him into going home now?"

'I'm trying to find him to get him away before there's big trouble. Frank West just got here."

"You don't figure Sam would start anything, do you? Not after—"

"Sam might not. Frank might. They've both said they're going to shoot the other on sight. Go around that way, Windy. See if you can find Sam."

Longarm started in the direction in which Belle had pointed. He pushed through the crowd, skirting the dance floor, but when he got to the side of the floor nearest the house, he saw that Belle had found her husband first. He walked up to them in time to hear Sam say, "I don't give a damn what you want me to do! If Frank's here and wants to settle things, I'm ready!"

"Sam, listen to me!" Belle was almost shouting. "I know you've got a good gun hand, but so has Frank!"

"Then we'll just have to see which of us is best!" Sam snapped.

Belle appealed to Longarm. "Windy, help me get Sam to be reasonable! I don't want him to—"

"No, Belle. You and Sam settle things between you. It's your family."

Sam said, "Windy's right. Damn it, Belle! Most of the time I listen to you, but this time I'm not going to!" In a calmer tone, he went on, "Frank's my kin, not yours. I've got to face him myself. You stay out of it."

A hush began rippling over the dance floor. The music faltered and died away. The dancers began moving off the board square, clustering at the corners. Longarm looked across the deserted boards. He saw a man—Frank West, he supposed—standing on the opposite side, staring fixedly at Sam. West was not making any threatening moves. He simply stood there, looking.

Sam said, "Windy, get Belle out of the way!"

"I'm going to stand with you!" Belle exclaimed.

"You are like hell! My people call me a squaw man! They'll start calling me a *squaw* if I don't stand up to Frank by myself!"

Belle tried to grab Sam's arms, but he was the quicker of the two. He shoved Belle into Longarm. Longarm grabbed her upper arms. Sam took a step or two away from them. His face was set. Longarm thought he'd never really seen Sam Starr until now.

Starr sidled along the edge of the dance floor, his stare matching that fixed on him by Frank West. Longarm didn't see which of the two drew first; he was watching Starr. Their two shots rang out at almost exactly the same time.

Sam's leg buckled, but he stayed on his feet. West was bringing up his revolver for a second shot when Sam fired again. West got off the round just as his body jerked to the impact of Sam's slug. West's bullet tore into Sam, who staggered.

Sam began limping toward West. He shot once more as West crumpled slowly. West still had enough strength for one more shot, and Sam went to his knees as the slug tore into him. His gun was still leveled. He fired, hitting West, who jerked and twisted to one side. Starr lurched forward on his face. He used his left hand to push himself up and get off a last shot before his muscles failed him.

Then both men lay prone and motionless as the echoes of their final shots died away and the clearing fell silent.

Chapter 16

Belle ran to her husband, who lay face down at the edge of the dance floor. Longarm was a step behind her. He could see at a glance that Starr was dead.

Across the bare planks of the deserted floor, Frank West's body twitched. Longarm went to check on him. West lay with his head twisted to one side. The eye that Longarm could see was sightless and beginning to glaze. West's arm was folded under his body; only the tip of his revolver's muzzle was visible.

Going back to Belle, Longarm said, "Sam sure did what he said he was going to. West's dead."

"So is Sam, damn it!" Belle's voice rasped in her throat.

"You can't do a thing for him, Belle. It's finished."

By now, others were beginning to gather around them. Longarm knelt beside Starr's body and turned it over. Sam's dead eyes were fixed upward, his lips twisted in death's grin. Belle took off her scarf and draped it over the dead man's face.

Longarm asked her, "Is there an undertaker here in town?"

"No. Folks in Eufaula take care of their own dead."

A ring of people had formed around them now, but none of them were talking. Across the dance floor, Longarm could see a similar circle around Frank West's body. As far as he could tell, the two groups were about equal in number. He wondered if it was a division by family ties, and if an argument was going to break out among the kinfolk.

Belle said, "Will you get Sam's horse from the glade, Windy? I'm not going to ask these people to lend me a wagon. I don't intend to be beholden to them for anything at all."

"You'll bury Sam at the Bend, then?" he asked. When Belle nodded silently, he said, "What about the law? A judge or somebody?"

Belle shook her head. "No. I guess the only ones who'd have any say are the Cherokee Tribal Council, and they're up in Talequah. That's a long way from here."

"I guess we'd better—"

Longarm was interrupted by a burly man wearing butternut jeans and a pink calico shirt, who detached himself from the crowd and strode over to them.

"Belle," the man said. He jerked his head in the direction of the bodies. "I see Frank and Sam finally found each other."

"Yes," Belle said tonelessly.

"And did what both of them swore they would," the man went on.

"Frank started the fight," Belle flared. "He called for Sam to come out and face him."

"That don't matter much now, does it?" the man asked.

"No. I guess it doesn't, Robert." She said to Longarm, "Windy, this is Robert West, Sam's uncle."

"Frank's too," West said. He dismissed Longarm with a jerk of his head, and turned back to Belle. "You going to bury Sam on his land?"

"Yes. We'll be going back right away."

"We'll see to Frank. Bury him this evening, I suppose. You won't stay for the funeral?"

Belle shook her head. "No, Robert. It wouldn't look right."

West nodded slowly. "I guess you're right, Belle, but I don't feel that way and neither will Sarah and the rest of the family. When will you be putting Sam away?"

Belle looked around the clearing. The sun was slanting below the treetops, and shadows were creeping over the dance floor, where a few people stood talking. She said, "We won't get back in time to bury him tonight. Tomorrow, I suppose."

"I'll bring the family out. Early or late?"

"I haven't thought about it, Robert."

"Sarah and Henry and John will want to be there," West said. "We'll bring our own tucker. Look for us sometime right about noon. You'll put us up for the night, I guess? It'd be too late for us to come back home after Sam's buried."

"You come ahead," Belle said. "I suppose Sam would have wanted it that way."

West nodded and walked back across the street, and Belle asked Longarm, "Can't we get started right away, Windy? I don't want to stay here any longer than I have to."

Longarm nodded. "Go on the porch while I get Sam's horse up here. It won't take long," he told her. "Unless you want me to come along and we'll bring back the mules too, and save stopping again."

"No. You go ahead. I'll wait."

Longarm walked to the glade and led Starr's horse back to where Sam's body lay. A small group had gathered around the dead man. Longarm started to lift the corpse, and two of the men stepped forward and helped him. Sam's revolver lay in the center of the blood-stains, his hat a foot away. Longarm went over and used the hat to pick up the blood-covered revolver, and tucked both in the saddlebags on Starr's horse. Across the dance floor, men were carrying Frank West's body into the house. Longarm watched for a moment, then went on with the job Belle had asked him to do.

With the sun slanting on their backs, Longarm and Belle rode back to Younger's Bend. It was a silent trip. Belle led Sam's horse, with the blanket-wrapped body lashed across the saddle, and Longarm led the mules, strung out behind in single file.

Belle spoke only once, when the trail widened and Longarm pulled up beside her to ask if she was all right.

"Yes. Sam's not the first husband I've had to bury, Windy. But I don't guess you ever get used to it."

"No, I guess a body don't."

"I should have stayed long enough to send a note to Pearl. And to Ed. They liked Sam."

"Your kinfolks will be out tomorrow; you can send whatever mail you've got back with them."

"Sam's kinfolks!" Belle flared. For a moment she was once more the Bandit Queen, short-tempered and snappish. "I wish I'd just told them to stay away from Younger's Bend! I don't want to have them around tomorrow, Windy. They'll blame me for what happened!"

"That was between Sam and his cousin, Belle. Hell, it wasn't your fault."

"They'll go back beyond the shooting. You don't know how the Cherokees think, Windy. Sure, it was Frank's fault for turning Sam and me in to the law. But they'll go farther back than that. They'll think that if Sam hadn't married me, he wouldn't have been doing anything the law would be after him for. They won't admit that Sam was outside the law before I ever met him. Hell, if Sam hadn't been pulling stagecoach and bank jobs with Jim Reed before I ever married Jim, I never would've met Sam."

Longarm finally got the sequence sorted out. He asked, "You're saying these kinfolks of Sam's feel like you set him outside the law?"

"They always have. And they'll be resentful because I'll inherit Sam's allotment land, instead of it going back to the family." Belle shook her head. "Cherokees carry grudges backward a long way. Robert didn't want to bring the family out tomorrow because of me. He just couldn't stand to see Sam's kinfolks disgraced because they aren't there when he's buried."

Longarm didn't bother to point out that Cherokees weren't alone in holding grudges. He remembered some of the feuding that went on during his own boyhood in the hardscrabble hills of West Virginia. He didn't think Belle would be much inclined to listen to anything he said, though. She was thinking her own thoughts. Ahead, the trail narrowed. Longarm reined in to let her ride ahead, and dropped back to the position he'd held most of the time since they'd left Eufaula, behind the horse bearing Sam Starr's body. Before they'd gone much farther, the rain began, a slow, irritating drizzle.

Belle took charge as soon as she dismounted at

189

Younger's Bend. She answered the questions that flowed from those who'd stayed behind, but cut her explanations as short as possible. When Floyd and Steed and Bobby tried to offer condolences, she brushed their efforts aside. Dry-eyed and determined, her thin lips pinched even thinner as she concentrated on what had to be done, she overrode the reluctance of the men to do household work, and kept them busy far into the night getting things in readiness for the arrival of Sam's kinfolk.

Laying out Sam's corpse was the first job. Belle did most of that herself. She had to have help in stripping away the bloodstained, bullet-torn clothes Sam had been wearing when he died, but she shooed the others away while she washed the body with vinegar water and dressed it in the best clothes Sam had owned. She brushed the dead man's hair and smoothed away the contorted smile that had frozen on his face during the moments of death. The only time she called on the others for help was when she was unable to force Sam's stiff Sunday boots on. It occurred to Longarm while he and Floyd worked at sliding the boots onto Sam's limp legs that he still hadn't seen Belle shed a tear over her husband's death, and her eyes showed no signs that she'd done any private weeping.

While Belle devoted her attention to the corpse, she put the men to work moving the horses and mules from the barn up to the corral. There was more room in the barn for mourners, and the rain-freshened air that circulated through the slat-rail walls made it a cooler place to keep the corpse than the small house. They raked the floor clean and smoothed it where necessary, then spread a thick layer of fresh straw. In the center they placed a pair of sawhorses with planks across them, and covered the boards with the blankets in which Sam would be wrapped for burial.

Only after these jobs had been finished did Belle allow them to stop for supper. Darkness had already come when they ate their pickup meal, standing around the kitchen table, munching whatever scraps and bits they'd been able to unearth of cheese, dry biscuits, a few pieces of hard corn pone, and some fried chicken that

190

had been sitting in a dish for two or three days. They washed it down with Yazoo's corn squeezings.

"I ain't much on cooking," the old man volunteered as they chewed, "but I can turn to in the morning and cook up some grub for the folks you said is coming tomorrow, Belle."

"They'll bring their own food," Belle said. "Enough for them and us too. Besides, you're not going to have time to cook tomorrow morning, Yazoo. None of you are. There's Sam's grave to dig and the house to clean up, and all that sugar to carry up to the stillhouse. There's more than enough to keep everybody busy. I want this place to be ready by noon, before Sam's kinfolks get here!"

At daybreak they started again. Belle had wrestled a breakfast of sorts from the kitchen range: soggy biscuits and bacon and coffee. She hurried them through the meal, urged them to haste in carrying the sugar and other items up the slope to the still, then designated Yazoo and Bobby to handle the housecleaning chores while Longarm, Floyd and Steed went up to the grove. They started the grave a short distance from the still-dark mounds of the other two so recently filled.

"For a hell of a lot less'n two cents, I'd call off this fucking job," Steed panted. They'd just broken through the hard surface crust; the rain had passed over during the night, barely moistening the earth. Steed took a swallow from the bottle they'd brought with them to ease the digging and went on, "Damn job's been jinxed from the start. McKee, then Taylor, now Sam. I can't keep from wondering if I'm next."

"That ain't no way to talk," Floyd told him. "The job didn't have one damned thing to do with what happened to them, Steed."

"So you say." Steed drank again and passed the bottle to Floyd. "Just the same, we're a man short again."

Longarm said nothing, but kept plying his shovel.

Floyd offered him the bottle, but Longarm shook his head. "Thanks. I'll wait till I can drink rye."

"Well, damn it, how do you feel about the job, Windy?"

"Same as always."

"Maybe you better tell us just what that means," Steed said.

"Means I don't give a damn. Call it off, go ahead with it," Longarm replied levelly. "I don't think it's jinxed, even if you do."

Longarm realized he was taking a chance in saying what he had, but it was another of those risks he couldn't avoid if he intended to keep up the front he'd been presenting the outlaws.

Floyd took a second swallow from the bottle and handed it to Steed, saying, "We're not calling off the job! If what Belle's told us about the bank layout is right, we can get by with one outside man."

"You mean Bobby?" Steed asked. He spat, then drank. "Shit! The kid's green, Floyd. We couldn't be sure he might not panic."

"Instead of us hashing this over, we'd be better off talking to Belle," Longarm suggested. He held out his hand for the bottle. Even though corn whiskey always tasted too sweet to him, digging was dry work. He took a sparing sip. "Maybe she'd know somebody who could take Sam's place."

"Not in the time we got left," Floyd said. He reached out his hand for the bottle and drank, then grinned mirthlessly. "I got a better idea. Belle's always bragging and blowing about how she's the Bandit Queen. Let's just tell her flat out she's got to take Sam's place."

"Me, go on a job with a woman?" Steed shook his head. "Not likely!"

"Wait a minute, Steed," Longarm said. "Floyd's idea might not be so bad. Belle knows the country. If she stood lookout with Bobby, we wouldn't be worried about him being green. She'd keep him on the mark."

It had suddenly occurred to Longarm that, with Sam gone, the use of Younger's Bend as an outlaw rendezvous would end if Belle was put behind bars. So would her payoffs. A bank holdup would bring a sentence that would keep her in the pen for years.

"See there, Steed?" Floyd asked. "Maybe you better think again."

"Thinking won't change a thing," Steed retorted. "I don't want any part of a woman on any job I ride out on."

"It wouldn't hurt to talk to Belle about it," Longarm insisted. "We're damn sure going to have to change our plans anyhow."

"Well . . ." Steed drawled out the word so that his doubts dripped from it almost visibly. "I'll go as far as talking, but sure as shit stinks, I won't change my mind."

They fell silent and finished their job. The morning was passing, breakfast had been skimpy, and they were anxious to be at the house when Sam's kin arrived with the food Belle had said they would bring.

A larger number of relatives than Longarm had expected arrived shortly after the trio returned to the house. The men rode in on horses; there were eight of them, and it seemed to Longarm that twice as many women were in the spring wagons that followed the horsemen. There were two of the wagons. The women sitting in them held plates and platters on their laps, and steadied big pots in the wagon beds with their feet.

Belle had stationed herself on the porch when she heard the wagons creaking up. She'd found time to change into a black velvet dress. It was ankle-length, like the green one, and very much the same in cut, with a high collar to hide the creases and loose skin of her neck. She hadn't put on her hat, but had arranged her dark hair in a curving bang that hid her high-domed forehead. In spite of the occasion, or perhaps because of it, she wore her silver pearl-handled pistols.

Yazoo, obviously drunk but still able to navigate, skipped out of sight into the house when he heard the relatives arriving. Longarm, Steed, Floyd, and Bobby retreated toward the cabins with their bottle, but stopped just beyond the well to watch the wagons as they pulled up and men swung off their horses.

There seemed to be a protocol the relatives observed. Robert West, uncle of both of the dead men, was the

193

first to step up on the porch. He bent over Belle, said a few words in a low voice, then stood beside her while the men filed past and stopped for a word or two before moving on. The women followed. They were a bit more demonstrative, but only words passed between them and Belle; there were no embraces or handclasps. The procession wound into the barn. When the last of the guests—a girl not yet in her teens—had disappeared into the barn, Belle rose and stepped inside the house. Yazoo came out with her almost at once. He carried a gallon jug of whiskey in each hand, and went into the barn.

Steed said under his breath, "When are they going to start dishing up the grub? I'm damn near starved."

"So am I," Floyd agreed. "You reckon they'll eat before the burying? Or wait till it's finished?"

"I'm as hungry as the rest of you, I guess," Bobby said. "What you reckon they got in all them platters and pots?"

"It'd better be food," Steed told him. He took another swallow from the almost empty bottle. "My belly thinks my throat's been cut."

Several of the older women came from the barn and sat down near Belle. They stared silently ahead. The other women began carrying the food from the wagons into the house.

"I sure hope that grub they got is fit to eat," Floyd said. He caught Longarm's eye and winked broadly. "Let's see, Sam was part Cherokee. Ain't it the Cherokees that likes dog meat, Windy?"

"Oh, most of the redskins I know about eat dogs," Longarm replied. "Sioux, Arapahoe, Cheyenne, Comanche. I guess the Cherokees do too."

"Dog meat?" Bobby gasped. "Is that what we're going to have to eat?"

"Oh, you don't have to eat if you don't want to, Bobby," Floyd said. "Or you can pass up the meat and fill your belly with bread and potatoes and garden truck."

"You and Floyd are funning me, aren't you, Windy?" Bobby asked. "Those folks don't even *look* like Indians. They don't really eat dogs, do they?"

"Well, they're all of them part Cherokee, Bobby," Longarm answered. "But I reckon they've given up a lot of their Indian habits."

"Dog meat or not, I don't aim to wait any longer for some grub," Steed said suddenly.

Longarm looked at the outlaw. Steed was weaving on his feet; the whiskey on his empty stomach was proving to be more than he could handle. Before anyone could stop him, Steed staggered over to the wagons. There was only one woman in sight. She was lifting out a heavy pot. Belle and the woman on the porch had moved into the house.

Longarm asked Floyd, "You think you better go bring him back?"

"Ah, Steed won't hurt the woman. He's just gone to find out when we're going to be fed." Floyd was feeling the liquor almost as much as Steed.

Longarm watched as Steed approached the wagon. The woman heard him coming up and half-turned, having balanced the pot on the edge of the wagon's side. Steed said something to her, and the woman shook her head. He gestured at the pot. His wild arm-waving overbalanced him, and Steed lurched heavily into the woman.

Longarm saw trouble looming and started to move. He got to the wagon just as Steed grabbed the woman's arm. She kicked at his shins, still trying to hold onto the pot, but almost dropping it.

"Don't put your hands on me!" she said as Longarm came up.

"Now, listen, you damned—" Steed began.

Longarm cut off whatever Steed had been about to say by grabbing his shoulder and whirling him around. "Leave the lady alone, Steed," he ordered sternly. "This ain't a time or place to stir up a ruckus."

"Let go of me, Windy, or by God, I'll—"

Longarm increased the pressure of his steel-hard fingers on Steed's collarbone. Steed broke off his intended remark to say, "Damn you, turn me loose! That hurts!"

"You've had a drink too many," Longarm told the outlaw. "Go on back over there with Floyd and Bobby and cool off."

Steed sobered up quickly as he got the message from

Longarm's hard voice and crunching grip. The memory of McKee may have helped speed his recovery. He protested, "I wasn't aiming to hurt her. All I want is a bite of something to stop my belly from griping!"

"Then wait, like the rest of us. Now come on. Let's go back over there with Floyd and Bobby."

Longarm swung Steed around. He hadn't really looked at the woman, intent as he was only on hustling Steed away from a situation that could create trouble. They'd gotten several steps from the wagon when she called, "I still don't know your name, but thanks for the second time!"

"You're welcome," Longarm replied. He turned as he spoke, and looked back. He recognized her then. It was the woman he'd bumped into at the shindy. As they had the day before, Longarm's eyes widened. Her face was one of the prettiest he'd seen in a long time, now that he got his first good look at it when it wasn't pulled into a grimace. There wasn't any special feature that drew his attention, just a general impression of mature beauty.

He said, "My friend didn't mean any harm, ma'am. We just put in a morning's work digging Sam's grave, and we're a mite starved out."

"There'll be plenty to eat as soon as Cousin Sam's buried," she said. "It wouldn't be respectful if we made him wait until after we'd eaten, though."

Longarm nodded. "We're not all that hungry. We can wait." In a lowered voice, he told Steed, "You were acting like a damn fool. If that woman had yelled, you'd have had all of Sam's men kinfolk piling out of that barn and onto you."

"Hell, I didn't mean anything, Windy. I only wanted to see if I couldn't get a bite to eat."

"Just the same—" Longarm began. He stopped as a drumbeat sounded from the barn, then another. He nodded and said, "I guess we'll be eating soon enough. It sounds to me like Sam's funeral's just started."

Chapter 17

To the measured beat of the drum, Sam Starr's body was carried from the barn on the shoulders of four of his kinsmen. The drummer led the way. His drum was small, less than a foot in diameter, and he carried it at eye level, bringing a surprisingly resonant note from it with his fingertips. The corpse lay on a single wide plank. The board was not quite wide enough to accommodate the dead man's shoulders, which protruded over its edges on both sides. Behind the bearers came the remaining men. All except Robert West wore hats. West had on a wide headband. As the tiny procession passed the house, the women trooped out and took up their places behind the men. Belle walked at their head, with a much older woman.

Longarm, Floyd, Steed, and Bobby followed some distance behind the women. Halfway to the grove, Longarm heard the scraping of feet behind them and looked back. Yazoo had appeared from somewhere and was following them.

Not until the men carrying the body reached the graveside and lowered their burden to the ground did Longarm see that Sam's face had been covered with a featureless mask, made of some sort of tanned animal pelts. The drumbeats stopped when the body touched the ground. Robert West leaned over the corpse and lifted the mask off. In the short interval that elapsed before West pulled around the dead man's face a fold of the blanket on which the corpse lay, Longarm saw that the face had been painted. A single band of black ran from ear to ear, covering both eyes and nose, and a pattern of thin red lines and small circles had been drawn over the mouth and chin.

After he had covered Sam's face, Robert West knelt. The other men followed suit. West said a few short phrases in a low voice, almost a whisper. He stood up, lifted his face and spread his arms, and raised his voice in a brief chant in Cherokee. He nodded, and four of the men lowered the body into the earth. All of the men then filed past the open grave, each of them dropping into it a small square of cornbread. West motioned toward the waiting shovels. The men took turns working with the shovels until the grave was filled and mounded. During the brief ritual, the women stood at one side, watching with impassive faces. Belle stood a little apart from the others. When the mound had been formed, West led the group back to the house.

"You reckon we're supposed to go in and eat with them?" Steed asked as he and the others fell in at the end of the straggling line. They carefully kept a bit of space between themselves and the relatives.

Yazoo answered him. "Yep. Belle told me to tell you to come on in and fill up after the burying. Them kinfolks of Sam's has brought enough vittles to feed a whole damn army."

"What—what kind of food, Yazoo?" Bobby asked hesitantly.

"Hell, I don't know." Yazoo was just drunk enough to be cheerful. "There's roasting ears and vension steaks and whole pots of stews and garden truck. I just got a look at it while they was unloading the wagons."

"Did any of it look like dogmeat?" Bobby asked the old man.

"Dog? I couldn't say about that, Bobby. You put meat in a stew, it all looks pretty much alike."

Bobby said, "I guess I'll pass up the stews, then. But that roasted venison sounds pretty good to me."

There was hardly room to move in the house. Belle was nowhere in sight, and the door to the bedroom was closed, so Longarm imagined that she'd gone in there. The food was plentiful, and he helped himself to venison roast, two ears of corn, and the only other meat he recognized, some pieces of fried squirrel. He took his plate outside and looked for a place to eat. Floyd, Steed, Bobby, and Yazoo had disappeared, probably to the cabins, Longarm thought. He wondered if they'd had the same feeling that had dogged him all the time he was in the house; Sam Starr's relatives seemed to be avoiding looking at him or getting close to him.

Wandering outside, Longarm walked over to the well and sat down on its curb. The thigh-high coping of planks made it a comfortable height for a seat, and the wide horizontal top board gave him a place to rest his plate. Longarm ate slowly, his eyes busy.

From the well, he could look into the barn. The men were gathered in there, and he saw the glint of the whiskey jugs being passed from hand to hand and tilted. He contemplated going to his cabin for a sip of rye, but the exertion of gravedigging had diminished his ambition to do much besides sit still. He finished eating and lighted a cheroot. A woman carrying a bucket came out of the house and walked toward the well. Longarm started to rise and leave when he recognized her as the unusually pretty one he'd noticed earlier. He changed his mind about leaving in favor of getting a closer look at her. As she drew near, he saw that she was a bit older than he'd thought. Her amazingly perfect cast of features masked her age effectively.

Longarm stood up when she reached the well. She said, "You don't have to move. I can draw from the other side."

"I've finished eating, ma'am. It won't bother me a bit to give you room. Here." Longarm dropped the wooden bucket that stood on the coping into the well and waited for it to fill. He drew it up, the pulley creaking from lack of oil.

She said, "I never did really thank you for taking your drunk friend away while I was unloading the wagon."

"I didn't expect thanks. All I was doing was trying to keep any trouble from starting."

"Yes. If the men had looked out and seen your friend, they'd have jumped to the wrong conclusion and probably would have rushed him."

Longarm studied the woman covertly while he drew up the heavy water bucket. Her face was a perfect oval, and her large brown eyes, fringed with long lashes, added to its symmetry. The line of her nose gave her face a squareness that kept it from looking too plump. Her lips were perhaps a bit overblown, her mouth a trifle wide, but this did not detract from the regularity of her features. She wore her hair long, in loose, thick braids that dropped down her back.

He swung the bucket over to the coping and lifted it to fill hers. She asked, "Are you one of Sam's friends? Or one of Belle's?"

"Neither one, I'd say. I never saw Sam or Belle until I pulled in here about a week ago."

"Then, are you—" She stopped short. "No, I mustn't ask you any questions. Cousin Robert said that was something we should be careful not to do."

"You can ask," Longarm smiled. "There ain't any law says I got to answer you."

"Of course. But it's better if I do what Robert says."

Longarm noticed that her eyes kept returning to his freshly lighted cheroot. He asked, "My smoke bother you, ma'am?"

"No. Just the opposite. I'm wishing I could have one myself. That's the kind I smoke. I stopped at the store as we passed through Eufaula, to buy some, but Eleazar said he'd sold out." Her eyes widened and she added "Why, you must be the one who bought them! You're the man who was with Belle and Sam yesterday!"

Longarm nodded. He said, "Yes. Too bad about your cousin. I guess the other fellow was a cousin of yours too?"

"Yes." She shook her head. "It's a little bit unnerving, two funerals in two days, and the long ride out here. Even if I didn't know Frank except to nod to, and met Sam just once."

Longarm took a cheroot from his vest pocket and offered it to her. "Maybe this'll help settle your nerves, then."

"Are you sure you won't run short?"

"Take it, ma'am. I bought all the storekeeper had. If you want another one or two, I'll be glad to—"

"No," she broke in. "This will be fine. Thank you."

200

She looked at Longarm questioningly. "I'm Jessibee Vann." She waited.

Longarm hesitated. It went against his grain to lie, and so far his deviousness with the gang at Belle's hadn't extended to outright lying. Rather, he'd just let them draw a lot of mistaken conclusions without correcting them. He didn't relish being called 'Windy,' but the name had attached itself to him and he'd been contented to let it stand. Jessibee Vann deserved better, though, he thought.

"Around here I'm answering to a sort of nickname," he told Jessibee. "But my name's—" he hesitated for only a breath— "Custis."

"I'm very grateful to you, Custis," Jessibee said. "Both for drawing the water and for the cigar. Perhaps we'll talk again before I leave tomorrow."

"I'd like that, Jessibee," Longarm said gravely.

"I'd better hurry back now," she said. "They'll be wanting this water to wash up with."

Looking at Jessibee's retreating form, Longarm tried to figure out whether she was full Cherokee or just part. She walked with an Indian's upright posture and straight-pointed steps, but there was something about her that didn't jibe with the idea that she was a full Indian.

He tried to recall what he'd heard, in bits and scraps during his wonderings, of Cherokee history. It seemed to him they'd been early to intermarry with white settlers, in their ancestral home in Georgia. And there had been some kind of split in the tribe a long time back that had brought part of them to settle along the Arkansas, even before the Cherokee Nation was carved out of the raw Western land. But that was years before Longarm's time, and history had never been his long suit. It had always seemed silly to him to study the past, when the present had so many things to keep a fellow busy.

After spending a few minutes trying to vainly to recall things he'd never really learned, Longarm gave up. The day was dropping down into evening, and he'd started early and worked harder than usual. He didn't have much taste for going into the barn; in fact, he had a feeling that he'd find himself an outsider at a family gathering. He wandered down to his cabin, slipped off his boots, and

201

poured a tot of his own Maryland rye into the glass that sat waiting beside the bottle on the table.

Longarm had long ago learned the wisdom of the old Indian axiom, "Never stand up when you can sit down; never sit down when you can lie down." He stretched out on one of the narrow bunks and lighted yet another cheroot, realizing ruefully that he'd been smoking a hell of a lot of the things ever since Billy Vail had put him on the case. He figured it was probably due to the strain of maintaining his facade as the close-mouthed Windy. Vowing silently to quit as soon as he'd wrapped up this whole nasty affair, he turned his thoughts to the business at hand. The crowd of Sam's kinfolk would be gone to-morrow and he'd need to think up some pretty convincing reasons to persuade Belle to join with the gang when the raid on the bank was staged. Sipping the rye and puffing at the cheroot while the sun dropped and darkness flowed into the bare little cabin, he noticed, not for the first time, that the pleasurable combination of his favorite liquor and tobacco had taken a few of the sharp edges off the world. He decided that maybe he'd been a mite hasty in his resolution to quit smoking. He'd definitely cut down, though—just as soon as he got back to Denver. Having thus appeased his conscience, he stubbed out the cigar and lay back. Then, after a bit, he dozed.

Longarm woke with a start and rolled from the bunk to his feet. He'd taken off his gunbelt and put it on the floor beside him. His hand moved as if by instinct to scoop up the Colt as he left the bunk. He was facing the door when a soft voice from the darkness said, "I hope I didn't disturb you, Custis, but you said to ask you if I wanted another cigar."

"Jessibee?" Longarm asked.

"I hope you weren't expecting someone else. If you are, perhaps I'd better go."

"No, no!" he said hastily. "I wasn't looking for anybody at all. And if it's a cigar you've come for, I've got plenty. Wait, I'll light the lamp."

"Don't," she said. "The moon's just behind a cloud

right now. We'll have all the light we need in a few minutes."

"If you say so. Wait, though. I'll guide you in and get you sat down. That is, if you've got time to visit a spell."

"I'm not in any hurry, Custis."

Longarm groped his way to the door, and extended a hand. He found her arm, warm and soft, and led her to the table, put her hand on one of the chairs beside it, and sat down himself in the other.

He said, "You sort of took me by surprise. But if you've come for a cigar—" He took two cheroots from his vest pocket and handed one of them to her. "Now shield your eyes so the match won't blind you so bad, and I'll light it for you."

Longarm took his own advice and closed his eyes until the first white flare of the match had subsided. He cupped the match in his hands and leaned toward her. Jessibee was just opening her eyes. They danced in the flickering of the flame as she puffed her cheroot into light. He lighted his own and blew out the match. The glow of the two cigars gave the little cabin a sort of radiance, a faint glow that was saved from being ghostly by its pinkish hue.

Jessibee said, "I couldn't sleep. I don't go to bed early when I'm at home, you see, like most of my relatives. They're ready to turn in when the sun goes down. Most of them farm, so they have to be up at daybreak."

"And you don't?"

"That's one of the good things about living alone; I don't have to follow anybody's schedule. If I want to read all night, I can. Or if I feel like getting up at three in the morning for breakfast, I can do that too, without disturbing anyone."

"A pretty lady like you are, I'd have figured you to have a husband by now."

"I had one," Jessibee said. "Until three years ago, when he died of pneumonia."

"Oh. I'm sorry to hear that."

"I'm over it by now, Custis. And to save you asking, I'm not looking for another husband. I get along quite

203

well alone, just as you seem to. You don't have a wife waiting for you somewhere, do you?"

"No. Never found time to get married, or a woman I'd want to tie up with for the rest of my life."

"Good. Then we don't have to pretend to one another, do we? Ask a lot of questions with double meanings, or say a lot of things we don't really mean."

"That's a habit I never got into," Longarm told her.

"It took me a while to break mine. But I feel a lot better if I don't try to put a false face up to someone."

A bit more light began to seep into the cabin now, as the moon came from behind the cloud that had shrouded it. Longarm could see Jessibee as something more than an occasional oval of blurred features in the sudden glow when she puffed her cheroot. Her eyes were deep pools in the bluish, uncertain light that turned her lips to a crimson so dark they looked almost black, accentuating their sensuous fullness.

He said, "Since you've got a taste for cigars, I'd imagine you might enjoy a drink of whiskey. All I've got is Maryland rye, if that'll suit you."

"It'll suit me fine. The whiskey that old man makes is good enough, but I had all I cared for up at Sam's house."

"Belle's house now, I guess," Longarm said as he poured their drinks. "I feel sort of bad about Sam. I was just getting acquainted with him."

"I never really knew him. Or Belle either. I wouldn't be here now, except that I was visiting Cousin Robert and he insisted that I come along." Jessibee sipped the whiskey. "It's very good." She drained the glass. "Whiskey's like a stallion mounting a mare. Quick and harsh. Brandy's more like a man with a woman, slow and lingering, but still with force and authority."

Longarm smiled. "That's as neat a way of putting it as I ever heard. But you didn't need to give me a message, Jessibee, except to let me know you're ready."

"If you are," she said.

Longarm stood up. "Maybe not quite, but I will be fast enough, if you're the woman I take you to be."

Jessibee came up to stand before him. She turned up

204

her face for his kiss. Her lips grasped his and drew his tongue into her mouth. He drew her to him in a hard embrace, and the warmth of her body began to bring him erect. Longarm ran his arms down Jessibee's sides. His fingers met only smoothness. She had on nothing except her thin calico dress.

"You got a head start on me," he said when they broke off their kiss. "Give me a little time to get off my clothes."

"We don't have to rush. But don't dawdle, either."

Longarm made quick work of undressing. He saw her pull her dress over her head, to show her body glimmering in the bluish glow that filled the cabin. It was as he'd thought: a woman's body, wide-hipped, full-breasted, with swelling thighs.

Jessibee moved to him. He said, "Those bunks are too narrow for us to be comfortable, Jessibee. Wait just a minute." He dragged his bedroll off and spread it on the floor. "Now. It won't be a featherbed, but we'll at least have room to lay down together."

Jessibee folded her legs under her and sat down in a single graceful sweep. Her arms were slender white columns raised to invite him. Longarm knelt beside her. Jessibee's hands were warm on his erection, which was beginning to throb to fullness.

"I was wondering if the light was fooling my eyes," she told him. "I didn't really believe them." She squeezed gently, both hands wrapped around him. "But I believe what I'm holding now."

Longarm found Jessibee's full, soft breasts and felt her nipples grow firm and lift to tautness as he rubbed and kneaded them with his calloused fingers. They stood out like small rough fingertips as he bent to kiss them and caress them with his tongue.

Jessibee leaned back and pulled him with her. She whispered gustily, "Come into me like a stallion, Custis. But then make love to me like I'm a woman."

Longarm moved his fingers to Jessibee's thighs, to spread them. She twisted her body on the rough blanket that topped the bedroll to bring herself closer to him. Her hands were holding his shaft tightly now. She rubbed its tip over her moist warmth and whispered, "Now, Custis! Go in now!"

Longarm buried himself in her hot depths. She rolled her hips from side to side as he entered, and sighed contentedly when he filled her. Longarm raised himself, almost leaving her, but Jessibee brought up her legs and wrapped them around his lower ribs and levered her hips upward to keep him in place. He thrust hard, a series of deep, swift strokes, then slowed to a more deliberate rhythm as Jessibee gripped him hard with her thighs.

"Don't hurry!" she whispered urgently. "I haven't had a man for a while, and I don't want to let go too soon."

"Let go whenever you feel like it," Longarm said. "I'll hold out for as long as you need me to."

"If you're sure you can hold out until I'm ready again."

"I'm sure. Go on. Enjoy yourself all you want."

Jessibee took him at his word. Longarm continued to go into her smoothly and steadily, with a hard, deep thrust now and then to bring her along more quickly. Jessibee's eyes closed as he continued his paced stroking, and he felt her body tensing. Longarm moved faster now, and thrust deeper.

Jessibee began to tremble, and when Longarm stopped for a moment, buried in her as deeply as he could thrust, she gasped, "Oh, not now! Don't stop now! Go faster, Custis, faster!"

Now Longarm started stroking with an intensity that set Jessibee panting and quivering tumultuously. He was buried in her to the hilt when she unlocked her legs from around him, spread her thighs wide, and began to gulp in a series of soft, sobbing cries. Longarm raised himself and then pounded into Jessibee with a succession of long strokes which he maintained until she shrieked deep in her throat and he felt her body heave convulsively and then go limp in a wave of relaxing shudders. He stopped thrusting then, and lay still, filling her.

Jessibee sighed. "Brandy and whiskey mixed, Custis. It's a combination I don't often find."

"We'll rest," he said. "Unless I'm too heavy for you."

"No. Don't get up. Stay in me. Now, especially. I haven't felt this filled for a long time."

Jessibee sighed and pulled Longarm's head down for a kiss. Their tongues met and slid together. Jessibee stirred. "Can you stay hard for a while?"

"Sure. As long as it takes. But if you're ready to start again, so am I."

"You don't need to hurry, if you want to rest some more."

Longarm responded by lifting himself and thrusting hard again. Jessibee drew a quivering breath when she felt his deep penetration, and raised her hips to meet him. The hot flood that he'd felt surrounding him when Jessibee climaxed had aroused Longarm. He wanted to feel himself sinking repeatedly into her ready body, and stroked with steadily increasing vigor. He was still holding back, and continued to do so until Jessibee began to grow taut again. He was building quickly now, but she was responding faster, too.

There was a time of suspended feeling as Longarm held himself above Jessibee, looking down at her face in the strange, filtered moonlight, watching her lips twitching, her head rolling from side to side. When she grabbed him and pulled him to her for a long kiss, he knew the time was close. He let go his control, pounding hard, while Jessibee rolled and thrust up to meet him with a wildness that set him to trembling. He reached the point of no return and felt himself draining in a series of spasms while Jessibee's throat pulsed with deep, sobbing moans. Then her body went soft and Longarm fell forward, growing soft inside her.

Jessibee sighed. "I've been without a man for such a long time! You've done me more good than I can tell you, Custis."

"You're a real pretty woman. Seems like you'd have a lot of men chasing after you."

"I don't let just anybody catch me. I do the choosing, not them."

"Like you chose me?"

"Exactly. I didn't see any way that you could come

207

looking for me. And I wasn't sure you would, or even if you wanted to. So I came to you."

"You're a right strong-minded lady."

"Most Cherokee women are. We run the families, you know. If we have a husband who doesn't live up to what we think he should, we divorce him. You whites haven't gotten that far yet."

"Are you a full-blooded Cherokee, Jessibee?" Longarm asked.

She chuckled throatily. "As much as any Cherokee is. We've always been tolerant, maybe too tolerant for our own good."

Jessibee stirred under him, and as much as Longarm was enjoying feeling her wet heat around him, he rolled off to lie beside her.

"Do you have enough cheroots so you can spare me another one?" she asked.

"Sure. You lay still. I'll get one for each of us." Longarm padded over to the table, where his vest hung on a chair, and took out two cheroots and a match. He asked, "How'd you get a taste for these, anyhow, Jessibee?"

"That's an easy story to tell."

"You might as well tell it to me," Longarm said, "unless you're figuring on going back to your kinfolks real soon. I hope that ain't in your mind, though."

"It's not. I know you can't stay hard forever, though, so we might as well talk while we're resting. But don't worry about me wanting to leave. As far as I'm concerned, I'm settling down for a very enjoyable night."

"I'll do my best to keep you full," Longarm promised. "And I aim to enjoy it as much as you do. But go on, Jessibee. Tell me how it was you started smoking cigars."

"I didn't start out with cigars. It was cigarettes at first. That was when I was going to Mills College. I don't suppose you've ever heard of Mills?"

"Can't say I have. Whereabouts is it?"

"In California, across the bay from San Francisco. It's a college that teaches young women such as I was then to keep just a little bit ahead of the times. It's what they call becoming advanced thinkers." Jessibee sighed. "That was quite a while ago. Just thinking back on it makes me feel old."

"As long as you don't look old, which you sure don't—you're pretty as any woman I've ever seen—and as long as you don't act old, then you ain't old," Longarm said seriously.

"That's a very nice compliment, Custis. But when I see all the changes that are taking place—" She shook her head. "I'm getting off the subject. Smoking was one of the advanced things I learned at college. Cigarettes, of course. But when I came back home, I found out that the storekeepers here don't balk at selling cigars or chewing tobacco or snuff, but they look on cigarettes as the work of the devil. So I switched to cigars. It's just as simple as that."

"Your folks must've been well-fixed, if they could send you all that way to school," Longarm suggested.

"They were. *Are*, I should say. My family got a head start here in the Nation, you see."

"Oh? How's that?"

"We're what the tribe calls West Cherokees." Jessibee caught the question before Longarm asked it, and added hurriedly, "That hasn't anything to do with the West family. I suppose you've never heard of Tahlonteskea?" He shook his head. She went on, "He was a Cherokee chief, many years ago. He saw that you whites were determined to take our homelands in Georgia, so he didn't wait for it to happen. He led a group of our people to resettle on the Arkansas River back in 1809 or 1810. So my family's been here for three generations. We were here long before the East Cherokees were resettled."

"What you're hinting at is that your folks got here first and sort of skimmed the gravy?"

"You could put it that way. My grandfather was an attorney. So is my father. Very good ones. They made a lot of money."

"So they could send you to a college where you learned to like cigarettes," Longarm said. "And being a pretty girl, you had beaus there, too. They took you to fancy restaurants like the ones I saw when I was in San

209

Francisco one time, and you learned how to drink liquor like a lady, too."

"Yes. And even if it's not considered ladylike, I learned to like what we just did, too. That's very important."

"At least you're honest and open about it," Longarm said. "Most women ain't. They act like they're just putting up with a man."

"I was open enough to come in here and practically tell you what I wanted," Jessibee said. "Why not? I knew you wouldn't come to me, not with my relatives up at the house. At least I've learned that if I want something, it's up to me to go after it."

She turned on her side and Longarm felt her hands surrounding his flaccid shaft. "Is it too soon for you to get hard again? Maybe if I helped a little bit?"

"You won't have to help a lot."

Jessibee began to squeeze and release him, her hand opening and closing in slow pulsations. "I like the feel of a man," she confided. "It does something to me for a man to swell up and get hard in my hands."

"It's doing something for me too," Longarm admitted. Then, as Jessibee massaged his beginning erection by rolling it between the palms of her hands, he added, "Especially when you do that."

"I like to feel a man's hands on me, too," she reminded him.

Longarm grasped one of her breasts in each hand and bent over to close his teeth gently on her stiffening nipples, moving from one breast to the other.

"It's not too soon, is it?" Jessibee whispered. She lifted a thigh high across his stomach and massaged herself with his soft tip. He could feel the moisture that still clung to her, and the tantalizing roughness of her pubic hair. She invited him, "Come into me, now. You'll get really hard when you do."

Longarm turned to her and Jessibee slid her other leg under him. She brought her knees high, up to his chest. Longarm felt her opening to him. Jessibee pulled his face to hers, and her mouth found his while her other lips were drawing him into her more deeply. He grasped her buttocks and pulled them to him. He was fully erect

210

now, buried deeply inside her. She sighed contentedly and rotated her hips with slow, studied sensuality.

"I can lie this way for hours," she said softly. "Will you stay with me, Custis?"

"As long as I can," he promised.

Time seemed unimportant as they lay interlocked. Jessibee moved occasionally to rub herself on Longarm's impaling member; her movements were slow and gentle. Now and then he pushed hard against her for a few seconds, and as time passed, she sought his lips or he found hers in a long, tongue-twining kiss. Jessibee lifted her shoulders from time to time to rub the pebbled tips of her breasts against the roughness of Longarm's chest hair. Once or twice, as their joining grew more prolonged, she slipped her fingers between their bodies to trace them around the tender flesh where they were joined, and brought herself to a small orgasmic shuddering. Longarm grew even more engorged and was thinking about thrusting when Jessibee's body suddenly began to tremble.

"Take me off," she urged. "Now! I can't hold back any longer!"

Longarm rose to his knees, with Jessibee's legs over his shoulders, her ankles locked behind his neck. He cradled her buttocks in his hands and held her body suspended; only her shoulders rested on the blanket. He drew out, then thrust deeply and felt her tighten around him when their hips met.

Jessibee moaned, "Quicker, Custis! Deep and fast!"

He was building quickly, but Jessibee was building faster. She writhed, her hips twisting, her full breasts rolling, her head thrown back. Longarm drove faster with each long stroke until he began to tremble too. Jessibee was whimpering now, a whimper that became a laughing sob and then a shrill cry as her muscles stiffened under his stroking and she shook with spasm after spasm, her taut muscles rippling. He could go no faster nor penetrate any deeper. He thrust again and again until his own orgasm began, and kept pounding until his strength drained away. He let Jessibee's limp body down, then dropped beside her and lay still until his rasping breathing slowed and he was able to move again.

Beside him, Jessibee exhaled in a long, contented groan. She said, "You're a randy woman's dream, Custis. I don't often meet a man who's built like you are, or one who can outlast me."

"I like to pleasure ladies," Longarm replied. "Most of all, ladies like you, who make it so plain you enjoy a man."

"I'm going to hate to leave you. If it weren't that this is Belle Starr's place now that Sam's dead, I'd stay and keep you company for a while. If you'd want me to, that is."

"Oh, I'd want you to, Jessibee. You've got whatever it is that grabs a man and makes him want to stay with you. I don't guess it'd work out, though, the way things are."

"No. It's too bad you're tied up with Belle."

"I ain't tied up with Belle Starr, not in any way, shape, or form. My business brought me here, and when it's finished, I'll go on my way and forget I ever seen her."

"I wish I could believe that, Custis. But from what the family tells me, Belle's got a way of holding men to her. Look at poor Sam. And everybody knows what her business is." Jessibee paused and then added reflectively, "Not that our people have much respect for white man's law. We've seen it change too many times, in ways that always seem to hurt us."

"Well, Belle's got no strings on me, Jessibee. And she never will have."

"You say that like you really mean it."

"I do."

"Where will you go when your business with Belle is finished?"

"That's something I can't rightly say, but only because I don't know myself right now."

"If you travel north, I live up by Talequah. That's just a little way from Fort Gibson."

"Are you inviting me?"

"If you're close by, it'd be unfriendly if you didn't stop

212

in." Jessibee stirred. "I guess I've got enough strength left to walk back up to the house. They'll be waking up before too long. The first rooster that crows will bring Robert and Aunt Sarah out. It'll save talk if I'm back before then."

Jessibee stood up and found her dress, where she'd draped it over the back of a chair. She drew it on over her head and came back to the bedroll. Longarm had risen to his feet. She kissed him quickly on the lips, then bent to give him still another fleeting kiss.

"Goodbye for now, Custis. I still wish I could stay."

Longarm watched her shadowy form as Jessibee went to the door, then outside into the gray false sunrise. He walked to the table and took a swallow of rye from the bottle, then he went back to the bedroll and stretched out and slept.

Whatever noise the visitors made when they left didn't disturb Longarm. He blinked awake in the sunrise and rolled to his feet. The woman-scent of Jessibee still clung to him. The smile brought on by the memory of the night stayed on Longarm's face while he took a whore's bath, moistening his palms with whiskey and rubbing them over his face and body.

Fully dressed, his weapons checked, another wake-up drink glowing in his stomach like the coal of the morning's first cheroot that he held clamped between his teeth, Longarm walked up to the house.

All the others were sitting at the table. Used plates in front of them showed that they were just finishing breakfast. The room was cool, and Longarm glanced at the stove. It had not been lighted. Judging from the food left on the plates, and that remaining on the platters that were in the center of the table, breakfast had consisted of leftovers from the funeral meats brought by Sam's relatives the day before. The platters held a few pieces of fried squirrel and the drumstick of a chicken, two small venison chops, and a little heap of drying biscuits.

Only Yazoo spoke. The old man said, "Morning,

Windy. You look like you didn't get much sleep last night." Then he cackled in a brief burst of laughter.

"I had all the sleep I wanted," Longarm said.

Belle smirked. "I told them not to rouse you, Windy. I saw that draggletail Cherokee chippy sneaking back up to the house from your place this morning before daylight. I thought you'd need all the rest you could get."

Longarm needed no interpreter to translate the jealousy in Belle's words; he'd seen enough jealous women. He said, "What I do is my own affair, Belle." He picked up one of the venison chops and a biscuit and began to eat, still standing.

"How was she?" Floyd asked. "Hot, like I hear these redskin wenches all are?"

"That's my affair too, Floyd," Longarm said levelly. He finished the little chop and reached for the other one.

"Don't get riled, damn it," Floyd said. "Hell, we're all friends together. You might've called us, though. She could've took on me and Steed and then give Bobby a turn, after you got through with her."

"Find your own women," Longarm told Floyd curtly. He faced Belle. "I guess Floyd and Steed said something to you about the talk we had yesterday?"

"About your expecting me to take Sam's place, and ride with you on the bank job?" she asked. Longarm's mouth was full, so he merely nodded.

Belle said, "They mentioned it to me."

"She ain't said she'd do it, though," Steed told Longarm.

Longarm asked Belle, "Well? What'd you decide to do?"

"I haven't decided yet. I'm still thinking it over."

"Looks to me like you better make your mind up in a hurry, Belle," he said. "This is the day we're supposed to leave, if we still figure on pulling the job tomorrow." He bit into a squirrel-leg without waiting for Belle's reply.

In the silence that followed Longarm's words, Yazoo stood up. He stretched and said, "You're getting ready to talk business, I guess, and it's business I got no part of. I'll be going. There's plenty for me to do up at the stillhouse."

For several minutes after the old man had left no one

214

spoke. Belle sat, her lips compressed angrily, a frown on her face. The others waited for her to reply to Longarm.

Finally Steed spoke up. He turned to Longarm and said, "Belle don't think it'll hurt if we put off the job for another day, or even two. Leastwise that's what she was saying to me and Bobby and Floyd, while we was eating breakfast."

Longarm looked at Belle while he finished chewing the mouthful he'd taken. When he'd swallowed it and she had still said nothing, he remarked casually, "Maybe, maybe not. The way I look at it, if Belle can't make up her mind, we'll be better off going ahead without her, or forgetting all about the damn job."

He was taking another risk, Longarm knew, but he counted on the greediness of Floyd and Steed to keep the risk marginal. Instead, it was Belle who objected.

"What do you mean, call it off?" she asked quickly.

"Just what I said." Inwardly Longarm breathed a sigh of relief.

"It's not your job to call off, Windy!" Belle said hotly. "I set everything up! Floyd and Steed and those two other fellows who had bad luck were supposed to fill out the gang, along with Bobby. Or did you forget that? You came tagging in at the last minute."

"You asked me to come in. I didn't offer or push in," he reminded her. "I've told all of you more than once, I just said I'd help out, and I didn't give a damn whether the job went off or not."

"That's right, Belle, he did," Floyd agreed. "And even with Windy in on it, we're still a man short, if you don't go with us."

Bobby spoke up unexpectedly. "Don't I have anything to say about all this?"

"Sure you do, Bobby," Longarm replied. "Just as much as anybody else does."

"Well, I think we ought to either pull it off or call it off," the youth said. "I don't know about the rest of you, but the longer we sit on our butts—"

Steed snapped, "That's enough, Bobby." Then he said to Belle, "I feel about like Windy does. We better go on and take that bank, just like we planned to. Hell, you said the other day you was sending word to them lawmen you're paying off, telling them when to expect us. What happens if we don't show up?"

Longarm welcomed the support Steed was giving him, but he didn't let it show. He told Belle, "You see, I ain't the only one that wants to go ahead the way we planned to. What's the matter, Belle? Don't tell me the Bandit Queen's getting cold feet."

"You know better than that!" she shot back. "I was hoping you men would be reasonable and let me have a few days to get over losing Sam, but—"

Longarm broke in, "Like you said coming back from town the other day, Sam wasn't the first man you ever lost."

"Well, he wasn't!" Belle retorted. "And he might not be the last! But that's no sign I can pick up and go about my business like nothing happened at all!"

"It'll be good for you to go, Belle," Floyd said. "Doing something ought to take your mind off your troubles."

They fell silent. Longarm started to say something, then thought better of it. He'd said enough, he told himself. The others had picked up what he'd started and made an issue of it. Belle was finding herself backed into a corner, and as far as he could see, she had only one way out. Before the silence grew too tense, Belle proved that his judgment to keep quiet had been good.

"All right," she said. "We'll go ahead with the job, just the way we planned to. I still don't think it'd do any harm to put it off a day or two, but it looks like you're all dead set on rushing along. We'll leave as soon as we get everything ready, and pull off the bank job tomorrow."

Chapter 18

Longarm didn't want to seem too eager, now that the decision had been made. He asked Belle, "You sure we can get to where we're supposed to camp tonight, if we start this late?"

Before Belle could reply, Floyd said, "Hell, it ain't all that late, Windy. And we won't need to do much but spread out our soogans when we get to where we'll be stopping."

Belle said sarcastically, "Maybe he's too tired to ride today, Floyd. Too much time in the saddle last night."

"I'll hold up my part of the job," Longarm said, trying not to sound too cheerful. "Give me five minutes to throw my gear in my saddlebags, and I'll be ready to pull out."

"It'll take us a little bit longer than that," Belle told him. "If I'm going on this job with you, I'll have to change my clothes."

She was still wearing the black velvet dress she'd had on the day before. She'd taken off her gunbelt, though.

"We might as well settle one more thing right now," Steed put in. "Something we never did get around to talking about before. I'll put in what I think right now. As soon as it's safe to stop after we've done the job tomorrow, we split up the take and part company."

"We can talk about that after we camp tonight," Belle said.

"No." Steed's voice was firm. "We'll settle it right now. I don't aim to lose my sleep or get all nerved up arguing tonight in camp. Let's get it done with before we leave, Belle."

"I'll go along with Steed." Bobby chimed in.

"Me too," Floyd said. "He's right, Belle. When we settle down tonight, it better be to rest up so we'll be fresh tomorrow. We don't want a lot of jawing."

"That suits me," Longarm told the others. "Makes pretty good sense, I'd say."

Belle could see that none of them was going to listen to her, but she battled to the finish. "Suppose there's a slip-up? What if a posse takes after us and we have to break up before we can stop to split the take?"

"Then we'll all meet back here," Longarm suggested. "But you're suppose to have things fixed so that won't happen, Belle."

"It won't. Or shouldn't." Belle was on the defensive now. "You can't control everything all the time, though. Something could go wrong."

"All right," Floyd agreed. "We'll do like Windy said, meet back here and wait until we're all together before we divvy up. But provided your setup holds good, and we ride away from the job free and clear, it's going to be one hell of a long time before you'll see me at Younger's Bend again. It's been too damned unlucky a place for me."

"Amen to that," Steed said. "I'll be riding on when the job's finished, too. How about you, Windy?"

"I didn't aim to stay this long when I headed here. Just a night or two."

"It's all settled, then?" Belle asked. She spoke tautly, and they could all see she was holding her anger in check. "If it is, we'd better get ready and go."

"All that's left is for you to tell us where to ride if we get separated after the job," Floyd told her. "You said you knew trails we could use to get to other hideouts, places where we'll be safe."

"I'll tell you all that tonight, after we're in camp," Belle replied. There's no use wasting time on it now. We'll be getting a later start than we ought to, as it is. I'll be ready in ten minutes. I suppose all of you can be ready then?"

They broke up at once, to make their individual preparations for departure. Longarm took fewer than the five minutes he'd told Belle he would require. All he had

218

to do was roll up his bedroll, toss loose items into his saddlebags, and pick up his rifle. Carrying the bedroll and saddlebags balancing one another on opposite shoulders, his rifle in his hand, he returned to the barn. He was saddling the hammerhead bay when Belle came in.

"It looks like you'll be the first one saddled up, Windy," she said.

Longarm turned to look at her, and his jaw dropped. Belle was wearing men's clothes, denim jeans tucked into boots, a flannel shirt, and a linsey-woolsey jacket that fitted loosely over her torso. She'd pulled her hair up under the low-crowned, wide-brimmed Stetson she had on, and her face under the brim might have been that of a callow youth, except for the age-lines it bore and loose flesh of her neck that showed above the loose shirt collar. She hadn't abandoned her pearl-handled, silver-plated revolvers, though. She still wore them as she had when she'd been in a dress, in front, ahead of her hips, as was necessary when she rode sidesaddle.

Longarm said, "I didn't look for you to be dolled up in an outfit like that."

"I've worn men's clothes before, when I was on a job," she replied. "That's why nobody credits me with a lot of jobs that I pulled off with Sam and with Jim Reed or Blue Duck." Then she remembered her old boast and added quickly, "And Jesse and Frank James, of course."

Longarm finished tightening the cinch around the hammerhead's belly and dropped the stirrups down to hang by the horse's sides. "I guess it'd fool somebody who just got a quick look," he said.

"That's not what I started to say, though," Belle told him. "You're all ready, I guess?" Longarm nodded. "Then will you do something for me? Yazoo doesn't know for sure we're all leaving. Will you ride up to the stillhouse and tell him? I want him to sleep down here while we're gone, and keep an eye on things."

"You expecting somebody to come calling?"

"No. But I wasn't expecting you, either, was I? You never know who'll be riding in, here at the Bend. If

219

Yazoo's asleep at the stillhouse, he wouldn't know it if somebody came and carried the damned house away."

"Sure, I'll tell him." Actually Longarm welcomed the idea of being out of the way of everyone else during the period that was going to follow. He knew that tempers grew short when men were preparing to ride into danger, whether they were outlaws or a posse or soldiers.

"Anything else?" he asked.

"No. He's got all that sugar up there, so he'll have plenty to do to keep him busy. You should be back here by the time we're ready to go. The others still have to get their horses saddled."

"If I don't get back by the time you're ready to ride, just go ahead. I'll catch up," he said. He led the bay out of the barn and swung up on its back. As he rode off, he saw Floyd and Steed and Bobby, loaded with their saddle-bags and bedrolls, heading up toward the house from the cabins.

There was no sign of Yazoo at the stillhouse, but the door was open and noises were coming from inside. Longarm went in, gagging at the overpowering smell of souring corn mash, old wood smoke, and the efflu-vium of whiskey that had soaked into the packed dirt of the floor. Yazoo was stirring a fresh batch of mash in a tub made from a sawed-in-half hogshead.

"Howdy, Windy." From the old man's speech, Long-arm judged that Yazoo had been sampling his product pretty steadily since breakfast. That didn't interfere with his work, apparently.

"Yazoo," Longarm greeted him with a nod. "Belle wanted me to give you a message."

"Decided to ride out and take care of that bank job, did you?" Yazoo nodded judicially. "I sorta had the idea you would, the way they was talking this morning at breakfast, afore you come in. You know, Belle was sure riled at you, Windy, for having that cousin of Sam's down visiting you last night." He somehow managed to chuckle and leer at the same time. "Not that I blame you myself. Only thing wrong with Belle is, she's jealous."

"I never gave her any cause to be."

220

"A'course you didn't! But Belle gets mad if every man that comes here don't fall for her." He dropped his voice to a hoarse whisper. "Belle's a whore at heart, Windy. Never did get over the days when Jim Reed used to give away a piece of her ass to cinch a tough horse-trade."

"I hadn't run onto that story," Longarm said. "But I'm ready to believe it."

"You can believe it, all right! I knowed Jim before him and Belle got hitched, and afterwards too. And Belle knows I know. I don't reckon she'd put up with me if I didn't know more about her than she does about me."

An idea struck Longarm. He asked Yazoo, "If you know so much about Belle, maybe you can ease my mind a little bit, Yazoo. She roped me into this job, and I said I'd go in because, from the way Belle talks, she's got strings in just about every town over on the other side of the Arkansas border, lawmen she claims she pays off to look the other way at her moonshining and selling stolen cattle. Is that just Belle blowing and bragging, or is it true?"

"It's true enough, all right. Shit! I could name you names and tell you places—"

"I ain't asking you to do that, Yazoo," Longarm interrupted. "I don't need to know anything except whether she's told me a straight story about the law looking the other way while we pull off this job. That's what bothers me right now."

"Well, maybe Belle don't pay off *every* sheriff or marshal or all their deputies from the Arkansas on up to the Neosho, and then on down to the Red. But she's got enough of 'em in her pocket so she can move around as free as she likes to, and get by with damn near anything she wants to pull."

"Thanks, Yazoo. You've made me feel lots easier in my mind."

"You don't need to worry," the oldtimer assured him. "Why, hell's bells, Windy! You don't think I'd be sticking around here if it wasn't the safest place I could find, do you? But I know, as long as I'm here at Younger's Bend, there ain't nobody going to touch me, because of Belle. And when a man gets to my age, he don't much like the idea of going back to the pen."

Longarm was absorbed in trying to formulate a plan. He replied absently, "Sure. You weren't as old as you are now, that last time you got sent up—" He stopped short, and tried to swallow the words he'd just let fall so unthinkingly. The minute he saw Yazoo's face, though, he knew the damage had been done.

Yazoo was staring at Longarm, the light of belated recognition dawning in his eyes. Longarm could almost literally see the memories flooding back into Yazoo's liquor-soaked brain.

"By God!" the old man said slowly. "That's where it was I seen you before! It wasn't in no outlaw's roost, nor in no saloon, either!"

"Now hold up, Yazoo—" Longarm began.

"Hold up, my ass!" the old man went on. He wasn't about to stop. "I seen you in a federal courtroom up in Wyoming Territory! Cheyenne it was, by God! The deputy that was guarding me pointed me out to you special! You're that federal marshal son of a bitch they used to call Longarm!"

"They still do, Yazoo," Longarm said. He wasn't worried about Yazoo jumping him. Age and liquor had robbed the old fellow of any real capacity to do any harm, and Longarm had never seen him wearing a gun.

"And you been skulking right here all this time!" Yazoo went on indignantly. "Acting like you was an owlhoot on the prod! Getting in on everything you got no business knowing about! You wait till I tell Belle and the rest of 'em! You won't last two minutes after they cut loose on you!"

"You're not going to tell anybody anything, Yazoo," Longarm said firmly.

He took a step toward Yazoo. The old fellow pulled out the wooden paddle he'd been using to stir the mash, and began to wave it threateningly.

"I might be old," he said, "But I sure ain't crippled. You'll have to kill me to take me!"

"Listen to me, old man! I'm not after you! I don't give a damn how much moonshine you stir up here.

But I've got to shut you up, keep from spilling what you've figured out to Belle and the others."

"Shoot me, then! That's the only way you can shut me up!"

Longarm had been edging closer and closer to Yazoo, and the old man had been backing off, waving the paddle. Longarm feinted a rush to Yazoo's left. The old moonshiner swung the paddle in that direction. Longarm stepped inside the swing with one long stride and grabbed the paddle. He wrested it away from Yazoo with one swift, twisting pull.

Yazoo struck at Longarm, who parried the wild swing with his arm. He grabbed Yazoo's wrist and yanked him forward. Yazoo, already unsteady on his feet, would have fallen if Longarm hadn't brought the arm he was holding up and around to keep him erect. He captured Yazoo's free wrist and clamped one of his big hands over both of Yazoo's.

"Now you keep quiet!" Longarm commanded. "They can't hear you down at the house. It's too far, so you might as well save your breath."

"What you aiming to do with me?"

"Damn little I *can* do with you, Yazoo. I'm not interested in taking you in; all I want to do is shut you up for a while." He shot a question suddenly. "Where's Belle planning to pull this job, Yazoo?"

"Damned if I know!" Yazoo blurted.

Longarm decided his reply came too quickly for the old fellow to be lying. That was all he needed to know. He said, "I'm going to tie you up now. Don't worry, I won't do such a good job that you won't be able to work free in an hour or so. By then we'll all be gone, and as long as you don't know where the job's going to be, there ain't a hell of a lot you can do to let Belle and the others know about me."

Longarm looked around for rope. He saw none, but Yazoo's bed stood in a corner of the stillhouse, a tangle of greasy blankets. Longarm pulled the old man over to the bed and sat him down on it. He ripped a blanket into strips and bound Yazoo, trying to tie him so that, with a little work and quite a lot of time, the moonshiner could work himself free.

Realizing that there was no way he could match Longarm's strength and agility, Yazoo put up no struggle. He said nothing until he saw that Longarm was preparing a gag, then he blurted, "I always swore I never would ask no favors of a lawman . . ."

"Go ahead and ask," Longarm told him. "Hell, I don't bear you any grudges, Yazoo. You've been real helpful to me."

"It wasn't because I meant to be," Yazoo grunted. "But except that you're a goddamn dirty sneaking conniving federal marshal, which makes you a first-class son of a bitch in my book, you'rt a right decent fellow, Windy— or Longarm or whatever you want to call yourself. You mind giving me a drink before you stuff that gag in my guzzle? My mouth's terrible dry."

"Sure. Where's your water bucket?"

"Water! Who wants water? Hand me that bottle of whiskey from over there."

Longarm held the bottle while Yazoo drank deeply. Then he finished the job of gagging him, and started for the door. Halfway there, he turned and said, "Oh, I nearly forgot, Yazoo. Belle said I was to tell you to sleep down at the house while she's gone."

Swinging into the saddle, he returned to the house. The others were just mounting. By common consent, they let Belle lead the way. She turned east as they came out of the long passage through the narrow ravine, and for the first part of the journey, the trail they took was one familiar to Longarm; he'd followed it before, when he came to Younger's Bend originally, then back and forth between the Bend and Fort Smith. They rode silently.

Noon passed without a lunch stop, and Longarm rummaged in his saddlebag for some jerky. His breakfast had been less filling than the one eaten by the others.

Belle led them across the ford above the juncture of the Arkansas and the Canadian. On the east shore of the Arkansas she struck off on a trail less clearly defined than the main route to Fort Smith. The sun had been at their backs for the better part of an hour when they

224

crossed the ford. It kept sliding down as they rode on in single file, until the thick maze of woodland through which they traveled took on the gentle haze that comes to such country in the period just before sunset.

Darkness was closing in fast when Belle abruptly turned off the trail. With the four men following, she wove her black gelding in and out among the tree trunks for almost a mile. There was no trail through the woods that Longarm could see, but Belle rode confidently, as though completely certain of the route. Suddenly the trees opened. A wide, shallow gully yawned in front of them. Belle followed its rim for a short distance, then urged her horse down its gently sloping side.

A tinkling white-water creek fanned over mossy rocks in the gully's bottom. The smell of woodsmoke hanging low to the ground reached Longarm's nose. In a few moments they saw light flickering ahead. A second light joined the first as they drew closer—the yellow, wavering glow of a lantern. The light shining in their faces hid what lay behind it until Belle reined in. Then Longarm saw that they'd stopped beside a slab-bark shanty, and that the man holding the lantern was dark and stocky. He wore overalls and an undershirt that, even in the uncertain light, was obviously long overdue for a visit to the washtub. His features were blunt and formless. He could have been Indian, Mexican, black, white, or any mixture of the four.

"Belle Starr," he said. He looked at the riders. "Where's Sam?"

"Sam's dead," Belle said. She offered no explanation, but went on, "I'll tell you about it later. We need supper and a place to sleep, and breakfast early in the morning."

"Sure," the man said. "Get off and come in."

"Chano will feed us," Belle told the others. "There's enough room inside for us to sleep. The horses will be all right out here." She dismounted. "We'll go over everything after supper."

"How far we got to ride tomorrow before we hit the town where the bank is?" Floyd asked.

Longarm had been wanting to ask that question himself, but didn't think it would have been wise for him to try to find out anything from Belle at that stage.

"Not far," Belle said. "We'll have to swing north a few miles to get around a big, sharp hook in the Arkansas. Then we'll just follow the river down—" She hesitated for a moment, then shrugged and added, "I guess it doesn't make any difference, since we're this close, whether I tell you now or wait until after supper. The bank's in a little town about ten miles north of Fort Smith, but on this side of the river. The town's called Van Buren."

Chapter 19

A bright midmorning sun in a cloudless sky sent sparkling glints from the surface of the river and defined the white-painted houses and storefronts of the little town ahead of them as Belle drew up and the others halted behind her on the riverbank.

"All right," she said as Floyd, Steed, Longarm, and Bobby pulled their horses up around the black gelding of the Bandit Queen. "There's the town. Take a look at it now, and figure out which way you'll be riding if something goes wrong and we can't get out in a bunch."

Van Buren was a bright town, Longarm thought as he joined the others in scanning it carefully from their vantage point, a high spot a half-mile from the first houses. They could see that the town's main street ran roughly parallel to the river. It was a long, narrow town, not a small, compact square or rectangle, but rather a crescent that curved along the course of the stream. Almost all the buildings and houses were white. A few were gray, and one or two of the stores had ventured into red or green paint.

Belle pointed to a buff-colored structure near the center of the main street. "There's the bank. It's brick, so don't worry about a rifle slug going through the walls if any shooting starts."

"There won't be any, if you done your part right," Floyd told her. He was edgy, as were all of them, and his voice showed it.

"I've done what I said I would, don't worry. Now study the way we're going out, then we'll ride in and do it," she said.

Before going to bed, they'd spent two hours rehearsing

227

their moves. Belle had given them the general layout of the countryside around Van Buren. If they had to scatter, each of them would take a different route back to Younger's Bend. If there was no trouble, they'd leave as a group and get across the border into the Cherokee Nation, stop as soon as it was safe, divide up the loot, and separate.

Longarm had his own ideas about what was going to happen if his own plan worked out. He'd been at the disadvantage of being unable to evolve much of a scheme in advance, before he'd actually seen the town and the bank. He'd decided that the best thing he could do would be to get behind Floyd and Steed as soon as the three of them were inside, immobilize them with the threat of his Colt, and then depend on the bank's workers to complete the capture while he went outside and took Belle and Bobby.

It wasn't much of a plan, he'd told himself while they were riding along the river an hour earlier, but it was about all he could come up with under the circumstances. He had to let the robbery actually get under way. Longarm looked on juries as highly unpredictable. He'd seen too many spellbinding lawyers convince twelve good men and true that a band of hardened outlaws entering a bank with weapons drawn had gone in only to make a deposit, that their intentions had been benevolent rather than felonious. This time he didn't intend to take that chance. He'd have hard evidence to back him up.

"If you've looked all you need to," Belle said, "we might as well ride in and get it over with."

They nudged their horses ahead. Belle still rode in the lead. Looking along the curve of Van Buren's main street as they came abreast of the first houses, Longarm could see only a few people moving around. In most towns that centered on farming areas, business in town waited until late afternoon. A rider was coming toward them, and Longarm caught the flashing of a star on the man's vest.

Look out, old son, he told himself. *Might be there's been some kind of slip-up, and they got a hot welcome all ready for us.*

As the rider drew closer, Longarm saw Floyd and

Bobby, who were riding ahead of him just behind Belle, move their hands unobtrusively closer to their pistols. He turned to look at Steed, who was behind him. Steed was watching the approaching man with slitted eyes, his right hand hanging casually at his side, inches from his gunbutt.

A moment or two slid by. The lone rider was only a few yards from the group now, and was eyeing them with a frown growing on his face. Then he looked at Belle closely. His features relaxed. He grinned and winked at Belle, then turned his eyes straight ahead and rode past.

Floyd turned in his saddle. His face was split in a wide grin. He nodded triumphantly at the others before turning back.

Longarm looked over his shoulder at Steed. There was a grin on the burly outlaw's face that matched the one Floyd had shown.

Ahead of them, the buff brick front of the bank loomed as they rode slowly down the curving street. A man was coming out, thumbing a wad of greenbacks. The bank had only two small windows in front, and a solid wooden door. There was a hitch rail in front of the building. The cross-street that Belle had described to them the evening before was visible now, but Longarm couldn't see whether there were any more people on it than there were on the main street. Far down, a buggy pulled into view, heading to the center of town. It carried a man and a woman. A horseman crossed the main street on the cross-street. He looked idly at the five riders, but went on his way.

Belle reined in at one end of the hitch rail. She did not dismount. Bobby pulled his horse around Floyd's and pulled up at the far end of the hitch rail. He stayed in the saddle too. Floyd pulled up next to Belle. Longarm took the next spot, and Steed went on and jerked his mount's head around to put himself between Longarm and Bobby.

"Don't just sit here!" Belle hissed. Her voice was shrilly nervous. "Get on inside, and work fast!"

Floyd was already sliding off his horse. Steed and Longarm followed suit, moving more slowly. Belle's plan, which she had explained to them the evening before, called for Floyd to saunter in and get to the back of the bank before Longarm and Steed entered. Then it would be up to Steed to handle the center of the building, Longarm to cover the door.

Floyd disappeared into the bank. Longarm could see Steed's lips moving as he counted to ten, then the outlaw followed Floyd inside. Longarm ticked off his own ten-count and went in. Just as he was going through the door, he saw a husky man wearing a gunbelt, carrying a white canvas money bag cross the room. The man wore a uniform cap with a badge of some sort on it; Longarm didn't get a good look at the badge, but figured the fellow for a guard.

As he walked the few steps to his position, Longarm had time to flick his eyes around the bank's interior. He registered the details quickly. A long counter stretched across one side. A wire grillwork rose from the top of the counter, broken by three arched openings. Tellers stood behind the windows, but only one of them was busy with a customer. The man carrying the money bag walked behind the tellers and entered the vault, which yawned open in the rear of the building, behind the counter.

On the opposite side there were four desks. The first one was a huge and ornate rolltop. It was backed up to the wall, and a gray-haired man sat in front of it, bending over a stack of papers. The second desk was a bit plainer; the man who sat at it was younger and was talking to an overall-clad customer who sat in a chair beside the desk. The other two desks were strictly utilitarian. The men who occupied chairs at them had ledgers in front of them and were bending over, entering figures in the ruled columns.

Floyd started the action as soon as he saw Longarm take his place and face the tellers. He whipped out his pistol and banged it on the desk nearest him. The sound echoed through the somnolent room. It seemed as loud as though Floyd had fired a shot. Everyone turned to look for the source of the unexpected noise.

"All of you stand real still!" Floyd commanded loudly. His voice had a jagged, nervous edge to it, but the pistol he was waving gave him all the authority he needed. Floyd saw that all eyes were on him and went on, "Just don't nobody move and nobody's going to get hurt!"

Nervously the tellers and others darted their eyes from side to side. They saw not just one gun leveled at them, but three. Longarm and Steed had drawn an instant after Floyd did.

His voice still pitched high, Floyd ordered, "All of you in behind that counter, get over here quick! And don't try anything!"

At the first desk, the gray-haired man slowly raised raised his hands. He swiveled in his chair to face the room and called, "Do as he says! Let's don't have anyone getting shot!"

Taking their time, the tellers began to file out from their positions behind the counter. They walked with their hands over their heads and took slow, careful steps, casting apprehensive glances at the three men holding guns. The lone customer who'd been standing at the teller's window backed across the room to stand beside one of the desks.

From the time the tellers had started moving, Floyd, Steed, and Longarm had been dividing their attention between the moving men and those at the desks. They failed to see the stealthy movement of the man at the second desk. He'd cautiously eased the drawer of his desk open and slid a revolver out on to his lap.

A loud, metallic clanging sounded inside the vault, and all heads turned in that direction. The guard came out. He saw the tellers with their arms raised, the men with guns standing across the room. He clawed for his gun, but Floyd's pistol was ready. Before the guard could draw, Floyd shot him. The guard slumped to the floor.

Seeing his chance, the man at the desk picked up the gun from his lap and levelled it at Floyd. Steed saw the movement, but Longarm got off his shot an instant before Steed's finger tightened on the trigger. Steed lurched forward to the floor.

Floyd's eyes had been on the guard. He turned in time to see the banker at the desk leveling his gun, knew that he couldn't bring his own weapon to bear, and dropped behind the desk by which he stood. The banker's round whistled through the empty space that Floyd had just occupied.

Longarm saw the banker turning in his direction. He wasn't going to shoot the man, but wasn't going to hold still for taking a slug himself. Longarm dived for the teller's counter and rolled behind it while the banker was still turning his chair around.

Floyd peered over the desk. Seeing the banker's movement in Longarm's direction, he brought up his gun and shot the banker in the back.

Longarm, unable to see from his position behind the counter, called loudly, "Don't shoot me, mister! I'm a U.S. marshal! Get down under your desk and let me handle these outlaws!"

Floyd's sudden rage at hearing Longarm's call immobilized and silenced him for a moment. Then he shouted, "You! Windy! Is that right? You been dogging us all along?"

"That's right, Floyd! You might as well drop your gun, or you won't walk out of here alive!"

"Like hell I will! You'll have to take me!"

Gunfire erupted outside the bank. The sound of pounding hoofbeats echoed briefly, then faded. The gunfire straggled away. Bobby crawled in through the open door, his belly hugging the ground. A bloodstain showed on his right shirtsleeve.

Longarm called, "Get over here out of the line of fire, Bobby!"

"Don't listen to him!" Floyd shouted. "He's a ringer! A U.S. marshal! Shoot him!"

Bobby's gun was in his hand, its muzzle pointing directly at Longarm.

Longarm said, "Don't do it, Bobby! Drop your gun and stay alive!"

Bobby's eyes rolled uncertainly for a few seconds.

Longarm held his fire, gambling that the youth wouldn't shoot. Bobby opened his hand, let his revolver fall, and crab-crawled to where Longarm lay behind the end of the counter.

Floyd fired too late. His slug tore Bobby's bootheel off, but by then, Bobby was shielded behind the counter.

Longarm asked him, "What happened outside?"

"Somebody started shooting at us from across the street. Belle took off."

"She got away?"

"I guess. I didn't stop to look." Bobby frowned, trying to straighten out his confused thoughts. "Are you really a U.S. marshal?"

"Yep. And you just surrendered to me, so you stay here out of trouble while I take care of Floyd."

Longarm inched himself into a position where he could peer around the edge of the counter. Tellers, bankers, and customers had all dived for cover when the shooting began. Longarm could see a foot sticking out here, a hand extended there, but he couldn't see Floyd.

He called, "Throw your gun out, Floyd! Give up!"

"Go to hell, you sneaking son of a bitch! It's me or you, Windy, or whatever your name is!"

Longarm located Floyd by the sound of his voice. He began crawling toward the last desk, where the outlaw had taken cover. He'd scrabbled half the distance when Floyd sprang up shooting. The instant's glimpse he had of Floyd's head rising above the desk gave Longarm the time he needed. Before Floyd could get his gun above the top of the desk, Longarm rolled, firing as he moved. At the same time, a rifle shot cracked from the door of the bank.

Longarm's shot and the rifle bullet took Floyd at the same instant. The outlaw's dying reflex tightened his finger on the trigger of his pistol as he was falling, but the slug plowed harmlessly into the floor a foot from Longarm's shoulder.

From the doorway, Andrew Gower's voice said, "Well, Long, I'm glad I got here in time for the cleanup."

Longarm took his time about getting to his feet. He asked Gower, "How in hell did you know where to come? I didn't find out this was the place until late last night."

"I didn't know," the chief marshal replied. "There were only two banks fitting the description you gave in your letter, this one and the one at Greenwood, so I sent some deputies I knew I could trust to cover both of them."

"You could've saved me a lot of trouble if I'd known you were going to back me up."

"No way to get word to you," Gower reminded him.

"Belle Starr got away, I guess," Longarm said.

"You mean that was Belle who rode off when we opened fire?" Gower asked. "Hell, I thought it was a man!"

"That's what she meant for folks to think."

"Maybe she hasn't gotten clear," Gower said. "Two of my boys took out after her. Maybe they'll catch her."

"If they don't, all you've got to do is have somebody waiting at Younger's Bend. She'll likely show up there. You got to send somebody to her place there anyhow. There'll be an old fellow there, answers to the name of Yazoo. He knows the names of everybody Belle's been paying off, and he'll talk if you give him a choice of that or going to the pen."

Bobby stood up slowly. "What's going to happen to me?"

Before Gower could speak, Longarm said, "You'll need this young fellow to testify against Belle, when you catch up with her. Think you could make things easy for him? Like a suspended sentence or a parole? I got a notion he won't be getting into any more trouble like this."

"No, sir!" Bobby said feelingly. "I've seen all I want of what it's like being an outlaw!"

Gower nodded. "I suppose something can be arranged, if you recommend it."

"Which I do," Longarm replied. He cocked his head at Gower. "Well? You think I can go back to Denver now?"

"As far as I'm concerned you can. You've done a good job, Long. I'll tell Billy that when I wire him."

Longarm nodded. Then he said, "You might tell him

234

not to look for me too quick. I left an army horse at that town across the river from Fort Smith that I'll have to ride back to Fort Gibson."

"Well, that'll take you a day or two longer than if you rode the train all the way," Gower said thoughtfully. "I'll tell Billy to allow for that."

"Now don't tie me too tight to getting back," Longarm told Gower. He thought for a moment. "You see, I've got a little bit of personal business I might need to look after. You know the Cherokee Nation better than I do. How far's Fort Gibson from a little town up thataway called Talequah?"

SPECIAL PREVIEW

Here are the opening scenes
from

LONGARM ON THE YELLOWSTONE

eighteenth novel in the bold new
LONGARM series from Jove

Chapter 1

It was a Tuesday morning and Longarm stood fully dressed before the open window of his room, looking down at the streets of Denver. The air was reasonably fresh and perhaps even invigorating, if one discounted the pungent fragrance of coal smoke and horse manure—and that persistent, mysterious smell of burning leaves.

Longarm turned away from the window. He had not slept alone the previous night, but in the predawn hours had returned to his room to freshen up and get ready for this day. His chief, Marshal Billy Vail, had been quite insistent the night before, when he had found Longarm at the hotel, in reminding him to show up on time this morning. As Longarm walked across the room to pick his hat off the dresser, he was an impressive sight.

He was a big man, lean and muscular, with a body any athlete would have been proud to inhabit. There was nothing young about his face, however. It was seamed and cured to a saddle-leather brown by the persistent suns and cutting winds he had experienced since leaving his native West-by-God-Virginia, where he had fought in the close late unpleasantness between the states. His eyes were gunmetal blue, his close-cropped hair the color of aged tobacco leaf, and he wore proudly his well-trimmed longhorn mustache. It gave his appearance a certain unpredictable ferocity he needed at times in his line of work.

Taking his snuff-brown Stetson off the wall peg by his door, he positioned it carefully on his head—dead center, tilted slightly forward, cavalry-style. He was wearing a brown tweed suit and vest, and a blue-gray shirt, with a string tie knotted at his neck. His cordovan leather boots were low-heeled army issue.

As Longarm squared his shoulders in readiness for the new day and strode toward the door, he moved with a swift, catlike tread, his tall figure seeming to loom in the semidarkness of the corner room. He was aware that his swift movements, combined with his height, tended to spook livestock and make most men thoughtful, but there was little he could do about that except continue to go where he was going by the most direct route, and not apologize.

He was just reaching his hand out for the doorknob when he heard a soft, insistent rapping on his door. He was instantly alert, and his eyes narrowed warily.

"Mr. Long!" he heard. "Are you in there?"

It was a woman, and Longarm just managed to remember her voice. It sounded as if she had her face pressed against the door. "Rose?" he asked, pulling his hand away from the doorknob. "That you?"

"Yes! Thank God I caught you before you left!"

"What's wrong, Rose?" Longarm was standing away from the doorway now. His right hand reached across his vest front and clasped firmly the grips of his double-action .44-40 Colt in its cross-draw holster.

"What's the matter, Longarm?" she whispered through the door. "You all wore out this early? I can't tell you through the door! Open up!"

Longarm was not usually this reluctant to let a young lady into his room. But his memory of Rose O'Brien was disconcerting, and he did not remove his hand from the Colt under his tweed coat. She had been annoyingly persistent the evening before as she pressed her charms upon him at the hotel bar while he tried to watch a most interesting poker game. Oddly suspicious of the woman—a stranger to him until that night—he had deliberately escorted another woman from the bar and left without allowing Rose to catch even a glimpse of his departure.

Now here she was, outside his door in the wee hours of a Denver morning. He thought that either he should congratulate himself on his awesome attractiveness to nubile females, or this young lady was up to no good. Besides, he had introduced himself to her as Custis Long, not Longarm. There were only one or two favored acquaintances of his in that bar who knew him by his nickname, and they would not have told it to *this* young lady.

"Are you alone?" he asked.

"Of course! What do you think? Please, Longarm! I must speak to you! I need your help!"

"All right," he said, pressing himself against the door and resting his left ear against the paneling. He thought he could hear a low, whispered instruction from someone standing beside the girl.

Removing his Colt from its holster, he stepped swiftly to one side of the door and yanked it open with his left hand, flattening himself against the wall as the door swung open. The ugly snout of a nickel-plated Smith & Wesson pocket .38 was thrust past the doorframe and bucked twice as its muzzle belched flame, its sharp detonations filling the tiny room.

Before its owner realized the Smith & Wesson had no target, Longarm brought the barrel of his sixgun down on the gunhand of the intruder. There was a scream of pain and the gun clattered to the floor. Reaching over with his left hand, Longarm grabbed the man's shirt and yanked him into the room.

Rose's accomplice was a ferret-faced, slant-browed sneak Longarm had noticed prowling the back alleys and sleazier saloons around the hotel. Longarm kicked his gun into a corner, then hauled the scrawny accomplice closer to him.

"My hand!" the little man bleated. "My hand! You broke it!"

With a grunt of disgust, Longarm flung the man past him onto the bed. He saw the fellow fly across the coverlet and heard him land with a crash on the floor beyond, but he paid no heed as he darted out of the room after the girl.

He still held his Colt in his right hand, and was in time to catch a clear glimpse of the woman's head and shoulders as she started down the stairs. He stopped and

241

aimed, then swore and holstered the gun. He couldn't see shooting a woman—not even this one—unless it was in self-defense. And even then he might find it impossible.

He raced down the dim hall, took the stairs in giant strides, and burst out through the front door and down the porch steps. The woman was nowhere in sight. Longarm's rooming house was in the no-longer-fashionable quarter on the wrong side of Cherry Creek, a rabbit warren of dirt lanes and sidestreets, back alleys and festering ditches. He looked up and down the damp cinder path that led to the Colfax Avenue Bridge, then gave it up as a bad job and hurried back inside the building and up the stairs.

He heard doors opening as he mounted the stairs, and saw his landlady's frightened face peering up at him through the bannister. "It's all right," he called down to her. "Stay in your room until I nail this jasper upstairs!"

Her face vanished and, as Longarm started swiftly down the corridor toward his open door, he heard a door below him slam shut, followed by the sound of a bolt being pushed home. He would have some explaining to do to his landlady and the other roomers before this day was out, he realized.

The fellow was on his feet behind the bed, holding the Smith & Wesson in his trembling left hand.

Longarm halted in the doorway and smiled. "Go ahead, you punk. Raise that gun and fire it again. Try it. I'd like to see that."

The menace in Longarm's tone sent a shudder up the man's spine. Longarm saw him shudder visibly and let his hand drop. The Smith & Wesson struck the floor a second time.

"You broke my hand," the man whimpered, his face screwing itself up into the semblance of a prune as he prepared himself to cry.

"Stow that," Longarm told him, striding into the room and picking up the weapon.

The fellow's narrow, pasty face lost its grimace as the man straightened and looked Longarm squarely in the eye. He was going to try to be a true Western Hero

242

now, Longarm realized as the fellow's mouth twisted into a snarl and his pale, lustreless eyes grew defiant.

"You ain't going to turn me in! What's the charge? I was just helping a lady, that's all."

Longarm's big hand reached out, wrapped itself around the fellow's face, and pushed. The man went stumbling back onto the bed. "What's your name, punk?" he demanded.

"Sammy. Sammy Wentworth."

"Well, Sammy, looks like your pal left you with your pants hanging down. Just helping a lady, is it?"

"That's right. That's all it was. You stole her money!"

"How do you know that?"

"She told me."

"And you would be the kind of man who believes everything a woman tells you."

Sammy lifted his right hand onto his lap with his left hand, and held it tenderly. His face was pale from the excruciating pain. "Jesus, she was so convincing," Sammy told Longarm, gazing up at him with a pathetic, woebegone look.

"What's her name?"

"Rose."

"What's her *name*, Sammy!"

The man appeared to shrink noticeably under the weight of Longarm's heavy voice. "Theresa Mirelda," he replied meekly, as he began to rock back and forth on the bed while holding onto his hand.

At once Longarm understood. This was the wife of a murderer he had brought back not too long before from San Francisco. The man had been a docile prisoner until he hit the city, at which point he broke from the train station. In the ensuing gun battle, Longarm had had to shoot him. He did not recover from his wounds. Someone on the train or on the platform had slipped Mirelda a gun—his wife, undoubtedly. And now she was after the tall lawman for killing her husband.

"Where does she live, Sammy?"

"I don't know."

"How did you meet her?"

"*She* met *me*. Last week. She had all this money and all she wanted, she said, was to throw a scare into you."

"Sure. What was the plan, Sammy?"

"She was going to come here with you last night, and as soon as you two were in the sack, I was going to break in—and scare you."

"Sure."

"Honest to God! She said she knew you from way back, and you'd laugh when we pulled this little joke."

"I never laid eyes on the woman before, Sammy. And you know damn well this wasn't any practical joke. Let's go!"

Like a whipped dog, and still clutching at his broken hand, Sammy slipped off the bed and proceeded ahead of Longarm out of the room and down the hall to the stairs. Longarm followed close behind Sammy as they descended. He was about to pull open the downstairs door for the wounded man when he heard the living room's sliding door creak back on its rail. He turned to see his landlady poking her head out.

"Mr. Long," she said, her voice quavering, "could you please come in here?"

"Later," Longarm told her, not unkindly. "I'll explain about this commotion later."

"Please," the landlady persisted. "I would like you to come in here for a cup of tea."

And then an incredible thing happened. The little old woman *winked* broadly at Longarm.

Swiftly Longarm pulled Sammy around in front of him and said loudly, "Of course, a cup of tea would be a pure pleasure right now, after what I've just been through. That's right thoughtful of you."

The landlady stepped back and opened the sliding door wider. Longarm pushed Sammy ahead of him through the opening. He saw Theresa Mirelda standing in front of the coffee table, a pearl-handled .32 in her right fist. *Christ,* Longarm thought swiftly, *what the hell did she need Sammy Wentworth for?* Even as he thought this, he ducked and, in the same motion, hurled Wentworth at Theresa. Her .32 went off just as Sammy went crashing into her.

Both of them went back over the coffee table in

244

a tangle, and when they came to rest, it was with an ominously quiet Sammy Wentworth sprawled on top of the Mirelda woman. Longarm unholstered his Colt wearily and looked at his wide-eyed landlady.

"How about sending one of the boarders after a copper—and an ambulance too, it looks like. Then maybe we can see about that cup of tea. Unless you've got something stronger."

The landlady whisked swiftly from the room, and Longarm looked down into the weeping face of Theresa Mirelda. She was weeping, he knew, out of frustration at not having been able to finish off the man who had killed her husband. She wasn't even thinking of the possibly dead Sammy Wentworth collapsed on top of her. Longarm was now thinking a bit incongruously, of how late all this was going to make him. Billy Vail was going to be purple in the face when Longarm finally strode into the chief's office.

Sammy Wentworth groaned and rolled off Theresa Mirelda's well-endowed figure. She still had the .32 in her hand. Longarm wrested it from her grasp, and bent to examine Sammy's wound.

It was well into the morning by the time Longarm left the police station and started up Colfax Avenue. The recently gilded dome of the Colorado State House gleamed proudly on Capitol Hill ahead of him. When he reached the U.S. Mint at Cherokee and Colfax, he turned the corner and headed for the federal courthouse. Inside, he elbowed his way through the lawyers with their briefcases, and climbed the marble staircase. He paused only momentarily in front of the big oak door whose gold-leaf lettering read, UNITED STATES MARSHAL, FIRST DISTRICT COURT OF COLORADO, then pushed his way inside.

The pale young clerk with his plastered-down, center-parted hair looked up from his typewriter and grinned. "Boy, Longarm, Marshal Vail is fit to be tied. He's been sending me all over looking for you."

"You ain't very good at finding people, are you?"

The clerk looked back down at his infernal machine.

"Nope. Don't look like I am. Finding people is *your* job, Longarm."

"*Mister Long*, to you," Longarm snapped.

Just then the door to Marshal Vail's office was flung open, and a very unhappy Billy Vail was standing in the doorway. "I thought I heard that growl of yours, Longarm! Where in tarnation have you been? I told you last night I wanted you here on *time* for a change. Get in here!"

"Only if you say please, Chief."

"Please! Now get the hell in here!"

With an aggrieved sigh, Longarm walked past Billy Vail into his office. As the heavyset man closed the door and hustled around behind his desk, Longarm slumped into the chief's red leather armchair. A glance at the banjo clock on the wall told Longarm it was close to eleven-thirty.

One bushy eyebrow cocked angrily, the pink-cheeked, balding official planted his elbows on his desk blotter and leaned closer to Longarm, his eyes fixed with irate intensity on his subordinate. "You have an explanation, I assume."

"I do at that, Chief."

"That filly you squired out of the hotel so sneaky last night, eh? She wore you out. That it?"

"Not quite. It was that other filly, the one hanging onto me when you first got there. You remember her, don't you?"

"Sort of. Look, Longarm, let's just quit this fancy footwork! You've got a long ways to go and one hell of a lot of details to swallow and you don't have all that much time. I'm going to have to brief you through dinner hour, it looks like, and *that* makes me *angry*. I told you to get here early!"

"Do you want my explanation?"

"You just gave it. A woman wore you out."

"Well, that ain't it exactly." Longarm was smiling broadly at the marshal by this time. "But if you don't want to hear it, that's all right with me."

"All right, all right, let's have it," Vail said as he began pawing through the blizzard of paperwork that covered his desk. He was going to listen, but not too closely, it appeared.

Longarm told Vail what had happened to him that morning following the soft knock on his door, and when he had finished with his story, including the part about the shooting of Sammy Wentworth and the ensuing events, Billy Vail was no longer poking through his paperwork. In fact, his mouth was hanging open just a little.

"You mean Sammy just up and vanished?"

"Looks like it. He's a pretty good actor. Slippery as an eel, besides. His hand wasn't really broken, I found out, and that bullet wound was an ugly-looking thing, but, like the doctor told me afterward, it was only a flesh wound."

"We'll pick him up, don't worry."

"I ain't worrying, Chief. Besides, we got the Mirelda woman. I hope you can put her away for a good long time. She's dangerous. Sammy was just a fool."

"I'm sorry, Longarm," Vail said, shaking his head unhappily.

"Sorry?" The note of contrition in Vail's voice surprised Longarm.

"Yeah, sorry. Wallace told me last week there was a woman in town looking for you, asking around at bars and such. He thought I ought to tell you, but it slipped my mind. I just figured it was your notorious charm."

Longarm laughed. "I guess I ought to be flattered."

"Just don't tell Wallace," the chief said, sighing.

"Now what's this big assignment, Chief?"

Vail leaned back in his chair and eyed Longarm appraisingly. "You ever heard of the Yellowstone Act?"

"The one that turned Colter's Hell into a national park?"

"That's the one," Vail replied, nodding solemnly. "That means since 1872 more than two million acres of untouched wilderness surrounding all those devilish geysers and springs have been set aside, protected from what the act calls 'commercial exploitation'—if you get my meaning. No prospecting, no cutting the timber. The land is set aside—" he glanced quickly at a government folder open on his desk— "'as a public pleasuring ground, for the preservation from injury or spoilation of all timber,

247

mineral deposits, natural curiosities, or wonders within this area and their retention in their natural condition.' "

Vail glanced up, and Longarm shrugged.

"I knew all that," he said. "What's the matter? Someone trying to cut that timber?"

"It's not as simple as that. We've got some very important people who want to do some of that 'pleasuring' the act set the Yellowstone Park aside for. But it might be the beginning of the end for this park."

"You better explain that."

"We got a passel of congressmen and their women who want to explore this new park. They want to see if this isn't maybe a waste of good natural resources. All that timber and mineral wealth being allowed to sit there just riles the hell out of these men, it seems. So here they come, Longarm, and you're the one who has to take them there and back."

Vail stopped abruptly and rocked back in his chair to let that sink in. His eyes were lit with interest. He expected his deputy to protest the assignment, Longarm realized. On the other hand, Vail was anxious for Longarm to take it because the old lawman was interested in the fate of the Yellowstone Park.

"Which side are you on, Chief?" Longarm inquired.

"You mean do I think we should go in there and rip up that park? Hell, Longarm, you've seen enough ghost towns, ripped-up land, and washed-away slopes, haven't you? Remember that bunch of loggers up in Digger-land and what they did to that valley? Christ, the way you told it, the whole side of a mountain came down on those bastards when they got through slashing off that covering timber. Hell, you know where I stand."

Longarm laughed, nodding. "I just wanted to hear you spell it out. So I'm to take those bigwigs from Washington up there and maybe lose them, is that it?"

"No, damn it! Now you know better than that, Longarm. That would only cause worse trouble—" Marshal Vail stopped in mid-sentence when he saw the look on Longarm's face and realized the younger lawman was pulling his leg.

"How many did you say?" Longarm asked, no longer smiling.

"A party of fourteen, all told. Five congressmen and their ladies and maids. A federal deputy has been assigned to meet you in Billings with a scout familiar with the territory."

"Who's in charge of the park?"

"There's a park superintendent; Norris is his name. A strange cuss, as I understand it from a letter I got here from Tyson, the deputy. The fellow is supposed to be hoping for hordes of tourists, and has already constructed a 'road of glass' on the way to Firehole Basin."

Longarm's eyebrows rose. "How the hell did he do that?"

"He wore a ledge of exposed black obsidian into shape by building fires on it, and when it was well-heated, he poured water on it. That's the way it sounds to me, but I'm no expert. You sound interested, Longarm," Vail said abruptly. "That so? You'll take this assignment?"

"Do I have a choice?"

"No, damn it, you don't. But I'd like for you to *want* to go. These people need the right handling, and if anything was to happen to any of them, the park would be blamed. That means a right nice idea would be down the drain. There's lots of other places out here that need protection from those Eastern moneylenders, but if this Yellowstone Park goes, there won't be much hope for any other parks like it."

Longarm nodded. He knew just what Marshal Vail meant. But shepherding a passel of congressional fat cats and their women into the wilderness west of the Big Horn Mountains was not going to be easy. And Vail was right; if any one of them got hurt or lost, the idea of a national park kept wild for visitors would be out the window. And in would swarm the nesters and lumbermen and gold-and-silver seekers. Longarm shuddered at the thought. He knew that Yellowstone country, and loved it.

"Fine, Chief," he said. "I'll go. And willingly."

"Good." Marshal Vail got to his feet and hurried around his desk. "I'm going out to tell my clerk I'm not to be disturbed. There's a lot I've got to tell you about this here expedition, and we don't have all that much time. You'll be leaving tonight, Longarm."

As Vail pulled the door shut behind him and started issuing orders to his clerk, Longarm took out a cheroot and lit it. He had been trying to cut out his smoking habit, and had been having moderate success this past week, but he needed something to get his brain cells to percolating. Vail had a lot to tell him, and there was a lot he needed to know.

For one thing, who was this Deputy Tyson? Longarm would have preferred Wallace, or at least someone he knew well enough to know he could be counted upon in an emergency. The way this assignment looked, there were sure as hell going to be enough emergencies to go around, what with him playing Mother Superior to five pasty-faced dudes and their hysterical womenfolk on a trip to the Yellowstone Park and back. The thought of it set his worry bells to clanging.

Longarm shook his head and inhaled deeply on his cheroot. He resembled a smoldering volcano when Vail returned.

Chapter 2

Longarm leaned back in his chair and studied Frank Tyson. The deputy had just introduced himself and sat down at his table. Longarm had arrived in Billings the night before, and had left word with the desk clerk at the hotel that anyone calling himself Frank Tyson could find him in the bar. Longarm had waited most of the morning. In a few minutes it would be noon, and his ass was sore from all this sitting.

But he kept his irritation in check as he looked over the man who was going to be his sidekick for the coming expedition up the Yellowstone. The fellow was lean. His eyes were a washed-out blue, his hair and eyebrows sandy, his face gaunt and drawn, with lines about his eyes and mouth that spoke of something painful that had worked itself down deep inside the man. He had spoken softly when he introduced himself, and had sat down carefully, as silently as a wet leaf settling on the ground after an autumn rain. Yet, despite the man's gentle, almost deferential manner, Longarm detected a latent wildness just below the surface—a fierce, bottled fury that the man kept under control only by dint of enormous effort.

The man's pale blue eyes met Longarm's, and he smiled. "Sorry to keep you waiting, Long. I was out looking for a guide, and seeing to our gear."

"You got my telegram, then."

"It got here day before yesterday. I just didn't think it would do any of us any good if I sat around on my duff to wait for the steamer to get in. Especially with those big shots due this afternoon."

"I thought I might wait and ride up the river with them on the *Far West*. Then I thought better of it,"

Longarm said, appraising the man coolly. "You've got some idea, then, what this is all about. That telegram didn't give me much room."

"Visitors. Sightseers. The West is filling up with them, now that the Indian problem has been solved." He put a sardonic emphasis on the word "solved."

"You don't think it has been?"

"To *our* satisfaction it has, I'm sure." The man's drawn face seemed to grow even sharper and leaner as he reached for his beer. "Nobody's bothered to ask the Indians, though."

"That's not very healthy talk in Billings, Tyson. You got any special reasons for feeling like you do?"

The man looked at Longarm sharply. "You mean beyond a wish for simple human justice?"

Longarm smiled. "Yes, beyond that, if you could maybe spell it out for me, though I ain't never seen human justice that was very simple or very just. It sure as hell was human, though."

The man frowned in concentration as he lifted his beer mug to his mouth. He cocked an eye warily at Longarm. "You seem like an honorable man. What I'm going to tell you is something I don't want generally known."

"If you mean do I blab, the answer is no, I don't. Let's have this big secret, Tyson."

The man put his mug down heavily on the table and looked coldly at Longarm. "I was married seven years ago to a Crow woman. I had two children by her. The three of them were killed by drunken cavalrymen who found them washing clothes on the bank of a stream. The two cavalrymen made themselves a little entertainment before they killed my wife and drowned the children. An old Crow woman crouching in the bushes by the stream saw it all."

"That don't make much sense. The Crow were allies of the cavalry. They've sided with the whites against the Sioux since way back."

Tyson smiled thinly. "You know those damn fool young punks that rode in the Seventh couldn't tell a Crow from a Sioux if their life depended on it."

"Did you report it?"

"All the way to the top. They let the cavalrymen escape. About that time, things began heating up around here, and they lost themselves in the area. Hell, half of this population is made up of army deserters, I'm thinking."

"If it was seven years ago, Tyson," Longarm said gently, "maybe you should think about forgetting it."

"Maybe. But I ran onto them a couple of years back. I'd nearly finished scalping one of them alive when the other came on us. I lost that skirmish, but I'll find them again."

Longarm studied Tyson carefully. He knew now the source of the man's deep anguish. But he had to figure out now whether or not he could afford such a man at his side on this upcoming trip into the Yellowstone country. A man bent on his own private vendetta could make very bad decisions at times.

As if he were reading Longarm's thoughts, the man smiled. "I know what you're thinking, Long. A man like me might go off at any moment on his own. You think I'm obsessed, that I lie awake at nights plotting ways to get those two. And if that's the kind of man I am, you don't think you can afford the luxury of having me with you on this trip with all those fancy congressmen and their women."

Longarm leaned back and sipped his Maryland rye. "Yep, Tyson. That's just about what I was thinking."

Tyson shrugged. "So what's so all-fired important about these congressmen coming to visit Yellowstone? Since when are a couple of deputy U.S. marshals needed to wet-nurse tourists? I should think we've both got better things to do with our time."

"Ordinarily we have. But this here's a different bunch of tourists, and I think maybe you'll agree that we got to do it right or this country hereabouts is liable to suffer."

"You'd better explain that."

Longarm told him the purpose of the congressional party's visit and the significance it could have in the future development of the area. When he had finished, Tyson was thoughtful.

"You think they might decide it's foolish to keep Colter's Hell a park. You mean there's a chance they

253

might go back to Washington and tell their buddies to open up this area to prospectors and the like?"

"Maybe, if something bad happens to one of them. They're coming out here to see what the hell we got that's so damn important we want to set it aside and keep it untouched," Longarm said. "I admit, it's a new idea to me. But I've been thinking on it since I left Denver, and damned if it don't seem to me like a very good notion at that."

Tyson nodded thoughtfully. "It's a good idea, all right. It's just a damn shame we couldn't feel the same way about the Sioux and the Arapahoe and the Bannocks and the Crow as we feel about the land we've taken from them."

Longarm took a deep breath and decided not to reply. He knew the pain inside the man was what made him go on like that, and he didn't necessarily disagree with him. But Longarm had seen all kinds of Indians, just like he had seen all manner of white folks, Mexicans, Chinese, and all the rest. There were good and bad to be found in every mix. These Indian wars now winding down had seen that mix on both sides. Not every raw recruit in the cavalry was a punk, and not every cavalryman took advantage of an Indian female when he found her alone. On the other hand, not every Indian woman who found herself in a recruit's arms wanted it any other way. He had seen at one time how eagerly some drunken Indian fathers had been willing to sell their daughters to a soldier for another bottle of hooch.

It just wasn't all one way or the other; the right and the wrong of it got terribly mixed up at times, and the law of the land that Longarm was hired to enforce didn't seem to be able to do much about pain and confusion and folks' needs.

Tyson finished his beer. "If you want to get someone else for this job, Long, you can. I won't complain. No sense in riding alongside a man whose prejudices you can't stomach."

"Don't talk like a damn fool," Longarm said softly. "I reckon there ain't one of us who don't carry a passel of false notions and angry judgments bottled up inside him everywhere he goes. The thing is, Tyson, I'd like your undivided attention during this trip into the Yellowstone. If you think you can manage that, I'll be proud to have you with me. Is that too much to ask?"

The man smiled suddenly, relieved. "Hell, no, Long," he said, the tension easing at once in his face.

"Good," Longarm said, extending his hand across the table. "Call me Longarm. That's what my friends call me."

Tyson was about to respond when a shot rang out in the street just beyond the batwing doors of the hotel bar. Longarm and Tyson hurriedly left their table and dashed out of the bar. On the boardwalk, they saw a crowd gathered around a lone Indian. Even as they arrived, one of the men encircling the Indian loosed another shot at the Indian's feet. Terrified, the Indian jumped and tried to break through the grinning circle of men. With a roar of laughter, he was flung back into the center of the circle and someone else aimed a shot at the poor fellow's feet. In his anxiety to jump away from the glancing bullet, the Indian lost his footing and went sprawling on his back.

"Just an afternoon's funning is all this is," said Tyson bitterly.

"He don't look like a Sioux," Longarm observed.

"He's a Bannock. He isn't any more welcome around here than a Sioux, and that's for damn sure."

The Bannock was on his feet now, crouching warily, watching the faces about him with a terror matched only by his seething fury. He was dressed oddly, in a buckskin shirt and pants with a battered cavalry campaign hat sporting a single feather on his head and a pair of battered cavalry stovepipes on his feet. Bigger than most Indians, he startled Longarm by glancing suddenly into the lawman's face. It was then that Longarm saw the bright blue eyes.

"He's a breed," said Longarm.

"Does that make a whole hell of a lot of difference?" Tyson remarked, stepping off the walk.

Before Longarm could hold Tyson, he had pushed his way angrily through the crowd. The last man he encountered tried to stop him. A swift backhand slap sent the man reeling into the arms of his friends. Tyson's sixgun was in his hand now as he turned swiftly to the Indian. Tyson smiled at the Bannock then, to reassure him—but the smile came too late. The Indian hurled himself at the gun in Tyson's hand and, with a powerful wrench, snatched it from him.

Brandishing the weapon wildly, the Indian shot into the crowd, then, with a shriek, he had dashed past Tyson and through the crowd that fell back in a panic before the Bannock's fury.

Down an alley toward the river the Indian raced. After a momentary confusion, the two men the Bannock had wounded were left to writhe in the dust as the rest of the crowd of enraged citizens, sixguns out and waving, took off down the alley after the fleeing Indian. Tyson was with them also, but his mission was obviously counter to that of the rest of the crowd, and Longarm realized, as he started down the alley after the mob, that Tyson was just liable to get himself killed. His interference had already caused bloodshed.

Since escape upriver was impossible, Longarm noted, the Indian was not trying to run in that direction, but was leaping into the greenery along the shore, stumbling, falling, sliding in marshy ooze as he neared the bank. Shots cracked. Longarm saw the Indian pause to return the fire, then struggle through the ooze toward the open water.

Longarm was gaining only slightly on the mob howling on the Indian's heels. As he ran past the Yellowstone Dining Hall, a crook threw a pail of slops into a tiny tributary of the river that wound under his establishment, narrowly missing Longarm as the lawman jumped over the narrow ditch and kept after the mob. The cook yelled after him, asking what all the fuss was about. Longarm did not pause to tell him.

Downstream now, closer to the Indian than the others since the fellow had backtracked to find more solid ground in his battle to reach the river, Longarm felt the sun thrusting its way through the willows bordering the river. He paused and, placing one hand on a willow trunk for support, yelled out to the Bannock and tried to tell the fellow he would be all right if he gave himself up.